I0628661

Accumulation

By G. Nykanen

~~~

Published by G. NYKANEN

Copyright © 2014 G. NYKANEN

ISBN: 978-0-9898784-6-3

0-9898784-6-5

This book is dedicated to TR.
Thanks for the wealth of material.

Somewhere in the beginning...

Separation

Chapter 1
Cold Fish

"**D**-ry? Dory, ar- you th-re?" A voice cracked distantly, as it strained through the receiver. "Did th- samples a--ive? I fou- - some - -ing else, - - - un- -pec-ed."

"What, professor?" Dory Wells struggled to piece together the fractured and frantic words. "I don't understand. You still want me to send out the samples when they arrive?"

"Se-d - -em ....."

I didn't get any of that, sir. Can you repeat it? How's Mongolia?" She was oblivious to the sounds of panic and upheaval swirling in the background. Her curiosity about the peoples of the region and her mentor's experience there was uppermost in her mind. As an anthropology student she yearned for the chance to be immersed in other cultures and was always eager to absorb new people and places, even if only second-hand from her esteemed teacher.

Professor Morton had been on sabbatical collecting samples for an anthropological experiment in hopes of tying the bloodline of Genghis Khan to the people of Iron Bay and the Bay Peninsula. He posited that there would be a link due to the heavy Finnish heritage of the area. He often explained his thesis at cocktail parties: "There's an Eastern tie to Finland via Russia, thus a tie to Khan. It's the only thing that explains the measured cruelty of my ex-wife."

Although his delivery of that line was always received with laughter, the real punch line was, he wasn't joking.

"CHAOS," his only clear and unbroken word. "Fl- -ts can - l-d."

"Your flight's cancelled, is that what you said?" Dory tried to make sense of Professor Morton's hectic and broken conversation. She rubbed the back of her short brown hair as she struggled to discern his message.

"Send it ----." His call was once again interrupted; pockets of silence garbled his words, his intention now diluted.

"Send it where, sir?" she was perplexed. "I thought we were sending it to Commerce City for testing like the others?"

"No ..."

"Sir? Professor?" Dory held the phone tightly to her ear, hoping to catch just one more syllable but the line had gone dead.

"Shit, clear as mud."

She leaned forward. The archaic office chair screeched as she shifted to make eye contact with a photo of Dr. Morton, which sat on one of the many wooden shelves adjacent to his antique desk. His curious eyes peered out from behind his wire rims as he towered above the children from the Yagua tribe in Peru. His pale complexion and light, wavy coif were in stark contrast to their deeply tanned skin and straight, dark hair.

"What do I do now?" her words were tinged with frustration.

"Who you talking to?"

"Jesus Christ," she swung around, the arm of the wooden office chair banging loudly into the edge of the desk. "Lance! You scared the shit out of me!"

"Having one of your conversations with the professor's photo again? I don't mind if you're a little touched baby, I still think you're sexy."

"Don't talk to me like that. You know I think you're repellant in every way."

"I'll eventually wear you down. I know you're not really a cold fish."

Dory sneered at his very existence. "Never!"

Lance Sisto had a master's degree in anthropology and was the assistant to Professor John Morton. He handled all the professor's business while he was away, not limited to, but including, teaching his classes. This gave him an inflated sense of self. She didn't understand why he was so cocky, as his hygiene and manner of dress were less than appealing.

His hair was slicked tightly to his scalp with the aid of some viscous product, the application of which made it impossible to discern what color it really was. He often sported LaCoste polos with popped collars in strange shades like puce and mustard, which seemed to accentuate the unusual yellow tint to his light-brown eyes. He tucked the tails of his shirts into his dark—*and entirely too revealing*—jeans, which he would cuff over his tasseled loafers. The oil he used to torture his hair caused his complexion to take on a waxy sheen, turning his nose into a greasy slope down which his designer glasses constantly slid.

"I could fire you, end your position here as the graduate assistant. You should be nicer to me. But I'll forgive you if you come hold that beautiful athletic build of yours against me."

Dory wasn't squeamish. She wasn't the type to get flustered by unwanted advances. Tall and beautiful since puberty, she had long ago developed the tools to defend herself and make boys cry.

"You're only an adjunct professor, Lance. You're about one peg higher on the totem pole than I am, so stop sexually harassing me, or I'll tell the Dean and end *your* position here."

"Touché," he winked flirtatiously.

"Yech!" The word was gargled loudly as though his presence had caused her throat to coat with phlegm. *Those expensive clothes are doing nothing for you*, she thought as she shot him a dirty look.

He was unaffected by her disgust and kept grinning, his thin lips pursed in her direction.

Dory redirected. "The professor was just on the phone. The call ended just before you came in and proceeded to ruin my day. He said something about the samples and not sending them to Commerce City."

Lance was flustered by the news. "Why not? That's where we've sent all the others. Why change location after we've already built a relationship with the lab and established a protocol?"

She shrugged her shoulders. "Beats me. He said something about cancelled flights and finding something else. Oh, and he shouted the word *chaos*. The line went dead before I could make any sense of it."

"Did you try calling him back?"

"No!" She was short with him, embarrassed she hadn't thought of that.

He rolled his eyes as he redialed.

"This call cannot be completed at this time. Please try again."

"I'll try his cell." He pried his Note from his pocket and selected the number from his contacts.

Dory watched as his face contracted, his attempt to reach their boss obviously a failure. "Well, it would seem the system is busy for some reason." Lance pushed as he tried to squeeze the device back into his snug jeans.

Smiling, she watched as he struggled. "Might I suggest bigger pants?"

He smirked in response to her clothing suggestion, and then, with a dry tone offered a scenario. "Perhaps this has something to do with all the shit they've been showing on the news? I heard that thousands have turned ill in China and India. Violence has run rampant."

"Maybe, but I doubt it. He's practically off the grid out there, I'm sure it's nothing serious. We'll just have to see if he left any instructions when the new samples arrive."

"They arrived last night, right after you left to grab dinner. I have them in the back room."

Dory rushed into Professor Morton's study.

The walls were lined floor to ceiling with industrial metal shelving, which were loaded top to bottom with volumes of books, periodicals, and artifacts from his many excursions. In the center of this cluttered yet studious room was a long rectangular table. Its aged and rugged wooden appearance clashed wildly with the modern lines of the professor's storage choices.

In the center of the table sat the box of samples. The package, a little smaller than a shoebox, had a paper covering worn and battered by its long journey. The many stamps and markings gave the otherwise drab, brown wrap an adventurous quality.

"What answers do you hold?" Dory carefully positioned the package. "It's postmarked five days ago. Takes a while to get from there to here, even in this era of next-day air."

"No such thing as next day when you live up here. This box went from one Sherpa to the next to arrive on this damn peninsula. I can't believe people live here on purpose, or stay for that matter. Once they're old enough to leave you think they'd flee in droves. You're like me: the only reason you stay is because of the university."

Dory corrected Lance. "Well, I like it here, it's fantastically unique. The people here are a breed all their own. This whole place is an anthropological experiment."

"I can agree with that. I've never met a population so physically and mentally removed from the rest of the world. I bet they all pay about as much attention to what's going on out there as you've begun to. Its like they believe there's a magic barrier protecting them once you cross the bridge."

"Perhaps the attributes of these local people have begun to rub off on me. *When in Rome...*"

He looked up at her from under his oily hair in a matter-of-fact gesture. "Rome fell." One saturated strand had come loose and now clung to his forehead.

"I'm going to ignore you now and open the box," she gave him a dismissive nod.

With the packing discarded she flipped open the top and eyed the many glass slides.

She investigated the contents of the small crate.

"They all look the same, usual packaging. I don't see a note or anything."

Lance pointed. "What's that?" A second, smaller box was barely visible beneath the hanging samples.

Dory carefully lifted the rack of slides and obtained the petite package, its size slightly smaller than a large box of matches.

A cardboard sleeve with a hand-drawn biohazard symbol was fit snugly over a dense foam inset.

Dory was perplexed. "Is this for real?" The seriousness of the symbol was eroded by the comical and childlike depiction.

"Maybe he was drunk and thought it would be funny; you know what a prankster he can be."

"I've literally never heard him so much as tell a joke." Dory slowly removed the foam from its sleeve. She placed the insert on the table. Licking her lips nervously, she lifted, pulling it apart. Nestled snugly inside was a vial.

"I think its blood." She investigated the glass cylinder, its tarry contents sticking to the vial wall. "It almost seems to be—quivering." She took a closer look, her blue eyes squinting. "I'm not removing it from its cozy foam bed." She was uneasy about the whole thing.

"That label, what does it say?" Lance was unwilling to handle it as well.

It was donned with the same type of label used on the slides, but, instead of the usual letters and numbers used to catalogue their contents, it read OID in bright red lettering.

"What's OID?" She doubted he knew either.

He shrugged off the question. "Let's just leave the samples at the work station and put the vial carefully in the fridge with all of the good professor's sardines. He was suddenly distracted by his employer's affinity for cold fish and saltines. "Why does he refrigerate them if they're canned?"

Dory's response was more question than answer. "Just likes 'em chilled?   ...So, with the professor's disgusting snack choices aside, I guess we'll just have to wait for good ole John to phone and tell us what's going on. Maybe we should Google what OID stands for."

In agreement on an Internet search for the mystery acronym, they moved toward the main office and Dory's desk. Her fingers began to strike the keys before her butt was even in the chair. Stretched over the desk, her rear end wiggled as she typed.

Lance admired her levitating backside.

Just as she was about to hit return, a commotion broke out in the hallway. A loud and steady rumble of voices filled the corridor.

"Who could be causing such a ruckus this early in the morning?" She glanced at the clock as she and Lance headed for the hallway.

"Classes don't start until nine. The only reason we get here so early is to score points with the professor."

Dory nodded in silent agreement to his admission as they peeked through the office door at what appeared to be a military-type patrol.

Several men in uniform scuffled down the hall. The jostling of their gear combined with the squelch of their radios added background to the rhythmic slamming of office doors as they swept and cleared every room in each corridor.

A voice screeched from the radio. "First floor clear."

"Roger that," the soldier approaching their door answered.

"Second floor clear," another voice provided, carried by the same radio noise.

"Roger that," the imposing figure answered again, members of his team in tow as their leader handled the radio chatter.

"Status?" a fourth voice questioned from somewhere beyond, all parties involved obviously spread throughout the building.

"Final door, Anthropology Department." Two fingers snapped forward, as he signaled the others to pull ahead.

"They're almost to us." Lance's vantage point was better than Dory's.

"What's going on?" She leaned trying to see around him. "Is this some sort of exercise?"

"I'll take care of it." Plucking up the courage to interrogate the armed intruders, he pulled open the door and stepped into the hall.

"Excuse me. Excuse me, but what's going on here?"

"You'll need to come with us," the soldier ordered before reporting his findings into the receiver. "Persons located, third floor science."

"Roger that, take them to staging with the others," a distant voice returned.

"Will do," he concurred.

Lance pushed. "I insist that you tell me what's going on."

"Yeah, what's going on here?" Dory was now irritated and in front of Lance.

"You're being escorted to the Paramount Room where you will await further instruction."

"Well, I tell you what," Dory jabbed the armed fellow in the nametag, "I'm not going anywhere until I get some answers. You can't just come up here with your guns and tell us what to do." She paused as she eyed his name—"Davies."

He grinned, not yet tired this morning of blowback from the frightened university population. Blake Davies was a good guy. He followed the rules. He was a solid soldier and a loving family man. He just wanted to safely corral these people and follow his orders. *They just keep busting my balls*, he thought as she scowled at him, her finger fixed in the middle of his chest.

"You will be given answers in due time." Davies smirked while he leaned over and pressed the brim of his hat to her forehead. "You *will* come with us, *peacefully,* and wait in the lecture hall. Don't make me get rough."

She peeked around, as she absorbed the reality of this soldier and his armed goons, and quickly decided to comply. She backed away and reached for Lance's hand.

She's willingly touching me, he thought. *It may have taken the fear of military force, but she's touching me.*

Chapter 2
Separation Anxiety

"**A**re the packages in place?" Governor Steve Landis queried into the receiver of his satellite phone, as the early light of day finally breached the backseat. He adjusted the front visor to diffuse the rays of the dull autumn sun. His hazel eyes squinted as he intently awaited a reply. With a swipe of his free hand he smoothed a stray hair on his precise dark coif.

"Yes sir, in place and ready for detonation," the command voice assured him from the other end of the device.

The time has finally come, he thought as he traced the letters embossed on the cover of the leather-bound book resting in is lap. The Griffin Survival Guide was passed down to him by his great uncle. Steve had followed in his footsteps, for he'd also been the governor, and he was the one who'd introduced him to the wonders of Lake Paramount and The Bay Peninsula.

Although the seat of government for the state was in Commerce City, the governor also had a summer residence on Paramount Island. So, as a child, Steve spent many summer days exploring the area and looking to the shore of the peninsula just across the straits where Lake Paramount converged with Empire Lake.

"Excellent," his attention now returned to the execution of his plan. He continued to give orders; his ear pressed firmly to the phone, while he soothed Mr. Mathers' frayed nerves. "It's all going to be fine; just sit back, relax, and watch me work." With a wink he gestured, his intention to put Mr. Mathers at ease.

"Have the trucks been dispatched?" the governor wanted to be sure all aspects of the operation were underway.

"Dispatched and en-route, sir," the confident voice concurred.

"Spectacular! Start the excavation on the west end, hold for detonation. I should be over in the next half hour."

"Roger that."

"It would seem our plan is poised for execution, Mr. Mathers, soon we'll be over the bridge and well on our way to a new life, cut off from all that would care to harm us." The governor rubbed his back. He arched, pushing into his palm.

"Oh you like that, don't you," Mr. Mathers, rested his head on Steve, responding to the affection.

The chauffeur (who was more bodyguard than driver) couldn't help but glance, his eyes darting to the rearview with curiosity over the bizarre behavior of this elected official. *My job has gone from high speed to weird indeed,* Deck thought as he watched the governor massage Mr. Mathers.

"Thirty minutes to the bridge?" the governor caressed his partner's chin, his voice still screwed up to the same pitch he was using to coo at his dear companion.

17

"Thirty minutes." Deck was unnerved by the haste in which they'd departed, not to mention the speed that his employer insisted he use; it had his gut in a knot. He thought about it as he hurtled up the interstate. *Why the rush...the middle of the night...* He couldn't help but glance repeatedly over his shoulder. The feeling that they were escaping something dreadful...that something was chasing them, crawled all over him.

"Very good," Steve's nerves were steady. "Say, how'd you get a name like Deck? Is it short for something or just a handle from your old life?"

"My first name is Ashleigh, Ashleigh Decker. It goes without saying that kids were particularly cruel. Deck isn't only short for Decker, but it was often my response to their relentless teasing."

"A nickname born from violence... I like it. What's your brother's name, Heather?"

"No sir, but I have a sister named Dylan."

"Your folks had a twisted sense of humor. Say, uh, Deck, are you married, do you have any kids?"

He didn't really care about the driver or his relationship status (he'd already callously left all of his acquaintances behind) he just wanted to know how steady Deck was, he didn't want to deal with his driver, slash muscle, trying to flee and return to his brood when the shit hit the fan.

"No sir, no wife or kids. I have dedicated these last several years to the service of my country."

"What exactly did you do for your country, or will you have to kill me if you tell me?" Governor Landis chuckled while he loosened the knot in his tie.

"If I had to harbor a guess, I'd say your build and demeanor suggest you were more than just a grunt."

Deck only nodded in agreement. His service years were not only secret but private. His missions and the sanctity of the bond he shared with his fellow soldiers were personal. *I would have to kill you*, he thought.

The governor pushed. "Ahh, a man of few words. Well, no military details, how about family?"

"It's complicated," Deck was uninterested in strolling down memory lane.

"Oh, playing hard to get. I'll have to pry the info out of you with a torturous line of questioning," Steve fired, trying to get answers while wrestling with the tie. "Are you close to your parents? Do you have any siblings you are particularly fond of? Perhaps an old sweetheart you might feel still have stirrings for?" As he rattled off the questions, he realized he probably should've vetted someone in advance. *But in an emergent apocalyptic scenario, perhaps you don't have time to find the perfect fit.* This internal rationalization was comforting and caused him to bob his head in a self-satisfied manner, his egotism still in place.

Once again Deck glanced into the rearview in a judgmental way. He decided to answer quickly before his thoughts became obvious via his facial expressions, just as his employer's had.

"My parents have passed and I have a sister, like I said, but we aren't close."

"Why not?" Steve pried as he rolled down the window, his loosened tie now grasped in his right hand.

Deck remained tight-lipped while he tried to find a way to avoid answering.

Still awaiting his driver's reply, he pushed, his voice now raised to combat the whistle created by the widely opened window.

"Well, one sister, dead parents: Why the rift?"

The crisp morning air carried the smell of impending snow as it whipped through the vehicle. It ruffled what little hair Mr. Mathers had, and sent the governor's tidy brown locks into a frenzy. Steve held his hand out the window; the blue and yellow silk flapped wildly in the cold autumn wind. He watched his tie trail along the outside of the speeding vehicle for a moment before letting it go. The useless piece of fabric was now a metaphor for what he left behind.

The governor continued to question with an insistent tone, "So, your sister," he rolled up the window; Mr. Mathers, now clearly irritated and shivering, scooted closer, leaning in for warmth. Steve received him and covered him with his coat, rubbing his delicate shoulders.

With his eyebrows raised at the bizarre relationship between his employer and Mr. Mathers, Deck returned his attention to the road. He began to divulge, in limited detail, what had gone wrong between his sister and himself. "Our mother died a few years prior to our father, who passed suddenly about a year ago. My sister had not only dealt with my mother's illness alone, due to my constant deployment, and my father's inability to face his wife's suffering, she also had to bear the burden of our father's death. She had her husband and kids, but still had to make all the hard decisions alone. I was unreachable. Off the grid so to speak, serving my country."

"So she resents you for being a soldier, for choosing country over family?" Steve contemplated the actions of his new employee while changing his clothes. He fished his survival attire from the black leather bag at his feet. *This guy might work out well*, he thought as he removed his dress shirt. *He obviously had no problem putting the mission first.*

"Sort of," the questioning irritated Deck, he didn't want to share family details. He drove on, his already troubled psyche now flooded with the memories he'd been trying so hard to avoid. *Why wasn't I there? Mom was in a coma, and Dad couldn't handle it... he avoided it... on a bender somewhere. Sis had to make the call... let her go. Dad slipped... a dark place ...they'd been joined at the hip since they were kids, childhood sweethearts... he couldn't deal with her being gone. I couldn't deal with it. Drinking, womanizing, baha-ing through the woods on his dirt bike like a drunken teenager. Poured one for the road and hit the trails... hit a tree. Once again, I was MIA, hiding behind my rifle. Dilly was left to pull the plug... I was selfish...Dad was selfish...*

It was this very stream of internal dialogue, this manic pattern of thought, that led Deck to realize he'd used his service to avoid the emotional discomfort of his parents' death, just as his father had used booze and denial to avoid their mother's. With this revelation, he'd left the military and returned to D.C., no longer wanting to avoid his family obligations. He tried to reach Dylan, but she'd moved. He questioned the neighbor, only to find that his sister had been ill and her husband had relocated them to the Bay Peninsula somewhere.

Unable to contact her, he landed a private security job in Michigan, intending to look for her in his time off. *My search will have to wait another day,* he thought as he sped up I75, hell bent for the Grand Traverse Bridge.

"They were looking for some peace and quiet, is what the neighbor told me... Came out here because she was ill."

I'm going to find them, he thought as he drove, now unable to get out of his own head. *If I could just see her...explain...*

"Wow, too bad about your sis. Under different circumstances I could have helped you locate her."

Deck was suddenly aware that his employer might not appreciate his past and how he'd left his sister hanging. *He's going to think I'm untrustworthy. Who could understand being absent when needed, not once but twice?*

"Well, I'm pleased you were so dedicated to your country. I was worried that you might want to flake out, head for your family when it started to get sticky, but you're battle-tested and steady. It's an honor to have you by our side." He gestured to Mr. Mathers, making sure that his companion knew he was speaking for both of them.

In a bit of a fog and overloaded by latent emotion, Deck slowly found the words. "Oh, yeah, thanks."

"So, are you familiar with Iron Bay and the Bay Peninsula?" Steve peered through the windshield as he finished buttoning the dark cargos, his clothes now changed, as the Grand Traverse Bridge rose from the road in the distance.

"Honestly, I didn't realize the state had two parts. My only previous exposure to this region was my brother-in-law's brief mention of being from here somewhere."

As they approached the towering expanse of twisted cables, Deck glanced back as movement on the road behind them caught his eye.

"Take it slow," the governor ended their exchange about the state. "Let my men get into position behind us." Steve rolled down the window, the cold air once again sending Mr. Mathers into a shivering frenzy.

Through the crack he waved. The gesture caused the two vehicles behind them to take action.

Deck eased the Suburban to a crawl. With caution he shifted his eyes from the road to the mirror and back again, trying to observe.

Two white pick-ups maneuvered abruptly, turning horizontally across the highway, where they came to a screeching halt. Once in position they flipped on the orange caution lights affixed above the passenger doors, as they created an impromptu roadblock. Two men exited each vehicle, dressed in a quasi-military tactical style. *Definitely not uniform*, Deck thought.

One of the men stood in the median, a department of transportation vest was over his uniform and with a hand held stop sign he halted the few cars that trickled toward the bridge. The others threw up four A-frame-type construction barriers, their orange and white stripes providing the appropriate and familiar warning not to cross. Behind these barriers they pulled a coil of double-ring razor wire. The outer ring stood five feet high and the inner ring about three, which made the obstacle impassible (well, without serious injury anyway).

With the roadblock convincingly erected, Steve was pumped and ready to roll.

"Step on it, Deck, we have a bridge to cross and time is wasting."

Deck picked up speed, as he followed his employer's orders. "What's going on here, sir?" Fear and suspicion plagued him. The men piled into one truck and pulled in behind them, leaving the other to flash its warning.

With his head swiveled Steve watched the Grand Traverse stretch out behind him, the growing line of cars no longer visible. "Sheeple," the governor was filled with contempt as he glanced back. "Programmed their whole lives to respect authority, no one behind that barrier will question it. They'll simply sit and wait for further instruction, or grow impatient and try to turn around. It doesn't matter that those are just trucks I purchased and topped with lights from Radio Shack. Or that those barriers and razor wire can be bought online by anyone. Poor stupid bastards have no idea what's in store for them, but if they wait long enough they'll get a hell of a show!"

Governor Landis the elected official existed no longer. The metamorphosis to self appointed commander-in-chief was complete.

Acutely aware now that this was no routine drive up north, Deck decided it was time to start acting tactically. "If I'd have known what we were embarking on, sir, I would have come more prepared. I only have my side arm, and the clothes on my back...not exactly supplied and sound by the way things are shaping up. Maybe if I had a bigger picture, I could start to get in the right head space."

"Everything we need will be on the other side. I have prepared for this scenario a long time, and believe me, being scheduled for work last night... well, you won the lottery. Maybe you saw some of the videos on YouTube? Anyway, we'll all come to a violent end if we don't remove ourselves from danger."

Deck shook his head. He hadn't had time for web browsing lately. As the new guy on the job (low man on the totem pole) he'd been on call at the security agency for the last two days.

"What about news reports? You think the media would've had a field day with this." He was perplexed by the lack of coverage something this serious was getting.

Steve tried to explain. "There've been reports of violent outbursts, but all under the guise of panic and scarcity of supplies... some common illness. I'm sure our president and the other many esteemed world leaders are being kept apprised of the situation. But remember, no one will want to overreact, and most people will minimize the already censored version they hear."

Deck nodded in agreement. *No one ever wants to believe it's as bad as it is. Coping mechanism,* he thought.

"I always keep my ear to the ground, gaining information, processing it, making sure to read between the lies our system generates to control the masses. This thing, this illness or whatever it is—it's catastrophic, and the powers that be *can't* and *won't* believe that it'll be as bad as I already know it is. It's too fast and too violent; we'll never survive unless we break ourselves off from the rest of the world. The life we know will be unrecognizable in forty-eight hours."

Deck was confused. "I don't understand, surely the federal government has a plan in place? What about the CDC?"

"There's no treating this, there's no time. The Office of Infectious Disease would need months to isolate the problem, if they even had the right samples, and I doubt we have days left, let alone the months it would take to design some treatment. All we can do is avoid it. Which I plan to do by crossing this bridge and separating ourselves from the threat."

Deck glanced back and watched the governor seek comfort from his companion. The pickup still followed as they approached the tollbooth. His stomach quivered. *What will this mean for me... for my sister and her children? We might be distant, but I don't want any harm to come to them.*

Deck worked hard to man up, to stifle whatever unexpected feelings had started to bubble up as the finality of what would occur seeped in.

Steve Landis held another one-sided conversation with his quiet counterpart. "Ahh, two dollars per axle or four per car. Seems like a fair price to survive the end of the world, don't you think so, Mr. Mathers? Yes. I think so too."

Needing the kick-off of his plan to remain discreet, the governor wanted to keep his identity hidden. "Stop and pay, just like anyone else; best not draw attention to the fact that I'm in here."

Once at the tollbooth, a pleasant, middle-aged gentleman greeted them. He was stout, with an accent as thick as his auburn mustache. "How ya doo-in tuh-day?" his vowels were long and trailing.

"Fine." Deck said the word, but was actually unsure how much longer that response would be valid.

"First time over da bridge?" the attendant questioned with his ever-widening smile.

"Yeah, first time." Deck wasn't sure what to think of this guy or the whole situation.

"Dat'll be four bucks den, eh." The jovial fellow extended his meaty hand, his palm outstretched.

"Yeah, sure." The character before him seemed so foreign, he felt like he'd crossed into another country, or world for that matter.

"Yeah, dat's perfect," he smiled as he grasped the singles. "You's have uh nice staaay now, eh."

Deck smirked and gave the guy a nod, fully aware that they'd all be staying forever now.

"We're over," Steve disclosed, his sat phone once again pressed to his ear. "Full speed ahead, Deck—let's put some space between us and the blast."

They reached full speed as the word *blast* dripped from the governor's bottom lip. The sound rolled in waves as the explosion tore through the cold northern morning. A long, low rumble crawled through the earth as Deck drove onward into uncertainty.

Chapter 3
This Is Not a Test

"I swear to god, if the two of you don't settle down right now, I'll feed your breakfast to Spencer!" Laney Riley jabbed the spatula in the dog's direction. Spencer, their twelve-year-old Labrador, remained curled by the back door, unaffected by the noise level produced by the Riley boys and their fed-up mother.

Ian and Sean, eleven-year-old fraternal twins, tussled violently (as usual) their highly physical play accompanied by boisterous chatter.

"Lick it! Lick it and looove it." Ian held the dog's freshly chewed and rather nasty rawhide to his brother's lips.

"I'm gonna kill you, Ian!" Sean wriggled, trying to turn his mouth away from the dirt and dog saliva mashed into the soggy beef hide.

"I'm gonna end you both if you don't cut it out," Laney was forceful, her spatula in hand as she scrambled the morning meal.

She glanced at the microwave's digital display. *Seven o'clock in the morning and I'm already exhausted,* she thought as she continued to poke at the wad of eggs slowly congealing in the skillet.

"Goddamn kids. Can't get a moment's peace around here," she took a break from stirring to contemplate pulling the bottle of Jameson from the cabinet above the stove and putting a little Irish in her coffee. Just the thought of the booze warmly traversing her insides as it journeyed to coat every frazzled cell brought a split second of peace, quickly followed by torment. *I will not cave to the temptation of self-medicating,* she thought as she pulled the bottle of Xanax from her sweater pocket. *I will not drink, I am not my father,* she insisted. *Just half of one, just half to take the edge off.* She popped the pill.

She flipped through the TV channels on the small kitchen set. *Why does the same news report have to be on every station,* she protested internally as she perused. *A few people are sick, it gets hyped, the media incites panic, and violence breaks out. Crap, I sound like my father-in-law.*

"Finally, a local friendly face," the morning news team provided a much-needed sense of familiarity.

"This just in," Cap Bozeman clutched the latest report in his boney hands. "We've just received word dat there's a state-ordered closure tuh-day for all Bay Peninsula county schools due to a health scare."

Laney looked at Cap. "You're the one having a health scare: pretty pale and thin today, Mister newsman."

"No playdates today, I guess Cap," the female anchors blonde hairdo was heavily sprayed and immoveable.

"That's awesome. A few people in the deepest recesses of the world get sick, so they close school here. A few kids get a sore throat... now the boys will be home all day raising hell." Laney dropped her head in defeat. *Best keep to routines*, she thought as she tried to find some strength before summoning her sons for breakfast.

She reluctantly made the announcement, "School is cancelled."

They chanted in unison, working up a lather, "Whoop, whoop! All right, free day, free day…"

"Hush." She held her palm flat, extended in that all-too-familiar stop position. "Would you please go get your sister, it's time for breakfast—and be nice about it." She worried they'd do something to set her off. *I don't need her lathered up too.*

As the boys worked their way toward the staircase, Elle worked her way across the front porch, pulling off her shoes to creep more quietly up the front steps. She winced as the cold wood hit her bare toes. Thoughts of Josh swirled as she cracked open the door. *Amazing night… Mom would be pissed…she won't find out.*

Now perched on the first step, they turned and watched as their older sister snuck in. She was disheveled. Her clothes were crumpled and her long dark-blonde hair was matted and sticking up in the back.

She set the shiny flats on the tile beneath the coat rack then lifted her finger to her lips. She ran her other hand past her throat in a slicing motion.

Ian and Sean nodded; they instantly understood that they should keep quiet or she would kill them.

With a judgmental finger pointed in her direction, Ian jumped from the step, headed toward his breakfast. Sean followed suit, chuckling quietly at the state she'd slunk home in. He added a few obscene gestures as he thrust his hips.

With her hand raised to hit her obnoxious little brother, Elle smoothed her hair as she walked toward the kitchen. With great focus she tried not to look suspicious. Sean ran ahead, wanting to avoid his sister's wrath.

"Boys, did you get your sister?" Laney started toward the front of the house to investigate. "Oh, there you all are."

The kids filed into the kitchen.

"You were so quiet, I didn't think you did what I asked." *Too quiet,* she thought as she served the eggs.

The three Riley children sat at the kitchen table, stoically chewing while Laney stared distantly out of the window. The sun had risen, but the deepening gray of the sky promised snow. Flurries from the day before had dusted the short mountain range that erupted from the back of the property. *I hate the cold and the woods,* Laney thought as she surveyed the landscape. *I miss the city.*

Elle flipped open the laptop and perused the Internet, hoping to further lay off her mother's suspicion by trying to act normal.

The click of the keys brought Laney back from her daydream and drew unwanted attention to Elle.

"Your hair's a mess." She eyed her daughter. "And weren't you wearing that yesterday?" Her irritation was now limited by the warm buzz of the medication.

"I overslept. I just grabbed clothes off of the floor and threw them on when the brats came to my door. I haven't had the chance to brush my hair yet," Elle searched her mother's face for acceptance. *I think she bought it.*

"I think you were out all night. I think you snuck out to see that boy again and your brothers caught you at the front door. I've sent them to get you for years, and they've never completed the task that quietly or quickly before."

"That's crazy," Elle tried to hold her ground. *How does she always know?* She was amazed by her mother's intuition.

"I guess I'll just have to interrogate your brothers, then."

Not wanting to make eye contact with their mother *or* sister, the boys looked straight down into their breakfast as they shoveled quietly.

Elle lifted her feet under the table, poking them both in the shins. *Just a gentle reminder to keep your mouths shut,* she nudged, as she dug the tip of her toes into their legs.

They feared their sister, but they feared their mother more. Elle's punishments were painful but swift. A punch to the arm or a pulled ear were a couple of the tools in her bag of tricks, but their mother, well, she had long-drawn-out punishments that would stick. She went for what really hurt, their fun.

Laney walked up behind the boys and placed one hand on the top of each of their heads, her eyes locked on her daughter. The computer screen was lighting Elle's youthful face as Laney peered at her from behind the boys. She ruffled her sons' hair, Sean's brown locks in her left hand and Ian's blonde in her right. She spoke at the back of their heads, her gaze locked on Elle. "If you value hockey, or video games, or watching television, I suggest you both get ready to talk."

All Sean did was glance, eyes only, ever so slightly to his brother, looking for that familiar agreement to roll on their sister. That tiny movement was *all* their mother needed.

"Uh-huh! I knew it! You were out all night doing god knows what with that boy. Why do you insist on making me crazy? Are you trying to get pregnant and ruin your life?"

"Ahh man, you two and your stupid twin telepathy."

The boys stood mid-shovel and backed away from the table. "Sorry, sis," they vacated the kitchen.

Laney glared at her daughter; the stress of the morning had built quickly. Once again she faced the digital display on the stainless steel microwave, which was mounted above the induction cook-top. With her hands planted firmly on each side of the stove for support, she eyed the numbers: *7:20 and already on the verge.* She studied her reflection in the microwave door. With professionally tousled hair and covered in the finest embellishments available for purchase at the local mall, her polished exterior was no indication of the mess that squatted within. She'd struggled, the last year or so, with some emotional issues. Her court-appointed therapist had suggested she visualize a gauge, "let's call it your snap gauge," she'd offered.

Laney Riley stood in her high-end kitchen, visualizing the needle on her snap gauge, which was already in the orange, as she struggled with the stress of her rowdy sons and the promiscuity of her teenage daughter.

Elle, who at seventeen had the attention span of a gnat, had returned to surfing the Net.

"Mom! Mom, come see this, look what I found on YouTube."

"You know I don't like to watch anything on there, and besides, you shouldn't be watching it either. I think restriction from the computer and a week of being grounded is on your schedule."

"No, really, it's crazy."

Laney approached her daughter. "Move over a scosche would ya', my ass is too big—I'll hang off the end."

Elle slid over in attempt to provide enough bench for her mother's behind. "I can't believe this footage."

"What's that? Oh my... is that a man?"

Mesmerized, they watched what appeared to be an African man in the midst of what seemed to be a series of seizures. He was lying on a dirt road, the fine dust clinging to his skin; it gave him a ghostly appearance. Several villagers had gathered around the poor soul. None of them came to his aid; they just kept their distance, simply spectators to the events that were unfolding before them.

Convulsions ripped through him in waves, every tendon in his body visible as his muscles tensed under the extreme strain of the violent episode. Dark, thick blood began to run from every orifice, cutting a path through the dust on his skin as he shook and flailed. With his back arched and his head thrown forward, he gurgled and groaned through his clenched teeth.

Laney was suddenly overcome with the impulse to shield her daughter's eyes.

"What the hell, Mom?" she swatted her mother's hand away from her face. "I'm seventeen, you don't need to protect me."

"I can't look anymore." Laney shut the laptop. "That's one Internet hoax that's gone too far."

"It doesn't look fake to me." Elle re-opened the MacBook with every intention of viewing the video.

Laney couldn't help but take one more peek herself. *I'm sure if I really concentrate, I'll find proof that it's fake.* "He does seem to really be suffering," she was suddenly uneasy at the thought that whatever was happening to him could be real.

Once again they were sucked in, mesmerized by what unfolded before them. They both watched as he underwent this horrifying and seemingly real metamorphosis.

"You know," Laney began to explain to her daughter, her head tilted to the side as she contemplated, "It kind of reminds me of those lycan movies... like he's shifting."

With his hands open and his palms facing skyward, he lurched and writhed as though he were pleading for divine intervention.

"Is that the sound of his bones cracking?" Elle gawked as his form twisted on the screen before them.

The bent and tensed fingers broke, each snapping loudly under the intense strain of the relentless spasms.

He was suddenly still, his joints bent and locked into configurations now more animal than human. His teeth were exposed to the gums, his mouth drawn into a snarl like some unknown force had pulled back his lips.

"Holy shit!" Elle cried. "You don't think that's what all the talk's been about lately, do you?"

Laney cringed. "Don't let your brothers see this."

Just when they thought it was over, he popped up, lunging forward; the crowd scattered.

Startled, they jumped, the intense moment palpable even through the computer screen.

With great speed and agility, he moved, as he swept a man to the ground and tore into his flesh with his jutted jaw and extended teeth. He snapped, his head popping back and forth from his now distended neck. The camera kept filming as this now-rearranged man mauled an onlooker. Flesh was torn from tendon, as bits of tissue and sinew stretched from prey to predator, each tear followed by a gush of blood.

Unable to contain his horror, the filmmaker gasped with his heavy British accent, "Oh my god!"

The creature, now crouched on all fours, snapped his head, and turned in the direction of the camera. That's when the filming stopped.

"What did we just see?" Laney sat mired in disbelief.

Elle was emphatic in her response. "I think we just saw a guy turn into something and then eat another guy."

"Nonsense. I won't believe it...I can't. It's just a farce, special effects."

"Well, I'm convinced," Elle crossed her arms at her chest.

"Convinced of what," a familiar voice called from the kitchen doorway.

Laney turned to find her father-in-law, the shock of his presence plastered on her face. "What're you doing here?"

Sue Riley, (Nan to the kids) crossed her arms and tapped her foot, already striking her judgmental posture.

Laney eyed her in-laws and then the dog. "Good job, if it was an intruder we'd all be dead."

Spencer was still sleeping soundly, his nose stretched and pressed against the crack under the back door.

"My gut was telling me to flee Vegas. Weird news reports, brownouts, watering bans, felt like they were building up to something, made my ball hairs tingle, I didn't like it. So I packed Ma into the car and started the drive north. I figured if the shit was going to hit the fan, this was the place to ride it out. I mean, could you imagine trying to survive out in that desert once the system broke down. The goddamn highway would be littered with bodies for miles. No water or air conditioning—certain anarchy."

Elle harassed her grandfather. "Is this another one of your conspiracy theories, Pop?"

Now worked up, with his eyes glossed over, he flexed the tendons in his neck while his stiff and wiry gray hair stood at attention. It was unwavering as he flailed and gestured (in his typically violent fashion) while he explained his theory.

"No. You know they never tell you the whole story; trying to control the masses, manage the chaos by keeping us in the dark, only out to save themselves. Why do you think they try so hard to discredit people who've had *encounters*?" His thin but muscular arms tensed as he made air quotes. "And even if they don't discredit them, they make them come off as crazy."

The five o'clock shadow that coated his tanned and wrinkled face darkened the deep creases activated by his overly animated expressions. "Besides, it seems we got here just in time. If I hadn't listened to that little voice telling me my government was lying to me, I wouldn't have been able to get into town. National Guard vehicles were setting up a checkpoint."

"What? What are you talking about? Why would they be doing that?" Laney's anxiety multiplied. *First the video, now a checkpoint, what the hell...* With her hand now jammed into her sweater pocket, she rolled the pill bottle through her fingers, the sound of the powdery white pills tapping against the amber plastic a soothing lullaby for her tired nerves.

"To keep people in, or something else out. Probably whatever illness, or virus, or whatever's been mentioned on the TV lately. Where is my son?" he transitioned abruptly as though it just occurred to him that he wasn't present.

"He's already down in his office. The ever-pressing needs of his job, I guess."

Doolin Riley had left his station in D.C. when he was granted a virtual position to move his sick wife to a quieter setting. So now he analyzed his slice of the bureaucracy from his basement office.

Laney wished he were upstairs now; she didn't think she could deal with the in-laws alone. (They made her self-conscious).

Both rail thin, she felt judged by them for her size and the size of her kids. They weren't fat by any means, just thicker than Pop and Nan who subsisted on coffee and cigarettes.

Suddenly a high-pitched alarm blared from the television, cutting through the momentary lull in the kitchen. Laney clutched her chest, startled by the sudden noise.

"This is the emergency broadcast system. THIS IS NOT A TEST.

Please stand by."

A clock appeared. It began to tick away; its digital numbers flipped rhythmically.

"Kind of cruel to make us wait like this, isn't it?" Elle was now clinging to her grandfather for comfort.

"My guess is some official will appear when this clock is done counting down, and tell us how they plan to protect us from whatever it is bearing down on us." With his hands on his hips, Pop broke into his sarcastic voice, which was just like his regular voice but high-pitched and mocking. "They'll probably say something like "stay in your homes," or "come to us, we'll help you."

Laney glanced at the computer, then at Elle, and then at her mother-in-law who was standing in the doorway, her judgmental arms still crossed.

Her blood pressure began to rise, along with her anxiety. *We did just witness some terrible illness transform a man into something unmentionable. There've been vague reports of illness and some hysteria in the far reaches, but wouldn't they tell us if we should be concerned? Wouldn't someone warn us if there was a situation? Pop is crazy. It's only been what, a few days since the first report. What could possibly move that fast?* She stood quietly as she contemplated, rolling the bottle, until the needle on her snap gauge drifted out of the red and comfortably back into that zone between yellow and orange.

"You should see this video on the computer." Elle beckoned to her grandfather. "It'll make you believe."

"Is that what you were talking about when I walked in—well, make me a believer my dear girl. Show old Pop what the media has neglected."

Elle hit play, once again enduring the horrific transformation, in hopes that her grandfather would believe too.

"Kind of looks like those movies where a guy turns into a werewolf for the first time."

"That's what Mom said, except more zombie than werewolf, maybe." She turned her head to the side while she tried to decide.

"No such thing," Laney was unwilling to accept any such analyses. "There is no such thing; you are talking about movie nonsense. Fiction!"

"Clearly he was infected by something," Pop posited, "who knows what, and, if they do know, they aren't telling us. Hey, maybe there are other videos."

"Yeah, something more clear." Elle quickly typed, hoping to find anything else.

"There, click on that one." Terry Riley was shoulder to shoulder with his granddaughter, eager to see what was next.

"It's the same, but it's so fast, they are turning so fast..." She was suddenly terrified. Elle looked to her mother, concern plastered on her young face as she watched those things attack and their victims spring up just moments later, they themselves now changed.

"This isn't just an illness... some freak occurrence. This is meant to spread. It's the form they've taken, the neck...the jaw... they are built to bite, to transmit. This is intelligent design." With a shudder Pop nodded, sure of his observation.

"Design by whom?" Laney had to doubt the theories of her father-in-law. He was notoriously given to bouts of conspiratorial whimsy.

Nan shot her a look of disapproval, clearly defending her husband.

"Don't start with me." Laney was now on the defensive herself. "I refuse to entertain you when you're hostile."

Nan stood, arms crossed, her signature scowl laser-pointed toward her son's wife.

Trying to ignore the rift between his wife and daughter–in-law, he explained who was responsible. "Nature, science, the goddamn government, who knows; but they are perfect machines, designed to attack, to bite, to spread." He reiterated his earlier observation.

"Didn't a guy recently get high on bath salts and then try to eat someone's face off on the street?" Laney was still trying to rationalize any scenario but the one they were faced with.

"Yeah, but you have to admit," Elle continued to plead her case, "it seemed like he died, right? I mean he convulsed and stopped breathing before he popped up. The way he was crunching, you'd think every bone was broken; how was he still moving?"

"That's what I saw," Pop interjected. "I mean, Christ, he, he was more creature than man by the time he jumped up." With the palm of his right hand he vigorously rubbed his bristly hair. "Looked like a howler; I don't know what explains that." He stood with his hand to his gaping mouth, for once in his life speechless. "One more time. I have to see it one more time, just so I can really absorb it."

Chapter 4
In the Zone

"I'm filing a complaint with the University when we get out of here," Lance clung to Dory. "Why would they let these goons come in here and manhandle us like this? And what's with the cameras?"

"Based on the faces I see in here," she paused as she scanned the auditorium, "The University had nothing to do with what's going on here. The Dean of Admissions is over there looking as perplexed as we are. As far as the cameras go, looks like they are setting up for a press conference. Minus the press, I guess. It's really just cameramen. It doesn't look like any reporters are here champing at the bit. I'm starting to feel a little irritated."

Lance whined, "Yeah, we've been sitting here for over two hours already, what are they planning to do with us?" He dug in his ear nervously as he mined for comfort. He swirled the waxy findings between his thumb and index finger, and then placed them under his nose and inhaled deeply.

Dory pulled away in disgust, losing what little respect she'd had for him. She sneered through her clenched teeth, frustrated by the lengthy wait. "What situation could warrant the military to sequester the University staff? What the fuck is going on?"

Just as she was about to leave her seat to approach Davies to go another round, a parade of people crossed the platform.

Lance watched two rather decorated officers take a position in each corner. "Looks like they're ready to get started."

They stood at ease, eyeing the crowd as two enlisted men rushed around, positioning the podium and a glass of water.

As the stage was set for Steve and his presentation, he camped in the lounge, sharing a moment with Mr. Mathers.

They were cuddled on the small sofa, its deep green a nice contrast to the red and brown of the brick walls, which displayed the age of the University with style and grace. Above the sitting area hung a painting of a grassy field. The hue of the foliage coordinated with the sofa, and its heavy wooden frame paired well with the wood of the other furnishings.

"Nice room isn't it, Mr. M. Very suitable for distinguished guests." Steve gripped his beloved's chin, as he looked deeply into his green eyes. "Well, this is it. I didn't think this day would ever come, but here we are, and I'm ready. I'll tell them what they need to hear and am prepared to do whatever necessary for us to see this through."

As the governor sat next to his counterpart and rubbed his back, he held another one-sided conversation (commenting for both himself and Mr. Mathers) while Deck stood guard at the door.

"How do I look?" "Fine, how do you like those new pants?" "Yeah, I like them. They're sporty." "I'll be lonely while you're out there, find me a companion."

"Will do."

Deck rubbed his forehead in disbelief. *This guy is something else. I can't believe he's an elected official.*

"Deck?"

He approached. "What is it, sir?"

"Pick someone from the audience to come and comfort Mr. Mathers. It's been a long morning and he's frazzled. I don't want him to be alone while I save all of us."

"What about one of the soldiers, they're already on the payroll."

"They make him nervous, too brutish, too much gear, choose someone who looks, well, you know what I mean... the opposite of you."

"Will do, sir."

Deck emerged from behind the curtain and stepped to the edge of the vast stage. He peered into the crowd, his hand above his brow, briefly catching Dory's eye.

Oh my, she thought. He was massive, at least six four, sporting a wide, muscular physique. His dark-brown hair topped a symmetrical face and chiseled jaw line. His dark-blue eyes scanned skillfully, taking in everything. *He's twice the man Lance is.*

While Dory eyed him, he eyed the faculty, searching for the perfect candidate. *Too bitchy, too old, too anxious... ahh, a meek geek,* he thought as his gaze landed on Lance. "You," Deck barked. "You in the second row, meet me stage left."

"I think he's pointing to you," Dory nudged Lance.

"No, it's you. It's you, he's pointing to you," he argued.

"Let's go, polo and glasses, I've got a job for you," Deck insisted.

"Ahh shit," Lance groaned quietly as he stood, "I don't want to."

"Let's go sir, a little faster. What's your name?"

"Lance, Lance Sisto."

"The governor needs your assistance, Lance."

Dory whispered. "Did he say governor? I'm really freaked out now. We must be up shit's crick if Steve Landis is holding us here.

"Did you just say 'shit's crick'? You really are becoming one with the local people," Lance slipped through the seats toward the aisle.
"Promise you'll come looking for me if I'm gone too long."

"Will do," she gave him a nod.

Dory looked up; she gave Deck a nod too.

Passing her a look of indifference, he backed up and turned to meet Lance. *Why would a woman like that be with this weasel*, he wondered as Lance approached.

"Follow me," he waved him backstage to the small lounge.

Lance swallowed hard, his hair on end as he followed Deck into the unknown.

Steve raved as Lance entered the room. "Excellent choice, he'll do nicely!"

Lance surveyed his surroundings. The governor was sitting on the green leather of the lounge sofa, with Mr. Mathers tucked tightly in his side.

The governor's enthusiastic demeanor confused Lance. "What's going on here?" He needed clarification.

"Oh, I realize this is sort of unconventional, and my relationship with this fine fellow is extraordinary, but he requested I find someone to stay with him, and I sent Deck and he chose you. Don't let anything happen to him. Keep him happy." The governor rubbed Mr. Mathers, who was now stretched out and chewing his nails.

"I'm going to take my notes and head to the podium." He ran his hand over his companion one more time. "Wish me luck," he requested of the Oriental short hair, before answering "thank you" and giving Mr. Mathers, one last nod.

Lance's jaw practically scraped the floor as he eyed the cat. "What the hell?"

Deck shrugged. "I know it's weird, but regardless of how bizarre your encounter just was, you will diligently sit and care for this fine fellow as if he were your own."

"Was he asking it questions, then answering for it?" Lance couldn't believe what he'd seen.

"Yes, but regardless of the governor's bizarre attachment to his unlikely companion, you are now in his inner circle and will act accordingly as far as he is concerned." He nodded in Mr. Mathers' direction. "I was weirded out at first too, just keep it to yourself."

"How long?" Lance had moved on from the shock induced by the behavior of his governor.

"Until I come to relieve you."

"My girlfriend might get worried."

"You and her?" Deck looked Lance over, skeptical that a woman like that would entertain a guy like him. "Well, I'll let her know where you are. Stay here."

Deck returned to the stage, thoughts of how ridiculous his life had become rolled through his mind, *governor's companion...fine fellow, I sound as crazy as he does.* He motioned to Dory.

"What is it?" She approached the left wing.

"I've assigned your boyfriend with a delicate task for the governor; he's in the back lounge. I imagine he'll be relieved from this temporary duty when the governor is done here today."

"Although I appreciate you telling me where he is, he isn't my boyfriend." She was adamant in her disclosure.

Decks tone was dry. "Yes, it did seem unlikely, but who am I to judge."

Dory eyed him then asked, "What's your name, so I know whom to blame if he turns up dead?"

"Ash Decker."

"Well, Ash, I'm keeping my eye on you." She stared at him until she reached her seat.

"Pssst, Pssst," Steve motioned to Deck to approach the podium.

"I'm ready to begin. Is Mr. Mathers comfortable, did he seem pleased with his attendant?"

"Yes sir."

"Excellent, let's get started."

Steve raised his hand.

The lights dimmed over the crowd. Silence fell heavily as the quiet chatter of the forced audience, ceased in nervous anticipation of what was about to occur.

A screen was lowered, and a map of the Bay Peninsula was projected. The land formation jutted into the waters of Lake Paramount to the north and Empire Lake to the south. The two waterways met at the peninsula's southeastern point. The Grand Traverse Bridge spanned the straights and connected the peninsula to the southern part of the state. The Transnational Bridge spanned a second narrower waterway at the northeastern border.

Above it was a definition:

Pen·in·su·la / noun

> **A body of land surrounded on three sides by water.**

"Hello, fellow Northerners. For those who don't know me, I'm Governor Steve Landis, and standing behind me to the right is General William Hatch, Commander of joint separation operations with the National Guard, and to my left is Colonel Harv McGovern of the Paramount County Militia."

General Hatch stepped forward and gave a nod. He was an imposing figure. Six foot four, and straight up and down, his physique was toned and lean. His high and tight was salt and peppered, and his stern gaze reflected a lifetime of service.

Colonel McGovern wasn't quite as polished as his Army counterpart. His hair was a little longer, he was a little softer around the middle, and he didn't share the general's height. But he had a pitiless glint in his eye that set the tone for his personality.

The governor continued, "I realize you're all a little unnerved by the actions taken here this morning, but I assure you it's for the best. The free-spirited, no-nonsense attitude held by the fine peoples of this northern peninsula is well known, and it is that very spirit I'm here to appeal to today. We are facing a serious threat from abroad, and as I am here speaking to you it is crossing our country's border and running rampant. I'm sure you've all seen the reports about illness and violence. Well, it's all true, and more. What the reports neglect to tell you, is that the illness causes the violent attacks, turning the healthy immediately into a host with only the desire to further spread the disease.

I am here to propose a plan that will ensure the safety of us all. As of this morning, I have declared martial law. The National Guard will be assisting me in separating this fine peninsula from the land mass to our west and ultimately creating a safe haven for us from what lies beyond. Colonel McGovern and the militia will assist with security and guarding the border."

The captive audience, already on edge, now shifted in their seats as they whispered amongst themselves.

"Ahem." Steve cleared his throat, his signal that the chatter should stop. "With the help of General Hatch and Colonel McGovern we handpicked a team that earlier this morning demolished the Grand Traverse and Transnational Bridges, removing our connection from the land masses to our east and south."

A collective gasp escaped the lips of all in attendance.

"With the demolition already concluded, we must now dig, finishing our separation from the land to our west. Given the lack of time needed to break us off from what is coming, one-third of the peninsula will have to be sacrificed. Instead of separating at the state line, we will excavate a trench from the west side of the highway here, south from the shore of Lake Paramount in Iron Bay, all the way to Empire Lake, ending in the town of Brookside to our south."

He pointed, highlighting the respective areas and the roughly sixty miles of land on the map projected overhead. "You can see that the land between the two bays is narrow and therefore a more feasible border than the one we share with our westerly neighbor. A watchtower and footbridge will be constructed every four miles for the guard units. Thankfully, our location is remote, and our outlying populations are small. General Hatch, Colonel McGovern, and myself feel most confident that those details will buy us some time while we construct our western border. School is cancelled, indefinitely, and all flights suspended, forever. From this moment on, no one from outside of The Bay Peninsula is allowed in; we are now static. Some rules and regulations will be broadcast, and informational kiosks will be located in each town center in the Static Zone. Please remain calm and in your homes. With a little cooperation, we'll all get by. I will allow a few questions."

The quiet chatter once again broke out; people swiveled in their seats to discuss what they'd just been told.

"What about the university students: Where have you placed them, and what if they want to return to their families abroad? Many are from out of the area."

The governor searched the crowd. "Who asked that, please stand up and state your name."

"Sheldon Marsden, Dean of Admissions." The insipid figure was as bland as his gray suit.

"Well, Mr. Marsden, the students have been instructed to remain in their rooms or held in the cafeteria just as the faculty was held here. As for being from out of town, or outside of the Static Zone," he pointed to the new territory highlighted on the map, "we'll allow people to cross into the Western Outlands for the next twenty-four hours. People will be allowed to leave however they see fit, starting immediately, bike, car, etc... Buses from the commons, at the center of town, to the border will be provided every hour starting tomorrow morning at six for those without transport."

"But what about the locals whose homes fall outside of your Static Zone?" Mr. Marsden's home was well outside of safety.

"Just as you may leave, you may cross into the Static Zone from the Western Outlands. Those citizens who find themselves outside of the zone can come to the closest checkpoint with proof of residency, and board a bus to the shelter that is being erected in the Paramount Dome here at the university."

"What gives you the authority to make these decisions!" Marcy Schmidt, the dining manager, shouted as she jumped up, her ample backside bouncing in unison with her massive breasts. "How do you know we're in danger? You're just the governor of one state, what makes you think you know?" Veiled with perspiration, her face was now the same beet-red as the large flowers on her blouse. She shouted and pointed her finger forcefully in the governor's direction. "I want some answers, we all want answers!"

"Yeah!" random shouts broke out.

"Well, I'm the governor, president of this state. My associate and I have long had a disaster plan in place, not knowing what or when, but knowing when the day came we would be ready. I may be *just* the governor of one state, but that gives me certain connections and I assure you, my actions in the last twenty-four hours are warranted, and have saved the lives of everyone now lucky enough to be in the Static Zone."

"Governor Landis, Dory Wells, grad assistant. How is it that you just happened to be the governor when the world decided to go to shit; isn't that a little too convenient?"

"I understand your skepticism; it probably seems like I've gone mad with power, but I assure you, the federal government wasn't going to act swiftly or with enough force. May I remind you of disasters from our past that have gone mismanaged. The U.S. border has already been breached. Based on my political connections, I still would've enacted a plan with the cooperation of whoever might have been governor at the time. Believe me, this is not just some mad plot I've hatched for my own entertainment." He tapped the cover of his survival guide. "I assure you that I'm acting in all of our best interests. I know you look at me and think I'm "the man" and I'm forcing your hand, but "the man" is the U.S. government, and believe me, it's in a chaotic freefall, and if we don't act, we will all fall victim to this terrible plague. We're no longer in Iron Bay. The government structures once in place and the boundaries once respected no longer stand. The life we all knew is over. This massive restructuring is designed to save us. Tomorrow when the border at the Static Zone's western edge is closed, we will need to work together to survive. We will restart our lives, and rebuild for a strong future. Thank you, no more questions."

Governor Landis closed his beloved brown book, tucked it safely under his arm, and departed. He stepped behind the curtain at stage right with the General and Colonel McGovern close behind.

They crossed the hall, and settled in one of the staff offices. Leaning on the desk, Steve briefed his chief officers on their current dilemma.

"We need a small crew, hand-picked by your best troops already on the inside. The regular grunts can handle crowd control and general day-to-day logistics, but we need a small unit to help handle thinning the heard."

"We are undermanned for that undertaking, uh, undertaking," McGovern joked; a smile crossed his usually austere face.

Hatch sniped, "Lovely. I enjoy your sick humor. Must be a real morale-booster for the militia. Can we be serious now?"

McGovern crossed his arms and nodded, his lips tightly sealed.

"It's an ugly business...Thinning. Whoever is chosen will have to want to survive over all else, or just lack all human decency." General Hatch speculated, "Perhaps some of these local guardsmen will be persuaded by the idea of keeping their families in electricity and food, while the rest of the world perishes in the dark."

McGovern jumped in, "Well, I know a few of the militia guys are survivalist nuts. They'll see the sense in limiting the drain on our precious resources. Even when the coal has run out and the food storage is depleted, survival could go on as long as the natural resources aren't tapped dry."

The governor made a suggestion, "What about Davies? He's been a real leader, keeping control here at the school while we rounded everyone up..."

Hatch shook his head. "No, not a good fit. He's a real boy scout, everything by the book."

The governor gazed from general to colonel and back again. "That's disappointing, but sounds like you two will enact suitable strategies for the acquisition of our Thinning team. We need to act fast, I'm sure lines have already started to form at the border checkpoints."

Hatch looked to McGovern, knowing now was the time. They needed to try and reason with Steve, streamline his grandiose plan.

"We would like to discuss with you the feasibility of some of your strategies. We have a few ideas to help simplify, thus stretching resources."

"Yeah, we can't possibly build a tower every four miles. You're talking fifteen towers, with drawbridges... I saw the plans... it will take months. The build is too complicated. We need something simpler. Also, there aren't enough men. We need at least four guards per tower per shift, three shifts a day, and that's at eight hours per, that's too long to be out in the snow when it's twenty below." McGovern was getting agitated, his demeanor unable to remain calm. Diplomacy was never his strong point.

"I think what he means is we need to focus more on the University, and the settlement here. It has its own power plant, we can use the coal from the city's plant to keep the U hummin' for a long time, especially if we cut power to all outlying areas. Maybe we build a tower every ten miles with a camp in between. The specs you sent us for roving units and snowmobile patrols, it's too much. Too many men, too much fuel, too many resources... just unreasonable."

"Nothing is impossible. Nothing I want is unreasonable. We've known each other a long time. You knew my father, your father knew my great-uncle, we go back a long way. Our families have been connected for decades. You know how important it is to me to follow my uncle's plan." Steve held up the book. "You know what it meant to him."

"Yes. And I agree it has its merits, but his plan was smaller, geared toward himself and very few others. What you want, this utopia, it's unsustainable."

57

McGovern watched Hatch and Landis as they sparred, Hatch getting a little hot now that he could see there would be no reasoning with his friend.

"Not to mention, the uprising you face when the fine citizens of your Static Zone get tired of struggling while you enjoy their fuel and food. Don't forget that confiscation, or as you like to call it, acquisition of supplies, is also on your list of to-do's. How many men will that take?"

"I'm sure you and McGovern, with all your military might, can manage. So, some men have fled, fewer mouths to feed. So I dream big; all successful people do. If you'd excuse me now, I have planning to do with Mr. Mathers."

Oh my god, Deck thought as he listened, his back against the closed door of the office. *Thinning? Thinning the herd. He said sheeple at the bridge. Sheeple is all they are to him. I'm working for a madman.*

Just as he contemplated dashing, the door opened, and the governor headed for the lounge. "I've had enough for the day. I just want to sit with Mr. Mathers and plan our apartment."

Deck followed him across the hall.

Lance was curled in the far-right corner of the green sofa, obviously cowering from the cruelty of Mr. Mathers, who was stretched out and methodically licking blood from his front paws, one and then the other, indifferent to the terror he'd inflicted on his sitter.

Deck handed him a tissue from the end table.

Lance proceeded to dab his scratched cheek.

The governor scooped up the cat and placed him over his shoulder. Slowly, he ran his hand over his gray and wrinkled skin. The feline nuzzled as he pressed his pink nose into Steve's ear.

With a coo he coddled the cat. "There, there, Mr. M, I missed you too."

Lance watched in horror as the governor massaged the fiendish thing, sweet nothings whispered into its pointed ear. "Did you watch me on the TV? What did you think? Yeah, it went well, I think so too."

With his question and answer session over, he turned his attention to Lance.

"So, Lance, as my assistant I'll need you to do odd jobs... laundry, cooking, care of Mr. Mathers from time to time..."

Lance was flattered. *The governor called me his assistant.*

"I also have some personal items I need set up. A few of my militia guys are delivering them, but I need you to oversee the execution. Find a space that will serve as an apartment. Maybe something nearest the nicest office."

"That would be the University president's office."

"Excellent! I trust you can make that happen. You look very capable. Nice polo, by the way. Daring color choice." Governor Landis knew all too well that he could make Lance his minion through flattery (he'd seen his type before). *I can get him to do anything with a few well-placed compliments, all sycophants have the same buttons to push, and that will come in handy.* Steve was pleased as Lance's ego began to swell. *I've got you now.*

"Show me to that office," he adjusted, as he hoisted Mr. Mathers back over his shoulder. "I'm ready to set up our new life." He walked as he rubbed the cat's back.

Lance practically sang as he led the odd couple out of the door. "Right this way."

Deck followed, waiting to make a run for it when the opportunity presented itself.

Dory was lurking outside of the lounge door, wanting to intercept Lance but he walked by as though she weren't even there.

"Huh, well, how do you like that?" she was perplexed by the cold shoulder.

"What's going on, Ash? You look like you've seen a ghost."

"We have to get out of here," he whispered from the side of his mouth.

"I knew it! He's a megalomaniac. I knew it, I knew he was evil. I could see it on his phony face. We need to warn Lance."

"Lance is smitten... lost to the allure of the governor's stature. Forget about him, we need to save ourselves."

With his eye on the group in front of them, he secured the perfect moment and grabbed her sleeve, pulling her around the corner and down the corridor. Their feet slapped at the commercial vinyl flooring, the subtle checked pattern running diagonally as they ran for the door.

"Where do you live?" He tugged her along, his swift pace only inhibited by his need to keep looking back.

She glanced too, "What are you afraid of, no one is following us."

"They will be when he realizes I know, and I'm not on board."

As they slipped through the door, progress was halted by a couple of guys from the guard unit carrying furniture.

"Oh shit." Dory hid her face in Deck's chest, her words muffled behind his sport coat. "That guy knows me, we had a run-in this morning."

"Yeah, he's one of the regular army. I saw him talking to General Hatch." Deck decided to shield his face as well, his nose now nestled in Dory's hair.

Oh my, she thought, her legs feeling a little weak as he nuzzled her, their fake moment feeling like more than a cover.

"You two get out of here," Davies walked by. "No loitering, take shelter."

"Will do," Deck shielded his face, his hand raised to muffle his voice.

With the men now out of sight, they continued to slink through campus, trying to make it to the city trails.

"The whole place is cut off. How do they expect you to get out of here, with that blocking the way?" She pointed to a large concrete barrier, backed by barbed wire and guarded by an armed patrol. Her yellow Tracker was imprisoned just beyond.

"Let's just keep moving." Deck once again tugged at her sleeve.

Chapter 5
Foul-Mouthed

"I'm not getting on a goddamned bus, controlled by the goddamned government! They'll probably drive us straight to the fucking gas chamber!"

Nan shot her husband a dirty look.

"All right, all right, I know, I need to simmer down...watch my language." Trying to check his behavior, Pop moved on to his granddaughter.

Elle scribbled frantically as she recorded the information streaming across the screen.

With one of his generic cigarettes squeezed between his lips he asked, "Get it all?"

"Yes, everything, Pop."

"Holy shit! Holy shit!" Doolin Riley bounded, climbing the stairs two at a time to emerge from his basement office. His hands were planted atop his wavy brown locks. His usually calm demeanor was flustered, but this had no affect on his attractive, outward appearance. Five' ten and fairly fit for a desk jockey, he was a nice match for his petite but pretty wife. "Did you see that broadcast? I can't believe... Holy shit!" he exclaimed again as he came face to face with his father. "What are you doing here?"

"You're gonna tell me that with everything that's going on in the world, you're surprised to see me. You've only been here, what, a little less than a year, and you're already are as oblivious as these locals."

"I was born here, remember. I'm just local by birth, I guess. That's not important right now," Doolin redirected. "We're on the wrong side of the highway. We need to pack up and find somewhere to hunker down. I don't think we should trust those buses."

"What did I just say," Pop threw his hands up. "Like father, like son."

Doolin stopped to welcome his parents, giving them both a large hug.

"Well, I have just the place," Pop patted him on the back, his attempt to reciprocate the warm greeting. "I have a cabin about five miles south-east of town. I bought it in the early eighties, right before we were reassigned to Washington, D.C. I knew this place would offer me shelter if the world went to shit. I've been saving it for a rainy day."

"I didn't know you were born here, Daddy." Elle was surprised. "I just thought Pop was from here or something, that's why you knew about it."

"No, I was born here when Pop was working out at the military base. We lived here for almost ten years."

"You were in the military?" The boys were impressed. "That's cool. Did you ever kill anyone?" Eager for a yes, they bobbed their heads up and down.

"Something like that," Pop didn't offer that his job was specialized and Cold War–fueled.

"Well, it's probably a wreck. The elements and wildlife have probably ripped it apart by now." Laney was flustered and about to dissolve into a full panic.

Her once-tidy appearance was as undone as she was. The layers of her hair now pointed every which way, its direction coaxed by her constant need to bury her fingers into the golden strands, palms to the scalp, and pull straight up. She wasn't pulling it out, just continually running her fingers through it, as though the repetition was somehow soothing. Her blue eyes were glossed over, coated by a combination of fear and anti-psychotic meds.

"Ahh, that's where you're wrong; I've been paying a cabin-keeping company to watch over it. Ma and I have even vacationed in it a few times over the years."

Laney looked to her mother-in-law, who was now at the breakfast table peering at them from behind the paper. She nodded, a gesture meant to confirm her husband's statement.

"What now? I, I don't know what we should do," Laney stammered as the panic took hold. Her meter had now swung wildly into dangerous territory. She placed her hand on the pill bottle in her pocket; its existence settling her nerves.

"Breathe, hon, take it easy." Doolin tried to soothe his anxious wife. "Try to hold it together, we don't want to have a relapse." He was acutely aware that she was losing it.

"Okay, okay." She placed her hands on her thighs as she bent over and breathed deeply. "Boys, go with Elle and gather some things, your sister will help you pack. Elle, make sure they have clothes. You know, underwear, pants, sweaters... Don't leave it up to them; they'll pack a snorkel and a change of socks." Laney joked from her bent position, "No one needs a snorkel in November to kick off the apocalypse."

"Take a look at this," Pop flipped through the news channels. "Nothing but chaos, from the East to West. There are reports of attacks along the Southern border and the Eastern seaboard."

The television flashed footage of crowds in select cities at the country's Southern edge fleeing with cars piled at intersections, looting and vandalism were rampant as panic ensued. Several major cities out East reported riots and mass chaos.

"This just in," the anchor announced, his usually pompous attitude diluted by manufactured concern. "A plane on arrival from Heathrow just crash-landed at JFK. Our New York affiliate is on location now."

"Yes, Chris, I'm here just yards from the tarmac. As you can see, a crowd has gathered, curious as to the cause of the situation. The crash is visible, with a debris field several hundred yards long. Smoke and flames are still billowing and rescue crews are en route to the aircraft, which is still obscured by the blaze and its resulting smoke cloud."

"Are there reports of any survivors, Charles? Can you see anyone?"

"No, Chris, as I said, smoke and flames are obscuring our visual, no, wait, I see someone. A figure has emerged from the smoke. Oh, oh my! It's a man, he seems to be injured. I think, yes, I think he is limping, and it would appear that some limbs

might be broken… his face is blackened by smoke… maybe burns. I think, yes… I can hear him groaning. "

The cameraman zoomed in, the injuries now nationalized and larger than life, his groaning and gurgling punctuated by clicking reminiscent of gum snapping.

"Well, that's exciting, Charles. It seems there are survivors after all."

They all gawked as he inched closer; the cameraman kept his lens focused. Desensitized and clueless, the crowd stood and watched as this twisted and broken man, teeth exposed to the gums, head thrust forward, (like the angled neck of a toothbrush) clicked and crunched his way toward them.

"The passenger is still moving toward us, Chris. He seems undeterred by his injuries. Blood is trickling from his ears and eyes. It would seem a few good citizens are running to his aid."

The camera panned, sure to capture every juicy detail.

"Hold on, man, we'll help you," one of the onlookers called as he ran toward the survivor. "Stop moving, we'll come to you," another shouted, as the three men ran unsuspectingly toward danger.

"These good Samaritans have just made contact, and holy hell! What the fu..!" he exclaimed, letting the end of the word trail off, still aware that he had an audience to cater to.

As Charles stood speechless the crowd lurched backward, screams rang out, as the camera became jostled; the survivor mauled the good Samaritans. His head swung forward violently as he snapped, his teeth distended. One of the men had fallen to the ground and was convulsing violently, while the others tried to fend off the attack, fleeing into the crowd. Already bitten, they too fell, convulsing violently as the crash survivor lunged, snatching his next victim.

"**Charles, Charles, what are we seeing?**" Chris asked from the safety and calm of the studio.

"**They are shifting... turning!**" Charles shouted over the roar of the ensuing panic. "**Animalistic... the cracking, I can hear the bones cracking! Oh my god, he's lunging... his legs are bent, almost canine in configuration.**"

"**Whose legs? The crash victim's? Charles? Charles?... We seem to have lost him. Please stay tuned.**"

"Let's turn that off and get out to that cabin," Doolin clicked off the T.V. "Best get moving, based on that bit of news. Pack all the food, toiletries, medicine... and I'll stop in the basement for a few necessities."

Laney was burdened with denial as she dug deeply for any kind of urgency. "I'll grab a few things and meet you in the van."

Frantically, she shoveled baby pictures and a few key pieces of clothing into her bag before she ran out to the driveway where the boys were already waiting.

"Good morning," George from next door lurked as she loaded the Town and Country. "Well, for a few more minutes anyway." He looked at his watch.

Laney grimaced, her back to the neighbor as she shut the tailgate. She dreaded the thought of turning around.

George was a stout man, middle-aged, with a strange yellow pallor. His round head came to an egg-like point and his squinty eyes seemed to struggle to open all the way from behind his wire-rimmed glasses. *Indication of his lack of intelligence*, she thought.

She took a second to muster a bit of consideration for him. She didn't think telling him to go screw himself while performing obscene hand gestures would go over very well.

"Hello." She faked a smile as she turned toward the exasperating little man. Standing on a small hill held back from her driveway by a short retaining wall, he weaved back and forth, his hands at his hips.

His no-doubt putrid breath rose in a white vapor as he spoke into the cold morning. "Off to practice?" He flicked his right index finger in the direction of the van.

"No," she wondered how he was unaware of what was going on. She was terribly annoyed by him and his lack of character.

He and his wife had moved next-door mid-July and Laney found him irritating immediately. Something about his personality clashed terribly with hers; the needle on her gauge floated into dangerous territory whenever he was present.

In fact, it was her inability to deal with irritating people like George that warranted court-ordered therapy in the first place.

"Can't believe October is over... and it's almost Thanksgiving. Where does time go?"

She worked to maintain her temper. "It does seem to fly by." She grinned smugly through clenched teeth, *not fast enough when dealing with you.*

"Just bought this new grill," he pointed toward his back yard, the finger once again wagging strangely. "You and the husband should come by sometime, I'll que' you some dinner."

"Yeah, that sounds good." She waited for him to get to it, certain he wasn't interested in small talk. *I bet he's laying the groundwork to borrow the mower.* She glanced at her wrist to fake as though she were checking the time: a subtle cue that she wanted to go. *If only the twins were acting up,* she thought. *I could use them as an excuse.*

Unfortunately for Laney, *this* was the *one time* they decided to sit peacefully in their seats.

"I see you gotta run." George flicked toward the van.

She found his constant use of bizarre finger movements as irritating as she found him.

"I was hoping to borrow the mower."

Finally, I knew it, he's such an ass! Her thoughts swirled angrily. **You just purchased a new grill, not to mention the two ATV's and the trailer you had delivered a few weeks ago; in fact, George, you've lived in the house for nearly four months, and still haven't found the time or money to shop for a mower, but have had plenty of both to purchase toys! Plus, it's November, everyone has stopped mowing, THERE'S FROST ON THE LAWN!**

Laney composed herself as she turned and walked toward the garage. With her movements sudden and deliberate, the small bits of snow lining the drive swirled as her boots hit the ground. She backed the mower out and pushed it toward the end of the driveway.

George came around and met her.   "I shouldn't need it too many more times, I imagine the weather will turn soon and none of us will have to mow any more."

Laney looked around at the bare trees as her breath swirled in the cool November air. *Did he just allude to its continued use? And does his car still have out of state plates? How does he get away with it? It doesn't matter, Laney,* she told herself, *you are fleeing this side of town because of some sort of epidemic, just let him use it.*

George continued to blather about whatever other nonsense he felt was necessary in order to rationalize his continued use of his neighbor's lawn mower.

She wasn't listening; she'd drifted into a trance. She had checked out.

Laney was now standing in the warmth of the summer sun. Her face turned toward the sky, as her nose caught the smell of the freshly cut lawns. She hummed a pleasant tune... and mowed George over. She backed up and gave his torso another pass, the blades grinding as they bumped over the hideous character. The rumble of the motor combined with the tune in her head drowned out his

screams as the blades diced him into small, manageable pieces.

A barrage of honks from her minivan interrupted her little daydream. She snapped to, and realized she was smiling widely. Worried it was a repeat of the last incident, she looked around to make sure she still had her hands to herself and George hadn't been assaulted in any way.

It wasn't that long ago that she'd had a break from reality, and while in the trance, actually acted out. Relief washed over her when she realized she hadn't actually tried to run George down.

"Hey, Doolin."

George's greeting went momentarily unanswered as Doolin trotted down the driveway afraid his wife would snap and assault their neighbor. He dropped the bag he'd packed in the basement and made haste toward his fragile spouse.

"Hey, George, he answered quickly, only interested in Laney's state of mind. He looked around as their other neighbors packed frantically, obviously aware that they were all on the wrong side of the zone.

"Uh, you all right, hon?" he leaned in to breach her line of sight.

She smiled flatly at her husband's concerned face. "Good, I'm good."
She turned and walked toward the car.

"Guess you need to get going," George offered as Ian honked.

"Let's go," Sean was excited about their upcoming adventure. His tone was tinged with impatience as he flailed his arm in a backward wave, its intention to draw his father toward the vehicle.

"Looks like you got some company," George flicked his finger toward Pop.

It's a miracle she didn't snap it off, he thought as he watched his neighbor's index finger wag.

"Yeah, my folks came to town. Listen, we'll be gone, so keep the mower; we won't be needing it anymore."

"Are you sure, where you going?" George's question was hollow; he was just thrilled by his score.

"Across town." Doolin was amazed by how obtuse his neighbor could be.

"Are you kidding me?" He had a gullible smirk on his rotund face.

"If you don't know what's going on already," Doolin motioned to the hectic pace of all their neighbors, "that's really the joke here."

Unable to continue the exchange with George, he turned and walked toward the car.

"I'll just be keepin' it, then," he called to Doolin's back as he walked away.

"Who's that idiot?" Pop gestured in George's direction.

"Just our new neighbor. He's irritating as all hell, but harmless enough. I think Laney is actually chemically angered by him... pheromones, but ones that cause hatred."

"I can see that. I'm irritated by him from here," he took another drag of his cigarette. "Who mows the fucking lawn at a time like this, and in November no less. Well, he'll figure it out, or he won't, but right now we just need to worry about us. Based on the chaos building in this neighborhood alone," he waved his hand erratically to draw attention to the pace at which his son's neighbors were loading their cars, "I think we should take the van as far as traffic will let us and then hike the rest. I don't trust the governor and his plan. And I'll be **God Damned,**" he swiveled his head in all directions, being sure to catch anyone within ear shot, "if I'm getting on one of their fucking buses!" He gritted his teeth, his face now red as the tendons in his neck flexed again.

"Let's load it up and get moving," Doolin shouted, trying to wrangle his mother and daughter. Nan and Elle slowly exited with Spencer close behind.

"Please, take your sweet-ass time, we're not running for our lives or anything," Pop used his command voice to motivate the dawdlers. "Move it! Move it! Move it!" he barked with his cigarette waving.

"Jesus, Pop," Elle rolled her eyes, his approach unappreciated. Nan gave her husband a glare as she took a seat in the Town and Country.

"What?" he asked his now-miffed wife, "No naughty time for me later? The baby door is closed?"

She stuck her tongue out at his vulgar response.

"Holy hell Pop, gross!" Elle was repulsed by her grandfather's innuendo.

"What, you think the stork brought you?"

"Doesn't mean I want to hear you talk about you doing it with grandma."

Sue shot her granddaughter a look, displeased at being called the "G" word.

"Sorry Nan." Elle went back to looking at her phone.

With food and baggage packed to the roof and the crew all strapped in, Doolin pulled slowly from the driveway.

The Rileys watched the house as they crept backward; they were all acutely aware that this moment would forever be marked by the crushing trepidation they felt.

"We're never coming back? This is it?" Laney trembled as they pulled onto the street.

Doolin responded gently, "Yes, I think so."

His wife smiled, her emotions confused as tears ran down her face. She turned her attention to their dense neighbor, who was preparing to mow his snow-dusted lawn. With the button to the power window pressed beneath her finger, she breathed deeply. The cold seeped into the opening as she cupped her hands to her mouth in a makeshift megaphone. "Fuck you and your weird finger, George!" She slowly rolled up the window as her middle finger wagged wildly in his direction.

Doolin shook his head in disbelief.

Pop congratulated her. "Might as well resolve old issues. Shouldn't hold onto stuff like that."

The boys looked at each other and grinned, greatly entertained by their mother's foul mouth.

Elle was, as usual, oblivious to the world around her, the phone planted in her hands.

Laney watched, tears streaming as her dream home slipped from view for the last time. Purchased with the life insurance left to her by her father, it felt like she was losing him all over again.

Doolin (Dooley to his family and friends) was a sensitive guy, keyed into the feelings of his wife. With one hand on the wheel and the other on his wife's knee, he tried to soothe her. "I'm sorry, hon. I know this is a lot to handle. We'll get to Pop's cabin and try to regroup. Find a routine, okay?"

Getting a little sick of being coddled, she thought, as she nodded in agreement, unable to speak as she held back the sobs of anger. She may have seemed sad, but that emotion had ebbed and was making way for fury. With her gut now twisted in a knot, her hand darted for the sweater pocket, which housed the coveted pill bottle.

She rolled it, and her anger ebbed as she gripped the cylinder in her hand.

"And I'm sure this won't be important to you right now, but I'm really proud of how you handled yourself back there with George. I hate that guy and his weird finger. I barely got out of there. Even I want to smack the shit out of him."

Laney smiled, her grin wide as she agreed with his feelings. *I won't tell him about my violent daydream or that I wasn't sure if I'd acted on it or not.*

She looked back at her children and took a second to be thankful that they were safe and healthy. The boys were quietly playing Gameboy, while Elle tried to text her boyfriend.

Now out of the neighborhood, they followed a steady stream of traffic. Cars, trucks, and trailers, piled high with gear of all sorts, inched southeast toward the lakeshore. "Can you believe this," Doolin threw his hands in the air. "We're held up, it's gridlock."

"Guess everyone's on the same wavelength," Pop's head and shoulders pivoted as he swiveled out of the large back window to survey the landscape. "Hey! Hey!" he yelled again as people looked out of their vehicle windows, his shouts clearly governing their attention. "Don't get on the buses. I guarantee it's a trap!"

"Just heading to camp... safety in the woods," one traveler assured him from the window of his red Ford pickup.

"Shut up Pop." Laney was embarrassed by his behavior.

"What? I can't warn these citizens that they are driving toward extermination?"

"You don't know that for sure."

"Uh, yes I do. The hair tingling on my right nut says I do. This might be a bad time to bring this up, Dooley, but did you remember the—extra bag?" He lifted his eyebrows as he said each word, being sure to non-verbally stress which bag he meant.

"Of course, but what about this." He motioned to the chaos.

"We'll walk it."

"I guess we're walking it." Doolin's eyes were on his wife as he exited the vehicle.

"All right!" the boys exclaimed, "Cross-country trek!"

Elle griped to her brothers, "You're so irritating. Who says that, and who would know to say it at the same time?"

Grinning at each other with confidence, they answered in unison, "We would."

"What?" Laney chimed. "We're just gonna abandoned our car? I love my car. This is my mom-mobile... my dream car." Laney pouted. "It has heated seats," she whined as she walked back to her husband at the tailgate.

Doolin tried to rationalize. "Pop left his car... and he loves his car."

"Of course Pop can leave his car, it's twenty years old. You can't even tell what color it is anymore."

"It's green," Pop interjected.

"This is just a van." Doolin placed his hand firmly on the Town and Country's silver exterior. "What's more important, surviving or stow-and-go seating?"

"Stow and go," she returned to the passenger seat.

Vibrating with anger, her hands trembled as she reached down to grab her tote bag when the glint of the boys' aluminum bat caught her eye. Wedged under the passenger seat since the end of the season, its very existence, at this stressful time, caused her great irritation. Now projecting her ill feelings on her sons, she slipped into a dark place. *I don't know how many times I told them to take this outta here.* She gripped it, her snap gauge swinging wildly.

The cold alloy met her palms and transported her to a cathartic place. She took a short swing, "Oh my," she gasped, suddenly rapt by the power she felt as she clutched the bat. Now in the depths of a violent daydream, she was shut off from the reality around her.

Wielding the bat she dished some justice to fellow hockey mom Liz Keating, who, last season, pulled out in front of her while she changed lanes improperly at the entrance of Northern Bay University. This maneuver caused Laney to swerve, running the curb. She'd narrowly avoided an unsuspecting pedestrian.

Liz exited her car and stood behind the door of her white Audi, her large designer sunglasses obscuring her pointed face. With one simple phrase, spoken in her signature snotty tone, she sent Laney into an emotional frenzy. "Watch where you're going!"

Now, with the chance to do it over, she wouldn't go home and stew for days; Laney would enact some justice.

She swung without warning, and split Liz's skull. Again and again, the aluminum met her cranium, punishing her vapid rival with impunity.

Liz's son screamed as he watched his mother's gray matter dribble onto the black top, her blood now splattered across the pearlescent coat of the pretentious sedan.

Elle looked up from her cell phone, curious as to the tune her mother was humming. "What song is that?"

Laney didn't respond.

"Mom! Mom! Laney Riley!" she finally yelled.

"What? What do you want?" Her trance was broken and the bat was now over her shoulder.

"What song was that?" Elle asked again.

"Song?" Laney was confused by the question.

"Yes, you were just singing a song, what was it?"

She spoke angrily. "I wasn't singing. Now, stop fooling around. Put your phone away and get the dog."

"But I can't reach Josh," her attention span was short and already diverted from her mother's catchy tune. "It's like the Internet is down or something."

"Lines are probably overloaded, not to mention the possibility that services have already started to shut down."

"You're a real ray of sunshine," Laney snapped at her father-in-law, still capable of protecting her children even while on the verge of a psychotic break.

Doolin was worried as he glanced around at the nameless faces inching toward the unknown. "Let's all just get our stuff and get going. We have a long walk ahead of us, and I want to be out of sight before tensions rise and people get desperate."

"Let's just take a moment to grab something from the bag, Dooley," Pop suggested with an eyebrow wag.

"Good idea." He met his father at the back of the vehicle for a private chat, the bag the only other attendee.

"Nice stash," Pop admired his son's firearm choices. "Kel Tecs PMR30, fantastic! Thirty rounds plus one in the chamber, less need to reload."

"I've got a stash of rifles, but these will travel better." Dooley checked the clip and stashed the gun in a shoulder holster under his jacket.

80

Pop did the same, "The holsters are a nice touch. Wouldn't want to keep this thing down my pants, might damage my favorite toy." Armed and ready to roll, he stepped from behind the vehicle. "Let's get humpin'."

Sean giggled at his grandfather's terminology. "Pop said *humpin',*" he nudged his brother.

He educated his grandsons, "That's a military term for a long walk, it's not just what the dog does to your leg."

"Lets dip into the woods and follow the trails to the highway. We should try to avoid crowds. Hopefully the traffic back here will be minimal." Doolin stepped off of the road and climbed through the ditch to a swath of forest that separated the street from the nature trails. The trail system was well established and groomed by the city. It would provide a less visible way around the crowds.

Pop followed his son, "Lucky there isn't any snow yet. It sure makes traveling these trails easier. I thought there'd be more by now. Couldn't believe how dry it was on the way up."

"We had a long, warm autumn. The temp just started to dip down this last two weeks. Hell, it was sixty on Halloween. We couldn't believe it."

"Means it's gonna be one hell of a winter." Pop now marched with his mind on the weather. "I lived here for a decade, and every warm autumn brought record snowfall."

Laney, bogged down with gear and stress, needed a goal to focus on. "How long will it take to walk there, Dooley?"

"Probably two hours, maybe three, depending on obstacles. I think we'll try to cross the highway and continue down the path along the lakeshore once we get past town. Don't worry, sweetie, we'll be there and safe by dinner."

Chapter 6
The Gas Chamber

"We need to discuss Landis."

"You mean his need for an extravagant apocalypse?"

McGovern knew that was what Hatch meant.

"I say we give him what he wants right here. Make it seem like it's done, and adjust in the field. He'll never know. He won't leave the U, let alone town. He'll never be the wiser. We won't build as many towers, we won't dig the trenches as wide or deep—we'll cheat."

"Roger that." McGovern was in full agreement. "I'll pass the word to the leads in the field."

As the decision to deceive Governor Landis was made, the men selected to manage the Thinning had arrived.

Hatch returned each salute as they filed in, their respect paid to the officer in charge.

Now at attention, they stood, waiting for Hatch to begin. "At ease, you may take your seats."

McGovern moved to the back of the room where he leaned against the wall with arms crossed. Only two of the twenty-plus men were militia; he wasn't surprised. Many of the militia guys had taken to the woods and the rest weren't interested in getting into bed with the establishment.

"You've been hand-picked because you possess the fortitude to do what needs to be done, and lack the moral indignation that might keep you from completing the objective. Consider your acceptance of this task a promotion. You have been elevated to the rank of the inner circle. For your diligence, you and your immediate families will be given sanctuary in the Static Zone settlement located at Northern Bay University. Many others, as you already understand, will not be so lucky. You will notice that a few of the original recruits are missing. They decided they couldn't go through with it. Loose ends and loose lips will be dealt with harshly and swiftly. We cannot risk word getting out; we don't need an uprising on our hands. Quick and quiet." General Hatch lifted his hand from the table and motioned to the twenty-five people in the room, "This mission begins immediately. The objective needs to be met in a timely and discreet manner. No unnecessary personnel are to be allowed into the area of operation. Any breach will be cleared with the deletion of the problem. To avoid the unnecessary neutralization of our fellow soldiers, be diligent in your efforts to keep the regular troops away. Please report to the team lead for your operation briefing. Dismissed."

The men stood and saluted before reporting to the adjacent room. A brief walk along the rounded second-floor corridor led them to the classroom slated for the meeting.

Desks sat in tidy rows and faced the head table utilized by the instructor. Beyond the table was a window that looked out onto the field. The dome of the university's sports-plex had several offices and classrooms tucked along the perimeter with a large athletic field in the center. The largest wooden dome in the world, it made for quite the command center for these military heads.

While General Hatch and Colonel McGovern discussed logistics with the other officers, the team was briefed on the Thinning protocol.

A man greeted them from his position at the head table. "If you don't already know, I'm Master Sergeant Brady. I will provide you with the information needed to successfully complete this mission." Brady ran his hand through his brown, thin hair. With a stern brow, he continued the briefing, his dark, serious eyes setting the tone.

A dry-erase board leaned on an easel with an illustration that depicted the buses and their alterations to provide them with a visual.

"The school buses, which have had the windows and emergency exits sealed, will collect the subjects at the border checkpoints and then transport them to the dome.

"On arrival, they will be waved through the gate, which will be guarded, and is separated from the docking area by concrete barriers. The exterior guards are regular army, and aren't members of the inner circle. They are under strict orders not to enter the A.O. Once the bus has been successfully docked, here inside the Paramount Dome," Brady motioned to the large window that over looked the athletic field, "the driver will prepare to depart by instructing the passengers to stay seated until called. While he is doing that, a canister will be placed under the bus and a line will be run through a port in the floor beneath the driver's seat. When the driver is clear, the door will be sealed and the bus will be filled with hydrogen cyanide. Once the passengers have expired, they will be loaded into shipping crates and submerged in the lake. Their vehicles and belongings will be inventoried and stored for later use if possible. All other items will be disposed of. Lake Paramount is just one klick from here, making disposal convenient. Any questions? Martin, go ahead."

Martin was ruthless. He was a dangerous ex-marine, ate up about being in the militia. He was perfect for doing dirty work.

"What is our recourse should the passengers make a run for it or try to break a window?" He stood and mimicked taking a shot, his imaginary gun mowing down everyone in sight.

"Gunshots will be hard to explain. Threaten, but only fire if it is the only means of control. This is a ruthless job, but one that needs to be handled delicately. Be purposeful, but be as considerate of their situation as possible. They shouldn't realize what's happening, until it's already too late. Anything else?" The men sat stoically, informed and prepared. "No more? All right. Break into five teams, and select a lead. Let's thin the herd."

"Sergeant Brady," McGovern called from the hall, "now that you're finished with the briefing could you please join the General and me in the other room?"

"Certainly, sir." He crossed the hall.

"We have a problem. Landis just sent word that his driver bugged out after our closed-door meeting at the University. He is worried that he *knows* and that's why he fled."

"Who was this guy? How'd he get so close without being vetted?"

"He was a recent security hire, the state's choice. Landis said he just happened to be on duty when the shit hit the fan. The General and I both know that Governor Landis, although fraught with resources both tangible and political, is indeed a little nuts, so this won't be the only loose end we'll deal with before this is over."

"I'll task a team to round this guy up, sir."

As Brady exited the General's office, Martin waltzed by, hell-bent for the john.

Martin is perfect, he thought. *The last thing I want is that guy dealing with people in the last moments of their lives. I'll keep him busy on a wild-goose chase.*

"Got a minute? I have a special task for you."

"Can we talk about this in the latrine, I have the heat." He gripped his abdomen, a clear indication that diarrhea was imminent. He trotted, unzipping his trousers as he walked.

With Martin now tucked in one of the stalls, Brady tried to task him with the search for Deck between groans and splatters.

"I can grab somebody to take a look, ahh man, sorry, so sorry," he apologized, his bowel movement now bordering on legendary.

"Jesus Christ man, what did you eat?" Brady was now shielding his nose with the lapel of his uniform.

"It's the chow... MRE's never agree with me. It's going to be a long apocalypse for my colon."

"And for your roommate. Are you married?" Brady suddenly felt sorry for his wife, if he had one.

"No, single. Like to play the field. Well, liked. Slim pickin's these days." His admission was followed by another gastric blowout.

"I'd really like you to take the lead on this. I'll leave the info on Decker in the briefing room. Grab a partner and patrol together. I'll check in."

"Will do," Martin groaned, as another spasm rocketed through his intestines.

Brady exited the men's room, gasping for fresh air in the hallway.

Chapter 7
On the Trail

*I*n any other situation, Dory thought as she walked the bike path toward the south side of town, *I wouldn't just tote some strange dude blindly toward my apartment, but I guess this is no longer a world where typical is a consideration... He felt really good.* Her memory of their close encounter was making her blush.

She glanced up at Deck, then ahead at the winding trail before them. The brisk afternoon air crept through the large knit of her cream sweater as the weak November sun lit the branches of the bare trees with a warm orange glow.

Lulled into a false sense of security by the seemingly pleasant stroll, they walked, almost able to pretend it was just another day.

"Oh my... Holy shit!" Deck clung to Dory's shoulder for support.

"Oh, he's a big one." A large skunk scurried over the path in front of them. It meandered, its striped tail twitching as it investigated the surroundings.

"Shouldn't it be hibernating?" Deck watched the creature, his nose tucked inside of his shirt.

"I would think so. I think they're nocturnal as well. Maybe he was displaced by the governor's excavation."

"Makes sense, turned out by construction of the border."

"Maybe we should have a talk about a man of your physical stature, and, no doubt, military training, being afraid of a little skunk." She found his childlike fear of the smelly but harmless woodland creature endearing.

"That is *not* little." He pointed to the skunk as it rooted near an upturned tree.

"How much farther?" Deck rubbed his arms for warmth as they tiptoed past the smelly obstacle.

"Not too much. My place is just on the south side of town. If we could cut through and take the sidewalks, it would be a little quicker, but the paths and trails meander; it adds time."

"I just don't think we should trust the established routes. He's up to no good." Deck wanted to stay out of sight.

"Do you think he'll really exterminate people? Maybe you misunderstood."

"No. I know what I heard. He was briefing his military heads. He said the Thinning, like it was an operation title, well, because it *is* an operation title. At the bridge he said *sheeple*... that the masses were sheeple. We're just cattle to be slaughtered."

"We need to warn people." Dory was sickened. "We can't just let them walk right into the governor's trap."

"What do you suggest? Going from car to car. Or maybe, start a whisper campaign, hands cupped to ears? They'll catch us and then we'll be eliminated." He exhaled, feeling stifled by the situation.

"Let's just sneak up to the last intersection in town, it's just a few blocks from my place, and see what our options are. We can't just let that nutbag get away with this." Dory hoped her traveling partner would see it her way.

"Just recon? I could go along with a little recon. But we don't act unless we have a clear plan."

Dory nodded. "Agreed. Are you going to try and get home, wherever that is?"

Deck sighed, his eyes darting from tree to tree while he decided what to say. Finally, with his eyes fixed on the path below, he answered. " My parents are gone, passed, you know, so I don't even know where home is anymore. I tried to get a hold of my sister when I left the military, but she'd moved. Funny thing is, the neighbor said they moved out here somewhere, but all of this happened before I could track her down."

"And she didn't tell you where she was going? That's harsh."

"She's mad at me, but I really hope she's someplace safe with her family. What about you?"

"I tried to call, before you snagged me back at the University. The lines were busy. I thought I'd head home, try to get downstate by going west then south-east, you know, the long way now that the bridge is totaled. But my car is trapped at the school, so now I'd have to hotwire something to get outta here. I don't know, my heart says run home, but my gut says stay put."

"Well, let's check out the situation. At the very least it will provide a distraction from the worry we feel over our families."

"Yeah, a distraction might be nice... you know, you're pretty sensitive for the beefy military type." She stepped over and playfully bumped his arm with hers.

"Yeah, I guess," he shrugged.

"Do you hear that? We must be close." She stopped their progress.

"Digging, maybe radios." He strained to listen to the sounds that drifted over the berm separating the path from the tree-lined hill below.

"Wait here." Deck hopped the path's edge and dropped to his stomach. He crawled, keeping low as he approached the crest of the hill.

"What can you see?" she spoke in a loud whisper.

He lifted a finger, a signal intended to keep her quiet.

Unhappy with that answer, she too jumped the berm and shimmied to his position. "Look at all the cars."

A steady stream rolled into the busy intersection, many headed out of town and into the forest, others, straight for the buses.

"They think they're all headed for safety." Deck shook his head.

~~~

As Deck and Dory were distracted by the mass of humanity that scurried below, Martin and his cohort got the drop on the target.

"It's him," he had a copy of Deck's file photo in his fist.

"Hey, you there," a voice called, accompanied by the distinct sound of a weapon being cocked, "Up and at 'em."

"I think they found you," Dory held Deck as they got to their feet.

"You are both to come with us," the armed goon commanded, as his sidekick frisked them both.

"Oh, look what I found, can't let you keep this." Martin took the 9mm and tucked it in his pants.

Deck observed, surveying the situation and all the variables. *Can't risk Dory being injured, shouldn't go for their weapons. I need a place to cause a diversion.*

"We will continue to the nearest checkpoint," his rifle was now in Deck's back. "No funny business. I don't want to drag your dead bodies out of the woods, you look heavy." Martin tapped Deck's shoulder with his weapon.

Deck and Dory walked hand in hand with the armed men close behind. "I'm scared," she squeezed his fingers tighter and tighter.

"I know, it'll be okay."

She looked into his face and realized he was plotting.

"Quiet, no chitchat," the ends of the rifles met their backs once again.

The stroll was no longer pleasant. Their ability to pretend was now destroyed by automatic weapons. Each step felt like an eternity as they reached the city walk.

"I see your bus."

Martin's joke was met with silence as they approached the checkpoint.

Cars were lined up for blocks. Whole families, people young and old, waited to be herded onto the Iron Bay school buses. The noise was stifling. Construction, crying babies, honking horns... Crowds of people were amassed and lurching toward the intake where the buses sat idling. Funneled by the lines of cars, the once-pleasant citizens of this rural peninsula were now seething, hateful, desperate people. It was clearly now every man for himself.

Deck took it all in, feeling confident that their armed goons were finding it difficult to keep close in this skittish crowd. *They can't possibly hear us,* he thought, wanting to pass his plan onto to Dory.

"All these people," Dory sniffed. "We're all going to die."

"We're not, not today. Follow my lead." Deck put his plan into action. "Oh my god!" he shouted. "Oh my god, that guy is sick!" He pointed into the crowd, trying to make a scene.

The horde of already lathered citizens shifted as they panicked, engulfing Deck and Dory, and separating them from their captors. Martin and his partner struggled to regain control. With rifles held high, they squeezed through the mob and toward their prisoners. Awash in a sea of scared and frustrated citizens, Martin struggled to stay on his own two feet as he watched them drop into the crowd and duck out of sight.

On hands and knees they crawled, hiding under vehicles and weaving through cars using the throng of people to escape their situation.

"We have to tell them!" She inched out from under the SUV currently providing cover, unwilling to escape before at least trying to warn them.

"It's a trap, the buses are a trap," she did her best to explain to the family in front of her, pleading with the frazzled woman, "You'll all die if you go." Afraid they'd lose their places in the queue, no one listened to the warning.

"You're just trying to trick us... to cut in line. She's trying to cut in line!" the woman focused the anxiety of the crowd onto Dory.

All in earshot snapped in their direction. "Come on!" Deck pulled her as he strong-armed the people in the lurching mass. The swarm pulsated, as they pushed against one another in a chaotic dance.

Deck trudged with forced until the crowd thinned and they were able to break into a run.

Gunshots rang out as Martin tried to quell the hysterical crowd. Everyone hit the ground, opening his field of view.

"Shit, they're gone." He shouldered his rifle.

"No matter. Can't imagine they'll try anything. Let's get outta here. These people are going to stand up and eat us alive."

The roar of chaos dissipated as Deck and Dory fled, each step putting distance between them and certain death.

"Holy shit. Oh, holy shit." Dory's breaths were rapid as she tried to gather herself. "I can't believe they're going to fall for it. As an anthropologist, well almost, I know people, and these northern folk are resourceful and far too independent to take the word of some stuffed suit from downstate."

Deck shook his head. "Did you see the look in their eyes? They were wild, lost to the panic. We barely got out of there alive as it is. They're lost... clearly lost."

Dory blanked, she couldn't linger on the topic of the buses, her brain wouldn't let her. "Did you know they call all the people from downstate trolls?"

"Why trolls?" He was eager for the answer.

"They live below the bridge."

"Huh, not anymore; I was there when it was demolished."

"Well, at least we didn't end up herded into the death mobiles with cattle prods." She was still catching her breath. "Sheeple prods, I mean."

Deck glared, her humor unappreciated at this time. "Where do we need to go? It's cold and I could really use a drink." His outstretched hand shook, his nerves were shot.

"At least you have your sport jacket on. I was ushered out of my office this morning without my coat or purse. Luckily I keep my I.D. and my bank card on this lanyard." She pulled a long cord from inside of her sweater. Dangling at the end was a holder that displayed her school I.D. on one side and her check card on the other.

"Although, the way things are shaping up, neither of these things will probably matter anymore."

"No government, no taxes," Deck smirked.

"That's a bright spot. Won't miss that," she agreed.

"Won't need this anymore." He had his cell phone in his hand. "Hasn't worked since lunch." He tossed the once-cherished and valuable device.

"So, if you look two streets in," she pointed, her apartment now visible, "I live in the one with the yellow door. I keep an extra key under the mat."

"Let's move." He waved his hand and snapped his fingers forward.

"If we're going to be holed up together during the apocalypse, or whatever this is, you'll need to teach me your signals," she mocked him, swirling her hands around nonsensically.

"Smartass."

"Better than being a dumbass." She falsely lightened the mood as they tried to cope with what had just happened.

Deck gave a short military answer, "I concur."

Maybe being stuck with him isn't so bad after all, she decided as they crept closer to her place.

"We'll need to rest then get equipped, find someplace more permanent to hunker down. I'm not feeling very secure about being in town. They said stay in your homes, but I don't trust anyone anymore." Deck had been in a bad situation or two in his time, and this definitely qualified.

"Why can't we just wait it out in my apartment?"

He patted her on the shoulder. "Big picture? We are talking about looting, food shortages, no water, no power or heat. Town will become a war zone at best. At worst, Mr. Landis will clean up and conserve resources for himself."

"No way. I can't believe these people would turn on each other, or stand for being bullied by the governor."

"People will do anything to survive. What did we just witness at the checkpoint? People crazed with fear and greed. The need to be saved overpowered all sense. I've seen it first hand. Men are capable of anything when they feel pushed and threatened. Even if folks around here are outdoorsy—resourceful, they'll be forced back into town when food runs out or medicine is needed. No one had warning. If they had months to prepare, perhaps everyone could stay tucked out in the woods indefinitely, but time was short and supplies will be, too."

"There are a few rental cabins just outside of town; they're managed by the guy who runs my building. We could sneak out there and see if one is empty. They're usually summer rentals... vacant this time of year. Probably secluded enough to hide in."

"That'll do," Deck assured her as they reached her door.

She rummaged under the mat for the key.

"Charming." Deck pointed to the small rug at their feet. It read, "Nice Underwear!"

She smiled as she opened the door, unapologetic about her smarmy welcome mat. "Sorry about the mess, I wasn't expecting company. Of course, I wasn't expecting it to be the end of the world today either. There's a few beers in the fridge if you're still thirsty. I'm just going to run in the back and grab some clothes."

"Okay." Deck strolled to the fridge, its avocado exterior plastered with magnets. "Huh," he chuckled; the menagerie was clearly an attempt to camouflage its dated color.

"My god, for a girl that fine she has a terrible diet." He was amused by the food that lined her shelves. Bologna and American cheese, leftover pizza, "Is that sausage and pepperoni?" He raised his voice, curiosity gnawing at his insides. "You work out a lot?"

"No, good genes I guess."

"Lot of junk food in here." He shut the door.

With the beer now in hand he took pulls from the bottle as he admired the eclectic decorating style of his new friend. She had photographs of places far and wide, villages and tribes, mountains and jungles, a plethora of people and places unvisited by the average traveler.

The pictures were displayed in frames with no rhyme or reason, big and small, mounted to the wall in a collage of anthropological glory.

Deck plopped down on the sofa, its cushions a welcomed comfort after the last eighteen hours. He ran his hand over the tan microfiber as he admired her colorful abode. The curtains and throw pillows were a blend of Eastern themes. "Looks like you bought out Pier One."

"Yeah, some of it, the rest I picked up here and there on my travels."

Deck stood and followed her voice. He walked slowly as he admired more photos along the way. "Is this your dad?" He approached the bedroom door, a family picture posted to its left.

"Yeah, that's him." He was tall and lean; she obviously inherited her structure from him.

"Great car." He admired the old Ford he was posed with.

"Family heirloom, I have it in storage downstate."

Deck turned and glimpsed her through the crack in the door. She was dressing, her bare back to the hallway. *I should look away,* he thought, his feet not responding. She began to turn and he quickly stepped away, silently sprinting back to the sofa where he sat, his legs crossed, trying to pretend he'd been there longer than he actually had. He took a long drink from the beer.

"Wanna get me one of those while I dig for some flashlights and outer wear. I could use a bottle of suds myself."

"Will do." He was relieved she didn't notice he was peeping.

"I've got a few clothing items left over from my last romantic mishap. He was a big guy, not as big as you, but close. Maybe you could find something that works. It's all in those shopping bags in the hall closet. He never came back for it, and I never got around to dropping it off at Goodwill."

Deck placed his beer on a cork coaster shaped like an elephant. It was nestled on the teak tray that served as the coffee table top, which was placed upon a large wicker trunk.

Dory was still collecting supplies while he perused his clothing options. "I think this sweater will fit, and these jeans might be a bit tight but better than the pants I've got on. Luckily I wore my good work boots; they look a bit dressy, but they are designed for running. In my line of work mobility is important. Can't run down someone in tasseled loafers."

"Not to mention how ridiculous you'd look in tasseled loafers." Dory recalled Lance's affinity for the hideous shoe choice. "You're more the steel-toed type."

"Yes, I am."

"I know you mentioned resting, but if we got going, we could reach the cabins before dark. Want to just push on?" She zipped the bag of necessities closed.

"Yeah, better safe than sorry. Does the path we were on get us out of town?"

"It leads to a trail system that cuts through the woods, and then to the lake shore." Dory packed another duffle with food while she gave directions. "A tunnel runs under the highway connecting the two. Maybe they haven't reached it yet. It's still a ways down."

"That's perfect. We'll take the path to the trails. We should avoid main roadways, they could still be looking for us."

"Pull that sweater on and let's go," she handed him a hat and gloves.

"More leftovers from the old boyfriend," he pulled them on.

"Yep." She placed the bag of food in his hands and walked out the door.

"I really enjoyed the photos of all the places you've gone. How many years have you been traveling?"

"Eight. I went on my first trip junior year of high school. My world history class took a summer trip to China. I stepped foot on the Great Wall and was hooked. I traveled every year after that, fascinated by distant places and the people who lived there."

Dory locked the apartment door and stood a moment, looking at the words on her welcome mat.

Aware she was dealing with leaving her life behind, Deck tried to distract her, "You're well traveled for someone your age." He tried to make conversation as they walked. "I, too, have seen my fair share of distant and exotic lands. Of course I wasn't there studying."

"Killing?" she raised her eyebrows.

"Extracting... sometimes peace-keeping," he offered.

"Oh, is that what they're calling it now...this way." She waved as they came to a fork in the bike path. "If we go right we'll end up on the wrong side of the highway... outside of the Static Zone."

"Well, we wouldn't want that." Deck followed as she veered left, past the tunnel that led under the highway.

"People bike this? Some of these hills are treacherous." He looked to his right at the steep drop to a rocky valley below. The large round boulders were covered in a bright green moss that contrasted with the orange and browns of the stark autumn backdrop. Trees lined the winding paths and crept down the hillside, their bare branches providing improved visibility.

"Yeah, hike, bike, ski, snowshoe, anything but motorized vehicles. Some of these trails are really only meant for the seasoned rider. I wouldn't want to bike out here." Dory cringed as she eyed the drop.

"Did you hear that?" he threw his fist up, apparently the sign to stop and listen.

"Didn't we already have a talk about you and your hand signals; I don't know what they mean." She slapped down his hand.

"Look," he hit the ground taking her with him, "I see something, people... kids I think."

"Don't run so far ahead," a woman's voice shouted from somewhere in the distance. "God damn it! Stop running!"

"It can't be," Deck whispered from their position on the ground.

"What? What is it, Ash?" she watched him, his face now twisted in a bizarre configuration.

"I think those are my nephews, and that is my sister yelling for them."

He stood. "Sean! Ian!" the boys were only fifty yards away, positioned on the path below him.

They stopped to look around, scanning the bare trees above for the mystery voice.

Just as Deck cupped his hands to his mouth to shout again, his sister emerged, no longer shielded by the hill.

"That's her, holy shit!"

Ignoring his own safety he dropped, sliding down the steep hill, through the trees to the path below. "Dilly!" he shouted. "Dilly, it's me!"

Dory ran, taking the long way down not feeling brave enough to scale the face of the hill like her partner had.

"Ash, is that you?" Laney had her hand over her eyes to cut the glare as the light fell through the barren trees.

"What are you doing here?" He threw out his arms and clung to her as she clung to the bat, the security of it hard to part with.
"My god, I was so worried when I couldn't find you."

The boys were clinging to his legs as their dad approached with Pop at his side.

"Holy hell, imagine meeting you here. What brings you to the north woods? Shouldn't you be in some hellhole somewhere fighting terrorism?" Doolin was happy to see his brother-in-law and vigorously shook his hand.

"Gave that up when I realized I missed my family. Went to D.C. to find you and tell you all about it, but you were gone. Thanks for letting me know where you were, by the way."

Doolin looked at his wife with concern. "We did send a letter to whatever 'stan' or 'bad' you were stationed in, but let's not get into that right now."

Laney was still holding it together, but barely. Her eyes had welled up; the tears were ready to spill as her bottom lip quivered.

"How?" she asked. That one word escaped her trembling lips as tears now glided down her cheeks.

"I got a job with a security company and the governor happened to be my latest assignment. So, here I am."

"Where's the governor?" Pop scanned the area for his presence, his hand on the grip of the pistol nestled in his jacket.

"Had to leave his employment. He was ..."

"Uncle Ash," Elle squealed as she rounded the bend with her Nan. She lunged at him, her arms now tightly wrapped around his neck.

"He was a megalomaniac," Dory jumped in. "Hi, Dory Wells." She waved eagerly, pleased to find a safe group and happy to see Deck reunited with his sister. *Careful, girlie, don't go getting feelings at a time like this,* she warned herself.

"We should get going; it'll be dark soon. We can catch up when we get to the cabin." Pop continued the walk.

He led the way, their line now two people longer as they wound their way through the woods and along the dirt trails that cut through the small mountain. *As if we weren't moving slow enough already*, he bitched internally.

"Are we there yet?" the boys dragged their feet. "We're cold."

"Almost." Doolin was agitated; the weight of the weapons had started to wear him down.

"Let me help with that." Deck took the extra bag off of his brother-in-law.

"Thanks, man. Uh, be careful with it."

As soon as he grabbed it he realized what it contained and why it was so heavy. "Guess we're prepared for anything." He hoisted the bag over his other shoulder, the food on one side the weapons on the other. "Good thing we have these, I was relieved of my firearm back on the other side of town."

"That sounds like an interesting story, why don't you tell us about it as we hike, it will..." Laney was cut off by Pop; he was tired of being slowed down.

"Why don't you shut your pie holes, conserve air, and walk. You can talk your lips off when we get there."

Now silent, they marched with purpose and made time, quickly nearing the forest that lined the lakeshore.

"Shhh." Pop raised a fist, his arm flexed, twisted in a halt position. He dropped to the ground; his hand gesture suggested they all do the same.

Bellies down, they ducked amongst the moldy fallen leaves. The earthy scent of the dropped foliage filled their nostrils, as they lay with their chins in the damp mulch of the forest floor. A thin layer of frost seeped into their clothes as their anxiety swelled.

What's happening, what's going on, Laney's eyes darted around trying to survey every angle as the men conversed.

"What is it, Dad?" Doolin crawled to his father's side.

"There." Another family was winding through the woods.

"I'm sure they're just trying to get to safety like we are. Wait, I think that's the Shaws; they live across the street from us. These trails connect to our neighborhood, maybe they just walked out."

"Yeah, come to think of it, I saw him eyeballing us when we were packing up, I remember because he was wigging me out a little." Pop adjusted as his ball hairs twitched.

"Don't be ridiculous, they're good people."

"None of us are good people anymore." Pop reached down and raked.

"It's true." Deck crawled closer. "Dory and I were almost mobbed today by the good citizens of the Static Zone. There was a panicked desperation in their eyes... a madness."

He's calling to us, he wants something... he's up to something, and the guys know it. Laney's mind wandered from one bad thought to another as she drifted to vivid visions of bat-induced violence. She reached for the pill bottle, and twisted the cap open inside of her pocket. She slowly slid the chalky tidbit to her mouth. Its bitter taste was a welcomed reminder that peace was just minutes away.

"Is that you, Dooley?" Shaw called from the adjacent path, his position just a hundred yards off. "I can see you."

Doolin stood and motioned to his family to do the same.

"Oh, it's just you, Jim. Can't be too careful right now, everything's uncertain."

Mr. Shaw held his family back, wanting to approach alone. He'd already bridged half the distance when he decided to break into a jog.

I knew it. I won't let you. Laney clutched the bat and tucked the boys behind her. "Go, get behind me, get behind Nan." She took another step forward, ready... willing.

Pop tried to enlighten the eager neighbor. "Whoa there, Jim, slow it down, it's a dangerous time to give someone the wrong idea."

"No, it's all good, just wanted to ask a question out of earshot of the wife." He was out of breath and pointing, his spouse and daughters still positioned on the adjacent ridge.

"What is it?" Doolin wanted to help if he could.

"I want that green duffle, you know, the military one filled with guns."

"You're outta your mind." Pop placed his hand on the PMR, the metal warm to the touch from being in his jacket.

"I saw you today. I saw you arming yourselves on the road." He held out a small handgun. "It's just me and them, no one else, no other men, or weapons." His gaze was cold, "I've already drawn. I could shoot you both before you even get those out of the holsters." He pulled back the hammer on the .22 revolver, his grip steady.

"Motherfucker!" Laney cracked him on the hands. He was so focused on Pop and his holster; he didn't see her cocking the bat.

The gun flew from his grasp, and he was brought to his knees by the force of the blow.

With a shriek his wife's voice echoed across the valley. "Jim!"

"Die, you bastard." Laney cracked him in the head. The aluminum sent a shock wave through her forearms as she nailed him again and again.

"Oh, Christ!" Doolin pulled her from behind, his efforts one blow too slow. Jim was unconscious and bleeding as he twitched on the damp and frosty ground.

"Sweet Jesus. Sweet ever-lovin' Jesus. Nice swing!" Pop turned and set his sights on getting to the cabin. "We needn't waste any more time on him, Laney sure took care of it."

The boys peered at their neighbor from behind Elle. "Is he dead? Did Mom kill him?"

"No, he's just knocked out; sometimes when you're knocked out your extremities twitch." Elle had learned that when her boyfriend and his buddy choked each other unconscious—of course, they weren't bleeding profusely from the head.

"He'll wake up with a headache." Elle rubbed their hair, hoping to erase whatever damage was done.

"Oh my god," Mrs. Shaw wailed as she ran. The little girls were close behind, their tiny frames trembling as they sobbed heavily.

She dropped to her knees. Her hands shook uncontrollably as she ran them over his still body. "What have you done, you crazy bitch! Jim! Jim, wake up." She rubbed his face; her hands smearing the blood from his cheek. "You bitch! You crazy bitch!"

Laney lurched and pulled free of Doolin's grasp.

"Shut your mouth, lady, or you're next." Her pitch was shrill as she charged, her bat at the ready.

"Mommy!" The tot squealed, as her large brown eyes pooled with tears.

The tear-filled eyes provided Laney with a looking glass. She glimpsed a monster, twisted and hideous, wielding a bloody club.

Laney lowered the bat, disarmed by the horror reflected in the eyes of the Shaws' small children.

Blood streaked the patchy dust of the last snowfall as she dragged the slugger on the ground behind her.

"Holy shit." Deck touched his sister's face as they hiked. He tried to comfort her, "You sure took care of him. He didn't see it coming."

"Takes one to know one." Her voice was quiet—raspy. "It was in his eyes, his voice. His steady hands...he was going to fire. Fire with my family in the bullet's path...my babies...husband." Her train of thought was fractured, her sentences choppy. She trailed off, with only the low hum of the familiar tune audible.

Doolin shot Deck a concerned look, his wife seemingly broken beyond repair.

"I see the turn-off, the house is just beyond that hill." Pop trotted ahead, checking for obstacles—dangers. *Clear the path*, he thought as he jogged, desperate for a distraction from the scene he'd just witnessed.

"Frrittt," he signaled all was clear.

Finally at the back door, the enclosed porch welcomed them.

The adults were still shaken by the gruesome act of self defense enacted by Laney, but the boys on the other hand, were unaffected.

"Diata--, Diatoma." Ian tried to pronounce the very long and multisyllabic word.

"Dia-to-ma-ceous earth." Pop sounded it out for his grandsons who stood in front of the bag, still

110

dumbfounded by the word. He fumbled with the key, the lock needing a little finagling to function. "Come on, you dirty whore," he jostled the key chain. It jingled in his hand.

"Christ, Dad, could you sweet-talk it more and talk dirty a little less?" Doolin was tired of the language battle and ready to let the boys absorb the foul education provided by their grandfather.

"Well, your wife is the one who set the tone when she dropped that F-bomb on your neighbor, not to mention, you know, what just happened back there. Besides, it's a new world, I think your tender offspring better toughen up."

"Not today... one hard lesson at a time. I think leaving their home and the F-bomb are enough for one day. Could you just open the stupid door?" Laney managed to skip over the brutal assault she'd perpetrated on Jim Shaw while compiling her list. As she shifted from anxious to angry, her hand cradled the pill bottle. *Everything's fine, everything's fine, everything's fine,* she repeated in her frazzled mind as she tried to keep her cool. *Don't lose it in here, not again, not in front of the boys.* She didn't think going off the deep end, wedged amongst survival supplies while elbow-to-elbow with her children, would be appropriate.

"Well, I look forward to tomorrow when I can teach them something really vulgar." He winked at the boys, a smoke already lit and between his thin lips; the resulting cloud polluting the enclosed porch.

Doolin rolled his eyes, sure his father wouldn't disappoint.

"What's it for?" the twins asked together; as usual their thoughts were in unison and focused on the bags of earth.

"Diatomaceous earth used along with activated charcoal can create a system for filtering water. We need to think about how we are going to obtain drinking water once the tap runs dry."

"Why would that happen?"

"Because, if I were the governor, I wouldn't be concerned about anyone but myself, and according to Uncle Ash's story, he lives at the University. So, I imagine, given a little time, all resources will be funneled there, leaving all of us out here high and dry."

"I thought this was out here, you know, removed from utilities and whatnot? Off the grid." Laney flexed her arms, as she borrowed Pop's air quotes.

"It is, in that it isn't in town, but it still has power and the pump to the well is electric. No electricity, no water."

"I think I saw a barrel behind that camp at the bend. We'll snag it after we get settled in." Doolin knew the plastic drum would be perfect to filter the water.

Pop finally opened the door.

"You do that, son, and I'll get a fire going. It's chilly in here."

Laney pushed past everyone, eager to see what awaited her. The cabin was small. There were rooms on the main floor, which consisted of a kitchen at the back of the house, a sitting room with a large stone fireplace in the front facing the water, and a small bedroom off and to the left. Stairs wound up the right side (if you were facing the kitchen) and immediately on the right, at the top was a tiny bathroom. A short and narrow hallway divided the second floor with a small bedroom on each side.

Elle bounded up the stairs, and began to screech. "You've gotta be fu... kidding me!" Her reaction was so impulsive she almost dropped an F-bomb of her own. "I can't share this bathroom with all of you. Is this some sort of joke? That's not a shower... was this tub once used to water farm animals?"

"Would you rather be dropped off at one of those buses?" Pop had his head pointed up the stairs. "The tub was never used for farm animals, but that was its intended purpose. This cabin was only equipped with an outhouse when we purchased it. We added the bathroom later, but the only way to fit a bath was the large galvanized tub. No other vessel had the right dimensions. It's that or bathing in a tub in the kitchen like the settlers. We'll probably be filling it with drinking water anyway. Soon bathing in it will be impractical."

"Fine," she huffed with her arms crossed as she descended the stairs.

Doolin watched Laney drop to the floor. "Laney? You okay?" She had her hands on the bat, which was lying in front of her. Its blood-stained surface rolled under her palms as she rocked.

"Hmm hmm hmm hm hmmmm." She hummed.

"What's that you're humming? Sounds familiar." He tried to make small talk, and not focus on the fact that she'd drifted off to some distant place.

"Yeah," Pop hummed along, "Hmm hmm hmmm," "What is that tune, Laney?" he was just as stumped.

"She was singing that same tune at the van before we left. She was just standing there, with that bat in her hands, humming it," Elle explained.

"The Carpenters," Deck answered. "Our mother listened to it all the time… 'On Top of the World.'"

"I think Mom's finally lost it. You broke her, Dad. Leaving the van, now having to spend the rest of our lives in this dump… she's gone bye-bye. Hell, I almost lost it myself when I saw the bathroom."

Nan gave her granddaughter a dirty look.

"We're going to adjust. We're together and alive, and that's what matters. Christ, just by some crazy dumb luck, we even found your uncle. What are the odds?" Doolin was desperate to keep it together.

"Luckily the water is still running, and I have a pile of wood that will get us started, but we need to prepare. Winter is upon us, and from what I remember, they are long and harsh." Pop placed his hands on hips and looked around. "Let's leave the women to unpack what we carried in and we'll hike out, see what else we can round up."

"We had snow in D.C.; how much worse could it be?" Deck was truly unaware of what they were facing.

With his trusty tendons flexed, the cigarette planted between Pop's lips quivered as he educated him. "Snow on the ground from November to May. No melt, no break, three hundred inches in some places, maybe more. Below zero temps, plus wind-chill, days at a time. We're talking about being snowed in… bound

114

by the elements. No end in sight." He concluded with his hands balled into fists and level with his ears.

"What are we waiting for?" Deck was now concerned for their safety. "Let's move."

"I can't leave Laney when she's like this."

Dory tried to comfort him. "Oh, aren't you sweet, such an attentive husband, but we can take care of her."

Nan nodded, her nonverbal agreement somehow sarcastic.

Elle tried to reassure her father. "Yeah, Dad, and I'll watch the boys. You go; it'll be fine."

The men filed toward the exit, and Deck, last in line, glanced back, his eyes meeting Dory's. She grinned. *He likes me*, she thought as he walked out the door.

"I think Uncle Ash was giving you the eyes," Elle teased, now acutely observant without the phone in her hands. "Josh used to look at me like that, I wonder if he's okay. I haven't talked to him in hours."

"I'm sure he's fine… Let's see if we can get your mother to come back from wherever she went."

Laney was still parked on the floor, rocking, the bat shifting in time. She was lost in a violent fantasy, as she strolled through town, her bat over her shoulder. She was going door-to-door, cracking skulls as she hummed her merry tune, each swing putting her gauge in the green.

"I think she's still humming that tune," Elle leaned in to listen; the sound was very faint.

Without warning she awoke from the daydream. "What are you doing!"

"Mom!" Elle was startled.

"Ahh shit!" Dory joined in, "You scared the hell out of me. My heart is in my throat." She bent at the waist to catch her breath, her hand to her chest.

"Oh, sorry," she cut to another conversation. "This place is...quaint, hey."

She was going to say "a dump," but wanted to spare the feelings of her moth-in-law, who probably chose the color scheme.

Nan knew she didn't mean it, the hesitation said it all. With her middle finger gently stretched, she feigned an itch and rubbed her eye.

Dory watched, entertained by the immature behavior of this older woman.

The space was pleasant enough in design. A large sandstone fireplace was the focal point of the small living area. Two sofas were centered in the room, one a green and blue check and the other a burnt orange. They faced each other and were positioned in front of the fireplace. The gap was bridged by a coffee table constructed of large barrel split vertically, which rested on a platform, topped by an antique door, bronze knob and all. The aged varnish had cracked, giving it a unique patina.

Dory looked around at the camp. Its exposed beams and trim had been painted white, giving the cottage a wonderfully airy feel. The rustic décor, although mismatched, was well coordinated.

"I've seen a lot of camps, and this one is pretty nice. Someone took great care to make it inviting."

Nan shook her head in agreement, her dull brown ponytail bobbing in time.

"She doesn't talk? You don't talk?" she re-directed to Nan, worried it seemed rude to ask someone else.

She gave Laney the nod.

"She's given me permission to tell you, that's what that nod meant. But first let me say, thank god she's mute. It's my one gift during this difficult time."

A robust and animated series of obscene hand gestures erupted from Nan.

"So, she wasn't always mute, she could talk as a child, but a severe case of strep went untreated and she developed rheumatic fever. After that she couldn't speak, might have caused some sort of nerve damage. Sometimes she can muster a low airy whisper."

Nan nodded.

"So, she doesn't talk and believe me, it's better for everyone," Laney stuck her tongue out in retaliation for the bird she had flipped. "I'm sure nothing of importance would ever escape her mouth anyway."

Nan gave her a dirty look, her nostrils flared.

"What you gotta say about it?" Laney offered Nan an ear.

Dory tried not to laugh; their exchange was quite comical.

"Wait, did you hear that?" Dory approached the windows. "Someone's outside?"

"Where're the boys?" Laney pointed at her daughter.

"Oh shit, it's probably them... up to no good I'm sure, and I was supposed to look after them."

The four women peeked outside. Laney took up the rear, bat in hand.

"I'll check upstairs," Elle didn't want to face whatever lurked outdoors.

"Thanks for nothing." Laney's sarcastic gratitude was aimed toward Spencer, who was sleeping heavily against the back door. She placed the bat on the floor before wedging both hands under him and sliding him out of the way. "Was it a long walk, you lazy old thing?"

With the exit now clear and her bat in hand, Laney jumped outside and quickly turned the corner, coming face to face with a thief. "What the fuck do you think you're doing?" She had the slugger at the ready.

"Whoa, honey. I'm just gathering some firewood. It's getting pretty cold out here and I'd already closed my camp for da season before all dis happened." He lied, trying to cover his ass. "I'm just a little short, is all." He hoped his fib would garner some sympathy and not violence.

"Put that back in the pile, every stick of it, do you hear me?"

"Is it just you... who else you got in dere? What else do you got in dere?" his eyes now grew serious.

"You better put that back and walk off." Her hands were steady on the foam grip.

"What's da ruckus, Elmer?" The wood thief's partner emerged from the shed, his wagon filled with pinched supplies.

"It would seem I've been caught red-handed, so tuh speak, and dis nice lady was just asking me tuh leave, but, I tink she wouldn't really use dat ting on me, and I tink dere might be some useful supplies inside."

"You see this, this is the blood of the last guy." Laney lurched as she swung the bat in his direction. She contemplated the situation, *I should just kill them, our own neighbor tried to kill us, what would stop strangers?*

"I felt da breeze off of dat swing dere, I tink she means business."

"*I* definitely mean business." Dory snapped the double barrel closed. "I think you should drop everything and get the fuck out of here." The stock was wedged in her shoulder, she raised the barrel.

"How long have you been behind me with that?" Laney turned to ask.

"I ran back to Dooley's bag and fished it out when you told him to put the wood back."

"Crap! I wish you hadn't done that."

"Why are you so pissed; these idiots were clearly plotting something terrible."

"I just really wanted to beat them with the bat." Laney gripped the aluminum tightly and hoisted it in a ready position. "I really, really wanted to crack 'em with it. Maybe you could just shoot the little one, and I can take out the stupid-looking one."

"Who are you?" Laney took a step closer.

"I'm Willy Jarvi and dis is Elmer," he gestured, his thumb pointing back and forth between them. "We're brudders."

That fact was obvious. They both had the same narrow nose, which came strangely to a bulbous end. Both were graced with the same thin eyebrows and both carried their weight in the same places, although Elmer, obviously the runt, was smaller proportionately.

"Well, Elmer and Willy, do you believe that I want to hit you?" She crept a little closer. "Do I have the look of someone vulnerable? Someone you could bully?" She'd snapped, her tone was sharp—her speech became pressured.

The gauge lurched. "I've seen some shit today, fellas, and I'm teling you, I'm not feeling too good about letting you go."

"We're gonna go, I promise we don't want any trouble." Willy dropped the wood and snagged his brother by the sleeve before breaking into a sprint.

"Cowards!" Laney shouted, "afraid of some little women!"

"Women with weapons," Dory had the gun over her shoulder.

"Where did you learn to handle that?" Laney was impressed by her new friend's skills.

"I've been involved with a few of these north-woods guys. I've picked up a thing or two."

They made sure the Jarvis didn't have any ideas about returning before they stepped back into the house.

"Huh," Laney shrugged. "Hope they were better-looking than these two."

"Yeah, more the hunky lumberjack type and less the Elmer Fudd type. Say, why all the weapons anyway?"

"Dooley collects, like to shoot things, it's a hobby. If you ask me, it's to release the aggression he harbors due to his upbringing."

Nan waved her hand dismissively, irritated by her son's wife.

"Who asked you, ya old hag." Laney shook the bat.

She didn't even flinch.

"Wow, bad blood between you two."

"Yeah, she hates me, always did. No one is good enough for her boy. Oh, I better check on the kids." She suddenly remembered that the boys were previously unaccounted for.

Relief washed over her as she reached the bedroom.

Elle was asleep, one of the boys in each arm. They snoozed peacefully, comforted by their sister.

"Everything okay up there?" Dory called from the bottom of the stairs.

"Yep, it's just like kids—they can sleep through anything."

Chapter 8
Guys' Day Out

"I hope the girls are all right," Deck worried as they peered through the windows of the rural county store.

"Let's hurry back. I don't feel too great about leaving them myself," Doolin commiserated.

"Stop your GODDAMNED whining and break a window already. My ass is cold and I'm tired of listening to the two of you share your feelings."

Deck and Doolin hesitated, so Pop elbowed the glass and flipped the lock. "Christ, do I have to do everything around here?"

"I feel bad breaking in like this." Doolin crunched across the broken glass. He hurriedly filled the canvas duffle bag with the few canned goods that remained.

"It's pretty scarce in here, think it was looted already?"

"Naw, no broken windows," Pop smirked, "Well until now. Dan probably used his inventory to stock himself before slipping out to camp. He and I have chatted here and there over the years. I would shop here with Ma when we would stay... good guy."

"I can't believe you've had that place all these years and never told me."

"I was saving it for a rainy day, and now it's pouring." Pop smoked while he looted.

"So what's going on with Dilly?" Deck was concerned about his sister. "Your neighbor in D.C. told me she was ill and that's why you moved."

"Kind of. She snapped, had a breakdown after your dad, well, you know. She was at hockey practice with the boys one day, I was working too much, and she'd been left to haul them and their gear. Well, boys will be boys, especially my boys, and they broke a kid's nose."

"So, hockey is violent. Maybe that kid was just a pussy."

"Pop, don't interrupt." Doolin continued his story. "Laney was on the ice, helping to break up the fight, when the mother started in on her about how the boys were heathens and should be locked up. They'd harassed that kid before, and anyway, the mother just kept bitching, and Laney lifted her hand and squeezed the woman's lips shut. Just squeezed. When she tried to pull away, Laney stepped on her foot and grabbed her by the back of the head, and kept squeezing. Well, she pressed charges, and Laney was ordered by the court to receive counseling. In the haze of it all I thought moving up here, where it's quiet, would be soothing. I arranged a virtual position and relocated. You don't have to be in D.C. to answer the phone."

"My god, it's all my fault. I should have been there for her. Dad abandoned her when Mom was sick, and so did I. Then I abandoned her when Dad died. I hid behind my rifle in another country..."

Pop added his two cents. "She's fruitier than monkey shit. Driven right over the edge. I don't think hauling her out to the north woods, and yanking her away from the city she loved...shopping and what not, was necessarily the right move. But you did what you thought was right... I've always liked her though; she takes my shit. She's tough... sassy. I like 'em sassy. You're mother is sassy, that's why they don't get along, too much alike."

Deck jumped in, needing to defend his sister. "It wasn't always like that. We weren't raised like that. You make it sound like she is some uppity suburbanite, but we didn't have it easy as kids. We lived in a small rural town. We were broke most of the time. Mom and Dad weren't what you'd call responsible. We knew how to rough it. Your son is the one who introduced her to a finer lifestyle. Don't let her fool you, she knows how to get her hands dirty."

"That's for sure," Pop lit up, "she beat the shit out of that moron in the woods today."

Deck appeared offended.

"Awww, let me dab your tears for you." Pop walked toward Deck, his sleeve pulled out from his jacket.

"That's enough, Dad. Now, it's great to chat like this, but let's grab what we can and get back. She could be on a killing spree with that bat by now." Doolin was worried.

"Dory will watch her. I'm sure they're fine."

"You seem pretty smitten with this Dory. How long have you two been together? She's quite the catch, I feel funny all over just looking at her."

"Christ, again with the girly talk, make sure to grab some tampons for the two of you. And weren't you just worried about your wife? Oh, but you'll set that aside to find out if your brother-in-law here has had carnal knowledge of that leggy broad back at the ranch. The nut doesn't fall far from the tree after all, does it? Deep down you are just as twisted as I am. Nice to know you'll carry on the family tradition of being a dirty old man." Pop wagged his wiry eyebrows, truly touched that his son had taken after him.

"Nice, Pop, always a charmer."

"Well, stop clucking like some old hens and lets get on with it. Deck can detail his escapades with Legs on the walk back."

"There's nothing to tell. I met her this morning at the University. Once I heard what the governor had planned, I grabbed her on my way out."

"Of all the people you could have saved from the governor, you chose only her? Wait, what exactly does the governor have planned?"

"He's going to kill everyone on the buses. He called it the Thinning."

"I knew it! The goddamn buses!" Pop glanced down at his crotch. "The hair knows."

Deck was embarrassed, his mind still on Dory. "I see how that looks…"

"You mean you saw how *she* looked and decided to snag yourself a piece of tail before the pickings got slim." Pop's eyebrows were now still and filled with false judgment. He lived to give someone a hard time.

Doolin shrugged in agreement with his father's observation.

"I think we got everything left that's usable. Is there another store nearby? Or empty houses—maybe other camps?" Doolin suddenly felt pressured to make a good haul; he had a wife and children to think about.

"Maybe we'll catch something else on the way back, okay, sonny." He recognized the look of concern on his boy's face. With a punch to Doolin's arm (his awkward but manly way of providing comfort) he acknowledged his son's feelings.

Chapter 9
Home Sweet Dome

"I'm home," Blake Davies entered the kitchen.

"What should we do?" His wife rounded the corner, worry resting heavily on her young face.

He held her in his arms, his presence a relief after the news of the day.

"I have to report to the University again tomorrow, but you take the babies to the nearest checkpoint and I'll just join you at the dome after my shift."

"Are they planning to house people there permanently?"

"I think everyone from outside of the zone is being funneled through there, but it seems that a more permanent settlement is being erected at Northern. I know it's hard to imagine leaving the house and all of our stuff, but we won't want to be stuck out here with the little ones when the weather turns."

"I'll just pack up the car and head over there after you go to work, then."

Blake was twelve years older than his young bride. He'd spent his youth abroad. Years of travel left little time for love, but once stationed at the National Guard unit as an active duty liaison he was finally stable and eventually found Julie.

Blake Davies, at thirty-six, with his military experience, seemed wise beyond his years. She trusted him fully.

He tried to reassure her, "We'll all be safe and together, you'll see. Hey, what's that delightful smell?" he fibbed with his nose in the air.

"I made a casserole for dinner, the one with the chicken you like."

"Great." He feigned a smile. *You aren't much of a cook, but you sure are beautiful,* he thought as he watched his wife pull the bubbling dish from the oven.

"I'll check on the girls while you set the table."

The Davies home was small. Its simple décor was splashed with warm colors and a thoughtful but eclectic collection of throw blankets and pillows, picture frames and knickknacks.

"There you are," he gushed as he reached into the playpen. Sitting happily inside was their eighteen-month-old daughter Lila. "Who's my Lila?" he asked, met with a wide and toothy, but drooly grin. She teetered as she found her feet; standing with her arms outstretched, she pleaded to be picked up with her favorite toy in her hand. "Who's my Lila?" he asked again as he scooped her up, his tone playful and loving. With her face buried in his chest, she kicked her legs excitedly as he rubbed his nose on her soft blonde hair.

She bounced her stuffed animal off of his head, giggling wildly as he sang the word *ouch*. "Oww, oww, ouch. You shouldn't hit daddy with Mittens Magoo."

The bizarre character was supposed to be an animal of some sort, knitted and stuffed by Julie's mom. The head was shaped like a mitten and was quite large in comparison to its tiny body, which had skinny limbs capped by bulbous hands and feet. The thumb acted as the nose, and it had eyes that seemed to pop from its head. The whole thing was knitted with a bright and random variety of yarn, and its thin black line of a mouth, paired with tiny black pupils, lent it a somewhat constipated expression. It had a Mr. Magoo quality in an abstract sort of way.

When it arrived in the mail, they had a good laugh, the note explaining it was supposed to be an elephant. Julie coined the name Mittens Magoo. Strangely enough, it was now their daughter's favorite item.

"I guess I see his appeal," he told her as she continued to bounce it off of his head.

"Baby," she said with her attention now turned toward her sister Larkin who was sleeping soundly in the bassinet.

"That's right, baby," he rocked her back and forth. "Baby's sleeping, so let's go to the kitchen and eat some dinner."

With Lila now safely anchored in the highchair, he took off his military issue shirt and hung it on the back of the kitchen chair.

"Rough day at the office?" Julie spooned some of the casserole onto his plate.

"A few of the folks down at the university gave me some blowback when I tried to escort them, but nothing serious. Once they realized it was just for the press conference, that they were safe, they settled down."

"I'm sure you were your usually gracious self. I'm a lucky girl, you're a wonderful man," she kissed him on the cheek as she delivered his plate.

He smiled at the gray mass centered on the china. "I'm the lucky one." He took a tiny bite, "Wow, even better than last time." *It actually is better*, he thought while nibbling slowly. *Not much of a cook, but I couldn't be happier. How did a schlub like me land a beauty like her?*

"What should I pack? How much can we bring?" she asked before taking a bite.

"Well," he paused to wash his casserole down with some water, "essential clothing and baby items, but not too many toys or household belongings. I just don't think there'll be room. People have been packing their cars full, but the military has been placing stuff in storage somewhere. Most of the people I've seen processed at the gates only had what little they could carry. I'm sure bunks and food will be provided."

"So maybe a photo album or two, a couple of the really important keepsakes?"

"Sure, whatever will fit in a few suitcases. I'll keep a couple bags with me, so you'll be able to squeeze a little more. As a matter of fact, I'll drop you off so you don't have to deal with the car."

"Oh, that's good, they'll probably be a little nicer if I travel light."

"Probably."

"Bah, bah, bah, Mama." Lila interjected, her meal now thoroughly squished between her fingers.

"I think she wants to join in the conversation."

130

"I think she wants a drink." Julie handed Lila her sippy cup.

"I can't believe how big she is already. No more bottles. No more baby food...soon she'll want to borrow the car." He wiped some chicken from her hair.

"Well, Larkin is only four months old, so she's still fresh."

"Funny. Very funny... Do you mean to imply that I talk about Lila as though she's passed her expiration date?" He stood and grabbed his wife around the waist.

He backed her against the counter and planted a kiss that was deep and passionate.

Julie smacked him on the behind, "You keep that up, and we'll be on our way to another Davies. You know Larkin is just about the same age Lila was when I got pregnant with her."

"Maybe this one will have your beautiful brown hair."

"Or your charming blue eyes," she included. "Maybe we'll have a boy, but I can't think of any good boy names that would go with Lila and Larkin."

"Well, he'd have to be named after his dear old dad of course. Blake Michael Davies." He slapped himself on the chest with pride.

Julie was charmed by the warmth of her husband and his commitment to the growth of their family. "Of course, why didn't I think of that."

"Let's clean this little girl up and pack some stuff before we get ready for bed." He tapped his wife's behind suggestively.

"Why Master Sergeant Davies, are you getting fresh with me?"

"Yes, ma'am, yes I am."

The witty banter continued as they flirted their way through packing and putting their precious girls to bed.

"I don't want to go to sleep. If we brush our teeth and go to bed, it means today is over, and tomorrow will mean leaving our home."

"We just have to look at it like a new beginning...an adventure."

With the covers now turned down, they climbed in, the cool sheets brushing their skin.

With the hem of the quilt to her nose she whispered, "I'm scared, Blake. I don't want to leave our home."

"I know, but I've seen things, heard reports. We need to be protected from what's coming. I only have our best interest at heart. I wouldn't uproot us if I didn't think it was the best thing. I promise," he rolled over his wife, nose to nose, his arms propping him up. "I won't let anything happen to you. As soon as I'm done with my shift tomorrow, I'll be right over to join you at the dome. And who knows, maybe things will pan out, and with time, we can return to the house. Maybe this is all just precautionary, the reports trumped up, and nothing will come of it."

Julie pulled up, her bright brown eyes filled with love as she kissed him, pulling him closer to her.

"Blake Michael Davies the Second," he whispered.

"Junior," she returned as she kissed his ear.

The uncertainty they both felt was minimized by their passion as they shared this intimate moment.

Julie held her husband's arm tightly as she drifted off. Her slumber was restless, filled with bad dreams about a crushing darkness.

The black void was filled with the fear of separation, her toddler's presence sensed but unseen; she was just out of reach. "Lila, Lila," she called. The abyss absorbed all sound, her voice unable to travel. She tried to run, but found she was restrained but no tether was visible. As she struggled a point of light drew near, warping... spreading. Through the darkness a lipless grin came into focus, its raw tissue and flaps of loose skin split and bleeding. Unable to avert her eyes, she watched in horror as the whole creature came into focus. With erratic articulation it walked lifting its twisted arms as if it were presenting a gift. In its grasp was her little girl, limp, lifeless, Mittens dangling from her delicate hand. Tiny drops of blood had collected on the monster's camouflaged sleeve. With eyes wide she followed the bent arm to the shirt's pocket. The nametag read 'Davies.'

"No!" she cried, her breath labored as she awoke with a start. "Thank god, oh thank god, it's just a dream."

"Waaaaahh." The wail of her little one drifted over the monitor.

"Want me to get her?" Blake rolled sleepily from his pillow.

"I was already up, go back to sleep."

"She almost made it all night." He lifted his arm to look at his watch. "It's five–thirty already."

"I know. We'd be getting up in half an hour, anyway."

"You feed her, I'll make some coffee." He climbed from the bed. The tired wood floor creaked as he walked to the upholstered chair in the corner, its seat a staging area for the next day's uniform.

"Are you sure, you could still get a few more minutes of shuteye."

"No, let's have one last breakfast together in our house."

"Thanks, Blakey."

"Ooh, I love it when you call me that." He tiptoed over and kissed her forehead while pulling on his pants.

"I'm coming, little miss." Julie rose from the bed. Her toes recoiled as they hit the cold maple. With a hurried shuffle she pranced to her baby's room.

"Good morning, lovely girl. Are you hungry?"

With the infant now cradled in her arms, she sat in the rocker, Larkin rooting for a nipple.

Blake dressed while he listened to his wife. Her gentle tune soothed their baby girl while she nursed, the sound of the rocker against the wood floor her accompaniment.

He finished buttoning up his BDU's and headed to the kitchen.

"Would you grab Lila on the way down?" Julie requested through the cracked nursery door, Larkin still feeding.

"Will do."

"Dadada." Her angelic voice drifted into the hall.

"Good morning, my Lila," he sang as he flipped on her light. She squealed with anticipation as he approached.

"What wonders await me in your diaper this morning, my dear girl?" he patted her behind as he picked her up. "Whoa," he grimaced, the disposable soaked and muddy. "Whew," he wrinkled his nose.

His comical reaction was met with boisterous laughter.

Julie smiled, endeared by the exchange between father and daughter.

With Lila clean and dressed, Davies wrestled her into the highchair and started hauling items to the car while he waited for his wife.

"Little Larkin," Julie cooed, rubbing the baby's cheek as she watched her eat. The now satisfied infant squirmed, ready to be burped. She hoisted her over a shoulder and patted as she headed downstairs.

"Was Daddy funny?" she asked as she entered the kitchen, Lila already in the highchair and working on a handful of Cheerios.

"Yes, I was," he answered for her, before kissing his wife good morning. "Let me hold her while you have a cup of joe," he picked Larkin from her arms.

"Mwaw, mwaw, mwaw," he smooched, the baby now smiling widely at him.

She beamed at her husband. "You're a nut, did you know that."

"Yes, but you love it," he reminded her.

"I put some stuff in the car already." He motioned to the black Volkswagen parked outside the back door. "Lila watched me go back and forth while she ate her cereal, didn't you, hon?"

She grinned in toothy response, soggy cheerios wadded in her palm.

Julie sipped her coffee, tears now welling as she knew the time to leave was upon them.

"I know," he said soothingly.

She nodded.

Blake helped to rinse the few dirty dishes while Julie bundled the girls against the brisk morning air.

With the kitchen clean, the car packed and the kids safely tucked into their seats, Mr. Mittens and all, they pulled from the driveway.

"You carried me over that threshold." Her memory was vivid as they passed the front door.

"Let's try to focus on something else, it'll be easier."

They made small talk as he drove toward the checkpoint, their house only minutes away. Today's crowds were considerably smaller, the limited population not able to support continued heavy traffic.

"They must have people squared away. It was a lot busier yesterday. I heard that some of the checkpoints actually had to implement riot control."

"Oh my, that's scary...but it seems okay now." She looked around: the lines were short and the numbers seemed manageable.

"Oh yeah, looks good," he assured his wife.

Chapter 10
No Escape From Reality

"Colonel McGovern," Brady saluted. "Here to check out the progress?"

The latest bus had just arrived, and they were ready to commence, the canister already in place.

"Had many dust-ups?" the Colonel watched as the team prepared to exterminate the many citizens aboard.

"A little crying... some fear, nothing worth reporting. Once the gas starts filling the bus, there's some panic, hands slapping windows, what have you, but waving the rifle around settles them down. By time we need to intervene, they only have a few breaths left." Brady had become detached, a shell. Fear for his own life was the only thing stopping him from deserting.

"Excellent. How about disposal?"

"Really easy. We carry 'em off the buses and stack 'em in these shipping crates, then the crates are stacked on the truck and driven out to the shipyard. The disposal team claims that Lake Paramount swallows them up without a trace."

"Very good. Oh, looks like we're getting a little panic," Mc Govern leaned in.

Hands had started to slap the windows hurriedly. The bus rocked; screaming was now layered over the frantic clawing of the bus's exits.

McGovern was amused, "They're really freaking out."

"Yes sir, fear of death," Brady stated.

The two watched as innocent people lost their battle with the noxious gas. Soon all was quiet.

"How long before they can open the doors?"

"Not long. The bus door is on a remote and there are large fans already incorporated in the building to vent the athletic field."

"This really was the perfect site for the Thinning. Landis knew what he was doing." McGovern was pleasantly surprised by the ease of the process.

The two looked on as the removal team approached the bus, gas masks donned for added safety.

"This is the part I find most difficult," Brady nervously disclosed as the masked men carried the limp and pale bodies from the vehicle. "It's the little ones that are the hardest to look at." He pointed to the corpse of a woman clutching an infant. One of the masked soldiers carried a toddler, her dead body losing its grip on her treasured toy.

McGovern rationalized, "Collateral damage... we knew what had to be done; it wasn't just going to be prisoners and the elderly."

The two men looked on as the bodies were stacked in the shipping crate, one on top of the other, no rhyme or reason. When the crate was filled to capacity, the end was held in place with construction staples; the recoil of the pneumatic nailer echoed through the athletic complex.

~~~

"What's that sound?' Davies approached the gate to the Paramount Dome.

"I'm not sure...Sergeant," the young private's eyes were darting nervously from Davies' uniform to his face.

"Doesn't quite sound like gunfire, does it?"

"No, Sergeant," he quickly answered.

"Say, I'm here to join my family, they were sent over from checkpoint Bravo. I just got off duty and am really eager to make sure they are settling in okay. My wife was pretty choked up about leaving the house this morning."

"I can't allow you beyond this point, Sergeant."

"Of course you can."

"No. Only special team members and selected officers, Sergeant."

"There must be some mistake, I thought all outside residents would be given shelter. I thought anyone from the peninsula could get on the buses and travel into the Static Zone, I put my wife and babies on that bus this morning."

"I'm not even allowed in, sir. They have us bunked across the way at one of the residence halls."

"Oh, maybe they were processed and sent over there," Davies coaxed.

"It's possible. Also, I've heard that a lot of military men and their families moved into a settlement on the main campus."

"Thank you, I'll head there now."

Davies fell out, leaving the gate at the dome in hopes of finding his wife and children bivouacked at the university dorms.

I was there all day, I didn't see any families, did I? He racked his brain.

Of course, they had me hauling furniture from one building to another, I didn't really see anyone at all, just common room sofas and tables.

As he strolled toward College Avenue, he strained to recall if he'd seen anyone beside Army or Militia members... *I was so busy I...what's that?* His thought was interrupted. "Screaming? Is that screaming?" He leaned toward the dome, now positive. *Faint but definitely screaming*, he hurried back toward the complex.

How to get in, he searched, finding cover and observing the buildings features. He circled the perimeter, seeking out the best entry point. Quarter of the way around, he found a single private guarding a door. He was shivering and had a distant look in his eye; he was lost in thought. *I wish I had listened to my mother and fled to the lake house. I'd probably be sitting down to a warm meal right now...* "Is this just fantasy, hmm hmm hmm hmm hm hm hm, no escape from reality...."

Davies slipped closer, creeping up on the young soldier's left flank. He was now just inches from the private's ear. He could hear his raspy tune.

"Is that 'Bohemian Rhapsody'?"

He turned abruptly, startled by the sneak attack. Davies threw an arm around his neck and wrestled him to the ground. The sound of the airy melody was now replaced with the scraping of the guard's feet as he struggled to free himself from Davies' hold. With his forearm pressed heavily against his trachea and his legs wrapped tightly around his hips, he squeezed the consciousness from the unsuspecting guard.

"Sorry about this," he hit him in the head for good measure.

After dragging him behind a nearby dumpster, Davies relieved him of his firearm and waltzed through the door.

The screams were no longer audible as he crept along the outer corridor of the circular structure. He took mental note of the directional marking over the entry he'd just used, *North East Entrance. This place could keep you running in circles.*

Davies' progress was impeded by two men as they chatted about their situation," The numbers are dwindling at the checkpoints, by General Hatch's estimation we should be done with the Thinning in the next two days."

Davies paused, frozen in the alcove of what seemed to be a supply closet. He listened intently to the conversation.

"Good thing, some of the men on the disposal team are looking pretty fried. The bigwigs stand up there watching, but they don't have to get their hands dirty. Some of these guys are finding out they aren't as hardcore as they thought... you carry a couple of dead kids to the crates and you start to question if it's worth it."

"I hear ya, but it's almost done and then we can all start the daily business of just riding this thing out. When I got to the settlement last night and found my wife and kids safe in their bunks, it was a little easier to swallow what we've been doing here. I saw some of the ground reports, the world is going to hell, it's gruesome out there, whole towns—cities burning, the sick making more people sick...NO, thanks! I'll live with a little guilt instead of watching my wife eat my kids any day."

"I guess so, I just want it over with. It's making *me* sick."

Davies shook, he was flooded with fear, anger, guilt... He was overwhelmed with emotion. *Oh my god, Julie, and the babies,* he thought as he tried to compose himself.

Tired of waiting for them to stop their gossip session, he turned and began to sneak back the other way. He was filled with dread over what he might find.

The gray cement of the industrial floor passed under his feet as he slunk along the outside hallway.

They could still be fine, maybe they weren't processed. He tried to remain optimistic. The concrete was soon breeched by a splash of light. Davies looked up to find he'd reached an entrance to the athletic field.

The voices of men echoed through the large venue, their tone hustled and task-oriented.

First checking his six, he continued forward, trying to get a closer look at what was going on. With each step, the picture grew clearer. These callous men worked side by side as they carried the bodies of the latest victims into the shipping crates. The crates were quite large, twenty feet long at least. The eight-foot-high openings allowed the dead to be hauled in, their lifeless bodies stretched between two men as they carried them by their arms and legs.

Davies watched as some loose change fell from the pocket of one of the deceased as he was carelessly flopped around, his body swayed recklessly on its journey from the bus to his industrial tomb.

"Stuff keeps dropping off the bodies," Martin commented from behind the gas mask as he kicked the loose items to the side. "Couldn't they have them empty their fucking pockets at the check point."

The change scooted across the concrete floor, landing along the wall's edge with other discarded items.

No, no, no, no. It can't be. Please, please, please.... He prayed as he noticed a familiar toy in the pile. *Oh no, oh my Lila—Mittens Magoo... Oh dear god.*

Davies stomach lurched; he doubled over, the horror of the scene too much to bear. *They're dead, they're all dead and it's my fault.* With each defeated thought, he dry-heaved, his insides trying to depart from his body.

Once again the recoil of the stapler ripped through the dome, its percussion carrying easily through the large space. Distracted by his tormented thoughts and the sharp repetition of the nailer, he didn't notice he was about to be infiltrated.

"You all right?"

Davies didn't know whether to start a killing spree or try to run. *Live to fight another day,* he thought, *cut the head off of the snake.* He decided in that moment; *the governor is the real target.*

He began to lie, "Just a little hung over, ya know, the Irish flu. Little too much camaraderie, I guess."

"Aren't you a little old for carrying-on?"

"Well, uh, Sergeant Brady," Davies fumbled as he looked for his name and any chance to escape this awkward situation, "Aren't I a little too old, and higher-ranked than you, to take your shit?" He noticed that Brady was only a sergeant first class.

"True, sorry about hassling you. Guess it's the stress of this place," Brady seemed truly worn. He didn't register that Davies was not one of the inside guys. "I'm just tired," he dropped his head before slinking away.

"I'll turn these guys against him. I'll build my own army and tear this place down," Davies scooted around the building. He watched for his North East entrance, eager to depart on his quest to exact vengeance for his wife and children.

Accumulation

Chapter 11
Going Rogue

"I can't believe how well things have gone so far." The governor looked down upon the settlement from his office window.

Military soft shelters bridged the four main buildings. The impromptu tent city, along with the occupants of the many residence halls and academic buildings, made for a population much larger than the governor had intended.

"The university proper, or U.P as the residents call it, is now a new town within the Static Zone. The separation, the thinning, establishing this," he gestured toward the window highlighting the bustling colony of his new constituency.

The tent city looked lived in, with its fire pits and picnic tables. The residents shoveled the snow and kept the common areas clear. People were gathered around tables and fires; they had even channeled their holiday spirit and strung lights along the corridor between the two rows of tents. With the snow-dusted trees and rooftops, it looked like a disheveled Christmas village.

"I underestimated the number of people I would need to pull this off, and the exponential growth that was caused by the addition of their families. I needed to entice loyalty by offering safety, but now I think I might be in over my head. And who told them they could waste energy by hanging lights? Come to think of it, if all my inside guys and their families have taken up residence in the buildings, and the army is using the dorms, who is living out there? "

Lance informed the governor, "Mostly militia guys who built and guard the trench on this end. Some started to stay once you turned off the power to the outlying areas."

"Why haven't we made them leave?" He was about to open the window and tell them all to get the hell out.

"At the time we were trying to keep a low profile, not anger the masses. The militia isn't as agreeable as regular army. They distrust easily and will abandon their posts, or plot to organize against you. McGovern suggested you placate them, that's why we let them stay and feed them twice a day. You need them at the trench."

"When did he suggest that?"

"In the weekly status briefing, about two weeks ago." Steve examined his cuticles, which is probably what he was doing two weeks ago when he ignored his military leader's suggestion.

Lance continued, "Everything will work itself out. You need the militia to guard the border and the guard to run the power plant and keep the University humming. The point was to survive in comfort, right... electricity and running water for you and Mr. Mathers, an army to protect your Static Zone? You need them, and to keep them, you need their families. You don't want to rough it, do you? You already shut the power off to the rest of the peninsula, which has angered some, but that's under control, and that decision alone should be able to keep the University in power for quite some time."

"I've received reports that more people sought cover in the woods than we originally thought, and desertion is at an all-time high." *I hope they stay out there.* Steve tried to stifle the deep fear that they would turn on him.

"So far the Army has retained the most; several of those guys are obeying orders. I think they just haven't caught on yet. But a militia by definition is purely voluntary, you're allowed to come and go as you please. Many of them probably just felt safer on their own, and word is some felt betrayed by McGovern's connection to you and left... probably aware that this operation was rogue."

"But the bus turn-out was still fair, right? I mean, by my estimation we thinned at least a third of the population, maybe more. I'm tucked safely in this lovely office. You have done a beautiful job with the apartment and Mr. Mathers... my closest advisors and their teams have settled in, their families' safe, everyone satisfied and continuing to do good work... I have been successful. Not one infected soul has breached our border. We are static and secure."

Lance rubbed the fresh scratch on his face, its sting a reminder to approach the subject of a promotion. "I would like to discuss with you, perhaps hiring another assistant to help with the day-to-day chores of the living quarters and Mr. Mathers, so I could assist you in a more official capacity now that we're static and established. I could be of great assistance while you govern our new settlement and the outlying areas of the zone. I have many clerical skills, not to mention a graduate degree in Anthropology. I could help you design strategies to control the masses. I could alleviate some of the concerns you have about your constituents and their behavior."

I was eloquent, it went well; he won't say no. Lance awaited the governor's reply.

"You're too valuable to me in your current position. Besides, Mr. Mathers couldn't possibly take as well to someone else."

Lance ran his hand over the countless scars that now graced his complexion. His blood boiled as he tried to agree with his gracious employer.

"Of course, sir, you're right. Mr. Mathers and I do get on quite well, and beside, who will get your shirts starched just right?"

"So glad you're pleased with your place. I need you to support me and Mr. Mathers during this monumental time in our lives."

Steve opened his trusty survival guide and flipped through the many aged pages, notes scribbled in every margin. "Here it is right here. Separate, establish, thin, survive. I can't survive successfully without you. Your role here is extremely important to me." Steve once again tried to use flattery to woo Lance.

Lance had wised up.

"I know you prefer to receive your suggestions from Mr. Mathers." The cat was now perched on the governor's chest, as he joined his master to recline on the office sofa. "But, if you're concerned about the number of people in the outlying areas of the Static Zone, you could send patrols out to eliminate the stragglers one site at time, or..."

"My great uncle, Harris William Landis," Steve interrupted, "who, if you didn't know, was also the governor of this great state, bestowed to me this book and all its secrets. My grandfather thought his brother was just some nut, filled with bizarre ideas, far-fetched and grandiose in nature. My father not only shared my granddad's opinion, but he was weak. He fell victim to the wiles of a woman, and the ties of family, just as my grandfather before him. He didn't have the constitution for the solitude, for the selfishness one would have to embrace in order to hold onto the ideals scribed in this book. I lived the life necessary. I continued the work my great-uncle started. He passed his connections down to me, his resources."

What does that have to do with anything, and what is really in that book? Lance had to ask, "Why? Why do it?" truly curious why he'd go through all the trouble. *Why would anyone limit his companionship to that of a cat?*

"To see if it could be done. And now, here we are, in the middle of it, and I have achieved and established." He looked to the cat and extended his gratitude. "Thank you, Mr. Mathers."

He thanked the cat? Lance stewed, anger boiling underneath.

"Would you mind whipping up some snacks for me and my little man. And could you straighten up my room, it's quite messy. You're a dear, Lance, really."

Son of a bitch never asks me for anything important, I'm just his butler.

Lance scooped up the cat, who protested loudly, his claws erect to emphasize his irritation.

"There, there, little sir," Steve scolded with pouted lips, "be kind to your friend, he cares for you as much as I do."

Mr. Mathers disagreed, his front claws planted firmly in Lance's forearms as his back feet kicked powerfully, leaving deep scratches etched in his chest.

"See, he loves to play with you." Steve was delusional and blinded by some strange affinity for the cat.

"Yes sir." Blood seeped through the torn fabric of his favorite polo. Lance ranted mentally, angered by the destruction of his mustard-colored shirt.

This was the only one left without holes. This was my favorite one.

Mr. Mathers continued to hassle his handler as he was toted to the kitchenette. It was adjacent to the office suite, which served as the governor's apartment. One room was staged with a sitting area and television, which no longer had a live feed but was still used to view DVD's. The adjoining room was the bedroom, which contained all of the luxurious furniture and bedding shipped in by Mr. Landis.

Lance set it all up. He orchestrated and oversaw the delivery and placement of every piece.

The kitchenette across the hall consisted of a fridge, microwave, hotplate, and a crock-pot that provided some slow cooking. It was acquired from the many personal items collected during the Thinning. A bar sink provided a tiny but adequate space for dishwashing and food prep. Not a gourmet kitchen, but given the circumstances, it sufficed.

Lance had polished his skills these last weeks, now able to prepare substantial meals with relative ease.

"What to have today?" he asked the temperamental feline who was perched on top of the fridge where he licked his hind leg judgmentally.

"Why are you always looking at me like that? Ahh Christ, now I'm starting to talk to you. Well, I guess it's okay as long as I don't think you've answered."

Unaffected by Lance's banter, Mr. Mathers licked on.

"Well, you spoiled shit, we're having chicken." He removed the poultry from the fridge.

Cooked the day before, Lance pulled the remaining meat from the carcass and prepared it as a cold cut, pairing it with crackers and some cheese.

"Smells pretty good, doesn't it, you bastard." The wrinkled and skinny creature ignored Lance and continued to groom his thin gray coat.

"Come on." Lance carried the tray filled with the governor's eats toward the office.

Mr. Mathers followed along, not out of respect for Lance, just for the chicken.

"How wonderful," the governor was pleased as Lance presented him with the meal. "You have such a way with food, you do so well at making do in these lean times."

"Thank you, sir, it does look wonderful. I'm quite hungry; I'm glad it shaped up the way it did."

Lance served his boss, then the cat. He began to place a reasonable portion of chicken and crackers on his plate when the governor made a request.

"Would you mind giving your chicken to my little man, he's eaten his already."

"But I haven't eaten today. There are only two pieces of cheese left, and they're on his plate." Lance tried to reason, his spirit just about broken.

"But look at his little face." Steve carried on with a pout as though that's what the cat was doing.

Lance placed his plate in front of the cat and watched as he chewed his chicken one strand at a time.

"I'm going to lie down." He stood to leave the room. "I'll be in my quarters if you need me."

Angered, he grumbled to himself as he stomped down the hall, "Giving my food to the cat... I promised myself the last time that I wasn't going to give my meals to that miserable varmint anymore. But I keep doing it. I keep caving to that nutbag and his terrorist of a pet."

As he reached his door the temperamental moment had begun to pass, and as he stepped inside he realized why he kept taking the governor's abuse.

The room was quite cozy, with a television equipped with video, a plush full-sized bed dressed in warm and clean coverings, and a window, which reminded him of where he could be.

"I'll just keep taking his shit and dealing with that cat, because living here beats living out there." He looked through his third-floor window down to the tent city that littered the courtyard.

It was filled with the flicker of firelight, as several of the tent sites enjoyed the warmth of small fires. Some were in portable fire rings, the kind you would find in the average backyard, and others were set in fifty-gallon drums.

"Looks like something out of a bad movie. Bums around fires in drums, just like the inner city."

As he gazed judgmentally at the citizens of the settlement, one in particular gazed back.

Davies had infiltrated, gathering intelligence, trying to find dissenters to man his new militia. He looked up into the windows of the university center, trying to catch a glimpse of the governor, wanting to map his whereabouts.

Lance made eye contact, and was suddenly stricken with a bad feeling. "What are you looking at?" He was pierced by Davies' gaze.

Davies pointed at his eyes and then at Lance's, the universal sign for "I'm watching you."

"Holy shit!" Lance looked away and quickly moved from the window.

Davies put his head back down; his hood obscured his face as he returned to his patrol of the settlement. He worked to blend in, trying to learn as much as he could.

Chatter had been quiet in the commons, but as he approached the tents at the far end, he overheard a few guys huddled around one of the burning barrels. They talked about missing family members.

Davies moved closer, throwing his hands over the fire, doing his best to act like he belonged. "Christ, it's getting cold," he tossed, hoping to be accepted.

"Yeah, the days just keep getting colder, my shoes squeak on the snow... Hey, haven't seen you around here before? You militia?" Johnson was leery of their uninvited guest.

"Naw, regular army. Oh, uh, just call me Mitt," Davies introduced himself.

"Well, I'm Bret Johnson, and this is my buddy Lewis Barker, and his son J.R. New to the settlement, Mitt?"

"Yeah, just got tired of trying to survive without power. I'm pretty angry." He fished for allies, ready to end the murderous thug who organized the mass death of the town and his family.

"You're not alone." Barker was a little angry himself.

"Sure, no power no heat, right? We had to stop living in our house, right here, just blocks from campus. No power, no heat leads to broken pipes. We couldn't even continue to squat in our own house. Luckily, I could sneak in here and camp with Bret."

Johnson gave his buddy a look of concern. He leaned over and whispered in his ear.

"Oh yeah." Barker looked green. "But I'm good. It's all good... happy to protect the zone."

Davies realized he had just been shut out. He placed his hand in the pocket of his Army parka, his finger now hooked on the trigger of his gun. *I'll just say it, and if they get hostile, I'll shoot and run.*

"Okay, I realize you don't trust me, so I'm just gonna go out on a limb here, because frankly," he sighed heavily, "I have wasted enough time being careful and am frustrated and ready to put an end to

156

the governor's reign. My wife and children, my little baby girls, were killed at the dome. I sent them there. I trusted the governor...my superiors, and sent them there." With a slight tremble he choked back a flood of emotion. "I saw evidence of it, concrete evidence." Mittens Magoo flashed through his mind. "I also saw bodies, from the buses, being closed into crates." He recalled the recoil of the stapler. "Help me. Help me get him. Help me make them pay for what they've done."

Ready to draw, he awaited a response.

Barker and Johnson once again whispered amongst themselves. An occasional glance was directed at Davies.

Looking relieved by Davies' monologue, Barker spilled. "That's why I said more than I should have before, you just seemed so trustworthy. Can't be too careful around here, though."

"Yeah, they want you to believe its only militia out in these tents, that we are the fringe, the nuts tasked with guarding the trench, but all sorts have landed here, and the regime doesn't like it. It's hard to control the masses at a time like this, a chaotic, displaced time. So, they have moles. People disappear, usually those who have voiced complaints about the zone or the treatment we've been given. It's just one more way to control us." Johnson became paranoid, his voice low as he continued to divulge, "All the uppity-ups are in the main administration buildings...large offices used as apartments. The dorms seem to be filled with regular army guys, mostly single; they don't know anything. They're just following orders. Some of the families have been stashed in the academic halls,

Science, Art, etc. Some are associated with special team members, but we aren't sure who or how many. We've discussed it, and from what we can tell, the majority of the people missing lived outside the zone, and trusted the buses.   Local guard troops who lost family members and complained, were either taken care of," Barker demonstrated for Davies by pointing his finger at his head, "or they disappeared into the woods." Johnson felt for Davies: his wife and son were safe in the tent.

"I've been searching for a month, trying to fill in the fucking holes; I want to take them down. I'm looking to recruit all those who want him gone."

"If my family went missing, I'd want revenge. Anyone hurt my boy," he ruffled his grown son's hair, "They'd be looking down the barrel of my gun."

"Arrogance," Johnson blurted. "He was blinded by greed, and figured he could just kill anyone who interfered.   He's a fool. From what I've heard, the trench to the south was half-assed. Dirt still piled everywhere... some of the towers weren't even built. The trench and towers on this end were perfected, giving him the illusion of completion while the other forty-plus miles were, well, let's just say if there's going to be a breech, my money is on the southern end. My inside guy says that the head honchos were just telling Landis what he wanted to hear, unable to fulfill his grandiose plans. Not enough men, or resources. Shit, just not enough time. Not to mention the buses. He didn't realize that only a select few of the team members would be able to handle that gruesome task. Even those with the hardest characters value their fellow soldiers, and take offense to killing their families. It's chaos. Landis thinks he's in charge but according to my source, Hatch and McGovern have policies and protocols in place behind his back."

"I, I don't even know what to say. He's crazed… placated by yes-men who lie to him and advance their own agenda. Terrifying." Barker rubbed his head, flabbergasted by their circumstances.

"Yeah, it is. But keep your friends close and your enemies closer right? That's why I'm camped here with my wife and son." Johnson motioned to the tent behind him.

"You said you were in the militia. Weren't militia families affected? Surely some of you were from outside of the zone?"

"Built in distrust of the government. Those who didn't volunteer for guard duty dispersed, finding shelter in camps and rural homes. A select few teamed up with the governor, but they were always the extreme members. Some of us were only drawn in because our Colonel asked us. Eventually we realized he was on the inside as well. Those of us still here only stay out of a selfish desire to keep the zone guarded. Well, and I have extenuating personal circumstances." He pointed to the tent once again, his sick wife in need of electricity. "We may dislike the governor, but he did have the right idea when he shut us off from the rest of the world." Johnson was worn thin, the weight of the situation tangible now that he was talking to Davies.

"How do you know your commander was in on it with Landis?"

Barker jumped in, pointing to the buildings behind them, the lights in the windows casting a glow on the tent tops.

"He's living one door down from General Hatch, who lives one door down from the governor."

Davies was skeptical. "How does your source know all of this? Why trust him if there are moles?"

Johnson tried to explain, "He's sick over what he had to do, once it started he was afraid, he couldn't back out. He wants to make amends for the wrongs he's committed. I believe what he's told me is true, and we all better take care, or we'll be gotten rid of as well."

"Do you know of any others who would join us? Clearly, it's not safe to just poll the settlement." Davies was desperate to build their ranks.

"There are some soldiers who've retreated to the woods, their families were lost or they're in fear for their lives because they voiced their concerns. They've organized an outpost. I'll give you directions. I'm sure they'd be willing to listen."

"Are you with me: Can I count on you to join me and turn this around...end the fear, the tyranny?" Davies was finally optimistic, his goal in sight.

The friends looked at each other.
"We're in."

Chapter 12
Behind Door Number Three

"So, here we are, a month in, Christmas practically here, and it really was the end of the world," Pop yawned over his cup of camp coffee. Nan shrugged in agreement, the warm mug wrapped in her cold hands.

"Hey, where'd you get coffee from?" Doolin's eyes were still half open as he eagerly poured himself a cup from the stovetop percolator.

"The cellar." Pop took another sip.

"What cellar? This place is so close to the water, there're no basements out here."

"Through the door in the living room," he informed him cryptically.

Nan smiled. She was excited about sharing the good news with her son.

"The only doors in there go to the yard or the bedroom."

"Suit yourself." He sipped again.

Doolin walked out of the kitchen confused. *There's a cellar and the door is in the living room.*

He stood and sipped his coffee facing the large windows that viewed the yard, hoping the caffeine would lift the fog. The front door was to the left of the windows, just below the stairs. *Bedroom door, front door, no cellar door,* he concluded.

The early morning light lit the snow that coated the bare trees surrounding the home. Lake Paramount was visible in the distance, the faint sparkle of the rising sun danced on its rippled surface.

"Find it?"

"No Dad, I didn't find it." His moment of peace was interrupted. He brought the cup to his lips again.

"Alright, well, I'm gonna head down and see where we stand with supplies. Pop walked around the sofa and stood at the coffee table's edge, it was a large and eclectic piece of furniture. He pulled a skeleton key from his shirt pocket, and placed it in the keyhole, which was located below the doorknob that was attached to the makeshift tabletop.

"I think you've finally lost your mind," Doolin assured his father.

He gave his son a wink before he turned the key and opened the coffee table. A wide grin spread across his face as he stepped into the barrel. He reached back and flipped on the light.

"No way, that's the door? And there's power. How is there power?"

"Solar panels. Didn't you notice them on the roof? Why do you think I keep shoveling it?"

"How long can they last?"

"Thirty years, give or take. If we're careful, mindful of use, we can have light in the shelter, that is if we ever need to be down here, or if there's a medical emergency."

"What about a generator?"

"Seems logical, wanting to generate your own power, but they are noisy. Even when we buried them

162

in the military, you could still hear it hummin' under the ground. Plus, if you think long-term disaster... no fuel for the generator, no power."

Doolin followed his father down the steep and narrow stairs. (Well, really more ladder than stairs).

At the bottom was a very small space, maybe six by six. At the far side was a hallway. It was very narrow, barely three feet wide. It ran fifteen feet to another door, dropping incrementally, the shelter clearly recessed for safety.

"Think Deck could fit through here?" he joked as he followed his father down the dimly lit throughway.

"He'll just have to turn sideways, should the need arrive."

They crossed through the second threshold.

The bunker was generous in size, as large as the house from the living room to the kitchen; at least seven hundred square feet.

"Holy shit, un-fucking believable. I don't understand," he gasped as he wandered the room. "How...when?"

"It wasn't easy. I had this bunker dug just a few feet from the house, but only after we pulled up half the floor and dug the landing and tunnel. Once the shelter was completed, they were tied together."

"So we walked under the house and out through the tunnel and this room is actually below the yard?"

"Yeah, incredible, isn't it? The tunnel and the bunker are recessed several feet under."

"I knew you were a conspiracy nut, but I had no idea you were a doomsday prepper."

Doolin walked around, admiring his father's commitment to doing it right. Three walls were lined floor to ceiling with crates of emergency rations. One wall was reserved for bunks, which were mounted in two rows, stacked three high.

"Been investing in storable food for long?" He ran his hand along the wall of plastic containers.

"Why do you think I've been driving the same car for last twenty years?"

"What's the shelf-life on this stuff?" He was mesmerized by the sheer volume of supplies.

"Twenty-five years, in the right conditions. Heat will shorten it, but luckily it's cold in the north woods, and the temp down here is steadily below sixty-five. I didn't tell you because I figured we'd eat what we gathered first, then move to the stuff down here only after I was sure, you know, that it really was over. So, now with the holiday close and things getting desperate I figure we'll start eating the oldest stuff first, rationing of course. I really wanted to wait, only dipping in once we were really sure it was our only recourse. I figure the winter months will require the most use, then we can hunt and garden in the warmer months. I have a case of heirloom seeds under the bunk."

"How old is the oldest stuff," Doolin wrinkled his nose at the thought of eating twenty-year-old noodles.

"Ninety-six, so about eighteen years, ever since the middle of the last democratic White House. I bought yearly, so it gets newer as you move down the wall."

"You bought into emergency food storage and built this bunker because of the last Democratic president?"

"Yeah, and look, we have another one, and it's all gone to shit!"

"Settle down, you're gonna blow an artery."

"I need a smoke." Pop walked toward the exit while jamming a cigarette between his lips.

"Can't smoke down here?" Doolin was surprised.

"Nope, could damage the supplies."

"Have you considered what you're gonna do when you run out of smokes?" He was unable to imagine his father smoke-free.

Pop turned, strolling back into the room. He stood in front of a footlocker. In a grand gesture, he flipped up the lid of a large trunk to reveal carton upon carton of white boxes neatly stacked inside. They were marked in black bold-faced type with one word: **Cigarettes.**

"Of course, you can't endure a catastrophe without being able to light up."

"If you think I'm high-strung now, imagine me sans nicotine."

"You have a point, Dad. No one should endure *you* in the midst of a nicotine fit."

Pop headed back toward the door with a box of oatmeal in his hands. "Grab a thing of powdered milk, the kids can put it in their breakfast this morning.

Tomorrow we'll reveal the bunker to the rest of the crew."

Doolin pulled the box of dried Carnation from one of the many shelves and flipped off the light.

With his father leading the way, they exited the secret passage.

"Always lock it when you leave." He handed his son an extra key.

"Can I tell Laney, she could use the good news."

"Sure."

He lowered the door back onto the barrel's side and twisted the key. The door locked with a satisfying click.

"Turn off the light," Pop reminded.

"Where is it?" He searched for the switch.

"End of the barrel, just below the tabletop."

With the door locked and the light switched off, Doolin carried the dried milk to the kitchen, still amazed by what he'd just seen.

"I can't believe it." He hugged his mother's shoulders.

With a warm smile she patted his hand, so pleased they had this gift to share with him.

"If you knew what I knew, saw what I saw, before the Cold War ended, you'd have the same bunker. Your mother thought I was nuts; she was not on board. Bet she's glad now."

Nan nodded, her affirmative.

"What are you talking about down here?" Laney's hair was on end and clearly expressing her worsening mental state.

The men became suddenly silent, afraid to set her off.

"Government conspiracy," Doolin offered.

"Oh, like the time Pop said that because he's a smoker, if he was run over by a bus, it would still statistically be considered a smoking-related death." Laney grinned. "Oh my god, is that coffee, and powdered milk?" She poured a cup before tearing into the Carnation box and using the dried dairy as creamer.

"You give me a hard time, but it would be; all they care about is their statistics."

"There aren't statistics anymore, we're at square one now." Doolin followed suit and spooned the powdered milk into his cup as well.

"So, what's our plan for today, old man?" His dad was now happily chain-smoking in the kitchen.

Laney shot him a look. "Pop, the kids."

He cracked the kitchen window and tried to blow the offending smoke outside.

"Well, firewood, and water. Since the pump quit with the power, keeping the tub full has been a full time job. Maybe take a hike and try to see what else we can round up." He was just about to discuss the holiday surprise when Laney piped up.

"Like the two brothers who decided they wanted to borrow some firewood and other necessities from our shed. I was about to beat the piss out of them with my bat, but Dory chased them off with one of the shotguns."

"What, when did this happen?" Doolin was upset.

"When we first got here, you were out looking for supplies."

He shook his head. "I knew something was wrong. I could sense it."

"Nothing was wrong, Dooley." Laney was irritated by his condescending voice. "We were perfectly capable of taking care of ourselves."

Her blood pressure rose—the needle nearing the red.

Suddenly overwhelmed, her voice became shrill; she yanked at her hair. "When will you stop treating me like a fragile child. I'm not helpless, or delicate."

"Sorry," Doolin called as his wife stomped off. "Wait, I wanted to tell you about..."

She was gone.

Chapter 13
Trench Warfare

"Frosty, ten o'clock," J.R. called from the tower. The afflicted, now contorted into its post-mortem, animalistic form, teetered forward, its pace sluggish due to the frigid December air. Freezer burn and the snow piled upon its head and shoulders gave it a flocked appearance, thus lending to the nickname.

"Roger that," Brady answered, Frosty now in his sights.

"It's a shame to waste bullets on 'em. They're moving so slow in this cold, seems like it would be more sporting to just crack 'em in the head with something, doesn't it?" Chalmers was bored to death and looking for some fun.

"I'm squeezing the trigger, one shot to the head," Brady assured his over-zealous associate.

Frosty slowly approached, his twisted frame burdened by the snow and cold. The ground cover was only about a foot deep but with a temperature steadily below freezing, it piled up a little more every day, covering the previously sniped snowmen with a thick white blanket. A few had fallen into the trench after being shot, and were now hung up on the many wooden pikes lining the bottom.

"Frosty down," Brady radioed back to the tower, its head burst and a spray of dark liquid discharged onto the snow.

"Anyone find it kind of ironic?" Chalmers asked, "That we are out here shooting Frosty, or whatever these things are, under orders from the governor. It's a lot like that show, where the governor ruled the little town during the zombie apocalypse..."

"Yeah, I saw that one," Barker chimed in, his rifle resting comfortably on his militia-issued beer belly. "Except he made himself the governor and all those idiots went along with it... but in our case, Landis really is the governor. We may not trust him, hell, I don't even like him, but his plan to separate has worked. Look, these things have just started to trickle in, and what, we're at the beginning of month two since the infection started, and we're all still alive and healthy. The trench and towers are doing their job. We're safe, well, as long as we guard this trench and keep our heads down... not question anything."

"Well," Johnson announced, "I'm thankful that my family is tucked safely at the University. If Landis is there and safe, it means I know where he is and we're safe. And sure, the other Static Zone residents are relatively safe in their homes or camps, but they're struggling through the winter without power or water, and we're rationed electricity and food. Our Christmas is about to be a lot merrier than theirs."

"But, how long do you think that will last? How long before we're given the treatment?" Barker once again demonstrated with a gun like finger pointed at his temple.

"You're right, you should be afraid." Brady was unnerved. "I've told you about his plans, his behavior. His top men think he's nuts. They are just playing along. I'm just waiting for the bottom to fall out."

"How'd you end up with this shit detail anyway, who'd you piss off?" Lee Chalmers and his snide demeanor were disliked by everyone, "Weren't you up at the dome all warm before? Why 'er you out here now?"

Scarred by the undertaking at the dome, haunted by the loss of life, Brady just wanted to be sure the border was secure, and no one died in vain. "Wanted my own two eyes on the front line."

"Oh... control freak, got it. Why didn't you want to patrol the straights?" His tone was grating on Brady's nerves. "I hear those guys are gearing up to spend the winter keeping the waterway open. They're afraid the infected are going to walk across the ice, if and when it freezes over, but I say, if they're moving as slow as Frosty over there was, no worries. Seems like an excuse to play with explosives."

"I'd be happy to request a transfer for you," Brady hinted that he should shut his mouth.

The truth was that he'd been stationed at the dome during the Thinning and was now damaged. He welcomed the clarity that protecting the Static Zone from Frosty provided.

"Okay man, I'll zip it...back to work."

"Has anyone implemented a clean-up protocol, we can't just let them pile up?" Barker looked at the bodies already dotting the landscape.

"There aren't that many, why don't we just torch 'em this spring?"

"That's just brilliant," Brady's sarcasm was aimed, once again, at Chalmers. "It's been what... four or five weeks, and there are one, two, three, four...twenty bodies out there, not to mention the stragglers at the other checkpoints. Do you really think it's smart to wait, there could be hundreds by then."

"Yeah, well I guess we didn't consider that. What if we wait until there are twenty-five." His tone was condescending. Lee gestured toward the watchtower. It was forty-feet high, with a wide set base, its design seemingly inspired by Eiffel, criss-crossed its way to a platform topped by a railing. "We'll drop the bridge and clean up every twenty-five, that'll be the protocol. Will that be all right with you?"

Attached to the front of each tower (one was supposed to be constructed along the divide every four miles) was a drawbridge released via a pulley system that allowed for passage into the Western Outlands, over the ditch which was approximately ten feet deep and ten feet wide, give or take, and lined with sharpened posts crisscrossed and wedged into the ground. If need be, the bridge could be lowered and accessed through the gap under the tower.

"What would be all right with me, is if we lower that bridge and force you to the other side." He was ready to exile Chalmers and his big mouth.

"Okay," Johnson intervened. "Let's not get ahead of ourselves." He approached Brady and placed his hand on his shoulder. "Would you mind if we talked privately?" He led him along the edge of the trench. He looked back and signaled to Barker to join them.

"We," Johnson gestured to Barker and himself, "met a guy named Mitt who is looking to get a group together to exact some revenge on the Chief."

Barker agreed. "Yeah, we sent him out to join the others on the fringe."

"Maybe the best way to put your demons to bed is take him down. You're already worried that he'll just start to thin us."

"Yeah or freeze us," Barker jumped in. "We're living in a tent. How long can that go on? My wife wants to move out to the woods, she'd rather take her chances in the wild."

"You said he pillaged the homes of all who were thinned. And we know that other houses were scavenged, some of the guys here on the trench were part of those teams. Fuel, food, blankets... hell, even snowmobiles. Where is all of that stuff? Who gets to use it? I'm pretty sure there's enough uncertainty fermenting under the surface to take him down. Maybe we should be thinning them for what they've done, or probably will do in the near future." Johnson wrung the barrel of his rifle, "revenge, or a preemptive strike, any reason will do."

"So many people... woman and children. I just watched it happen... just watched..." He clenched his fists, the look in his eyes distant. He paused, lost in his own thoughts as he wrestled with his past. Brady's voice was deep and haunting, "They all deserve to die."

"Okay then, let's get this thing organized, maybe work for a date after Christmas." Johnson was excited; he was ready to turn the tide. His wife needed special care...electricity. If he couldn't trust that Steve Landis would continue to provide it, he needed to go.

Chapter 14
New Member

"Finally," Blake Davies was relieved. The trek to the outpost had been lengthy, and the cold had taken its toll. Although it was early afternoon, the skies were dark with the steely gray of inclement weather. The glow of lamplight was visible through the outpost windows, and was a welcomed sight as he traversed the last few yards. Tents and campers littered the property, positioned to create a corridor that led to the front entrance of the main dwelling.

"Johnson sent me." Davies spoke through the sliver in the door.

"What's your name?" only the suspicious nose and one eye were visible.

"Mitt."

The door slowly opened as the occupants filed forward to get a look at the newest member of their morbid club.

"Come in," they invited. "Johnson radioed, said you were coming."

Davies heard shuffling on the porch roof above. He shifted his gaze skyward to find the barrel of a rifle visible from his vantage point; it was aimed at his head.

"Home security system?" he joked trying to lighten the mood.

"Just making sure we get them before they get us," the greeter asserted.

Davies made his way in, the men parting as he walked through. He took a seat at a pine picnic table, which was positioned alongside the fireplace. Chilled by the long walk through the dark winter morning, he welcomed its warmth. With his gloves now discarded, he rubbed his hands near the flames. "The temperature is dropping, I think snow is on the way. I'd say it looks like we'll have a white Christmas, but there is already snow on the ground."

No one was amused by his humor.

He took a moment to survey his surroundings. A map of the area was spread out on the table: key points, mostly near the university, were highlighted. Supplies were stacked in corners, canned goods, sleeping bags, and gallons of water...

Shame, he thought, *this would be a nice place to stay under different circumstances.* It was like rustic living met modern man cave. The walls were covered with wood planking that ran the perimeter of the structure. An impressive array of signage and license plates, not to mention old oilcans and bar mirrors, dressed the walls in a masculine display. *Designed by men for men,* he thought as he admired the worn leather sofa against the back wall.

He looked up from his visual tour of the room to find he was surrounded; the men lurked silently.

"So, I see you've been planning; what's the story?"

The room was still, the crackle of the fire the only sound. Davies scanned their faces. The once proud military men gathered there were now jaded, disenfranchised by the very leaders they'd obeyed and trusted. "The governor took them, killed them all."

"He did," Davies assured them. "I got inside, I saw them stacking bodies in crates. They're all dead. That's what led me here."

"Let's make him pay." The room erupted, the men now shouting, as they shared their thoughts.

"Let's take him down."

"Yeah! Let's pick him up in one of his buses and drive him straight to hell!"

"Johnson knows a guy from the inside... knows exactly where the governor roosts, what his schedule is like... he can assist us." Davies was relieved. He'd wandered, searched these last weeks, trying to find his way...he was finally on his path to revenge.

They were just out here plotting... waiting. Davies was thrilled.

"What's the plan? Any ideas?" He'd waited a long time; he was ready to go.

"No plan," a gruff voice barked. "If we plan, the more likely they'll find out. I think we should just amass as many disgruntled citizens as we can. After five weeks of roughing it, that shouldn't be too hard. I think we hike and gather, growing as we roll, until we pull into town and just start..."

"Wing it? You want to wing it?"

"Quiet, Nick, who asked you."

"Who beside you, Walter," Nick Jeffries scoffed, "thinks it's a good idea to wing it?"

"Well," Davies interrupted, pausing the heated exchange, "short organization and a surprise element definitely would have its benefits. Besides, do you want to spend any more time out here looking at this map and eating canned pears?"

"We've got weapons."

"Who are you?" Davies was somewhat overwhelmed by the number of displaced soldiers.

"Elmer and Willy Jarvi." He pointed to himself, then his brother.

"How many weapons?"

"Oh, somewheres around one-fifty, well, firearms, dat is. Dat doesn't include da crate of F1 Limonka's we managed to pick up at a swap meet last summer out in Nort Dakota, eh."

Davies was floored by the thick northern accents; it was a brogue like no other.

Willy nodded enthusiastically while producing one of the Russian grenades from a worn leather satchel hanging over his round frame. "Isn't it pretty," he commenced to stroke the ordinance, its smooth shell pressed against his face.

"Holy shit!" Davies lurched, his instinct being to move away from the device.

The occupants of the cabin took a step back, hoping that a bit more distance would save them from whatever mishap was about to occur.

"Okay, that's a good start," Davies was trying to sound positive, waving his hands in a gesture meant to goad Willy into putting the grenade away.

"Yeah, we were in da militia until we saw the Colonel hob-knobbin wit da governor. No good, I tink, dat dey are in cahoots."

"Dat Landis tinks he's safe. Dat his plan was a success... he's wrong."

"He sure is," Elmer once again piped up. "Willy and I have been crossing da border, searching empty properties for supplies out here for weeks. Half of da guards aren't doin dere jobs, and those dat are don't care if other militia guys come and go."

"Yeah we've been crossing to rummage and occasionally we'll go plinking and pop a few of dose Frosty in da head for fun."

"A few what?" The brothers were difficult to understand. "And how do you get across?"

"Frosty is what dey're calling da dead or infected or whatever, cuz dere frozen and covered is snow. Oh, and we get across just by climbing over da dirt pile, trew da ditch and around da posts. Some parts are shallower, sometimes narrower dan others. I guess dey got a little hasty during construction. Anyways, our buddy out at station Foxtrot told us dat dey have da highest volume of infected. We were fixing tuh go out dere on our Ski-Doo's and see how many we could exterminate."

"Are the snowmobiles here now?" Walter didn't fancy the idea of a long walk in the snow and cold of a north-woods December.

"Heck no, eh. Gotta conserve fuel. Only emergencies and, well, the up-coming hunting trip."

"You betcha!" Willy added, excited about their pending adventure.

"You saw one, in person?" Walter pushed his way through the crowd to get the answer face to face. "What do they look like? What...are they fast?"

The crowd leaned in.

"It's sorta like, if a hairless werewolf, and a zombie had a baby." Willy chuckled, amused by everyone's curiosity.

"Well, except covered wit snow, eh, and frost. Oh, except da one we saw da udder week during that warm spell, right, Willy, he was a bit drippy."

"More like a slushy than a Frosty," Willy added a punch line.

His analogy struck his brother's funny bone. Elmer laughed deeply. "Oh dat's a good one Willy." His hysterical reaction caused him to bend over from the stitch in his side.

"What are you doing? You could infect us all. What if one attacked you?" Davies was flabbergasted. "You could destroy everything."

Elmer answered with exaggeration. "No way." Dose tings move sooo sloooww."

Willy once again shook his head as he agreed with his brother.

"Alright, so, where are the weapons?" Davies was tired of their antics, his patience for the Jarvi brothers was wearing thin.

"Dey're at our place." Willy pulled a Blatz from his satchel.

"Whoa." Davies stepped toward Willy, "No more grenades." He reached to disarm him before he blew them all sky high.

"Hey dere now, no worries. Brain grenade, not a real one."

With the top now popped, he sipped loudly.

"How's about a cold one for me?" Elmer held his hand out.

"Last one," Willy took another sip of the beer before passing it to his brother.

Relieved, Davies stepped away. He watched as they passed and sipped when he recalled a key statement. "Wait, what are you doing here if you're militia and these guys are clearly only harboring their own?"

"Oh, we were stealing da firewood and dey caught us, eh. I'm pretty sure dey were just about to beat us senseless when you showed up. We figured if we were helpful, dey might let it go."

Davies looked around the room. "What do you say, think we could forgive them if they lend us a hand?"

A rumble of scattered and random approval moved through the room.

"I guess that's a yes." Davies stood and put his gloves and hat back on. "I'm psyched. Let's get this show on the road. I don't know about all of you, but I'm ready to put an end to those sons of bitches."

The cabin was suddenly a flurry of activity as everyone scramble to bundle up and collect whatever paraphernalia they wanted or required to get that bus to hell rolling.

Davies watched as they all jumped to, suddenly filled with purpose.

"Well, just follow me and Willy, we'll lead da way."

"You heard em, fall out," Walter Briggs shouted.

"You can take the man out of the military, but you can't take the military out of the man, hey Walt." Nick Jeffries zipped his jacket.

"We'd still be in if we weren't stabbed in the back by General Hatch and the governor."

"Don't forget dat prick McGovern," Willy reminded.

The men filed out of the back door, the Jarvi brothers in the lead, their hunting sleds in tow and piled high with contraband.

Davies grabbed a cup of cold coffee from the table and threw it on the fire before walking out. The men traveled in pairs, chatting to one another as they meandered through the shallow snow. Their breath swirled in the cold air as they made their way toward the Jarvi's cache of weapons.

They wandered between trees and through fields as they followed their guides along the path they'd previously cut through the fresh powder.

"How much farther?" Jeffries was already whining, his feet becoming cold and stiff. "I think I'm working on frostbite back here."

"Two miles, give or take."

"We've already walked two or three."

"More like one and a half," Davies corrected.

They passed rural homes and camps, many the brothers obviously had visited to lift supplies, the trail of their larceny stamped in the snow.

"I see you have been to all of these properties, leave anything for the owners?" Davies observed from the back of the line.

"Finders keepers," Elmer called back.

182

They kept trudging, the cold now eating into everyone's outerwear.

"If you must know, we didn't get anyting from dis place." Willy pointed to the Riley's camp, the glow of its windows visible through the trees, as they now followed the lakeshore to the Jarvi's house.

"Why not, seems like you pillaged every residence for last five miles."

"We tried, but dey, much like dese fellas, didn't take too kindly to us helping ourselves."

"Yeah," Willy joined in, "dey were armed to da teeth."

"Looks like we're in for a humdinger of a storm," Elmer pointed, bringing the guys' attention to the sky. Lake Paramount was calm, its glasslike surface reflecting the dark gray skies of impending snow.

"What's dat?" Elmer's attention now focused on the water. "Sometin's floatin."

With the line halted, the troop of displaced soldiers turned their attention to the form drifting in the frigid lake.

"It's moving, sweet Jesus it's moving!" Walter got closer, his toes now in the water. "Quick, get a branch, I'll try to pull it in."

A few scrambled, foraging in the snow.

"Here, got it." Jeffries passed a large stick to Walter, who had moved farther into the drink trying to reach the target. He slapped at it, trying to hook the fabric floating on the surface.

"Is it a person?" someone called from the beach, cautious to not get to close.

"I almost have it," he grunted as he struggled, the object heavier than he expected.

With it in reach, he snagged the wet mass of fabric, not sure what to expect. Now pulled into the shallows, the horrible truth was revealed.

"Holy hell! Holy ever-loving hell!" Walter Briggs jumped back, immediately vomiting. He violently heaved as the others moved in to investigate what he was so upset about.

"Its brain is hanging out. Right? That's its brain hanging out?" Davies looked around for confirmation.

With the jaw gone, and the tissue surrounding the neck shredded, the woven ball of gray matter was slumped over, hanging on what used to be its chest.

"Yeah, still attached to the spinal cord I guess," he turned his head sideways, trying to make rhyme or reason of the jumbled, displaced, interconnected parts. "And maybe some entrails, I think those are intestines or something." Jeffries poked at it with the stick; the stumps where the arms used to be twitched in response.

Nibbled by fish or eroded by the perpetual motion of the lake, this infected soul was now just a quivering glob of gelatinous anatomy.

"For Christ's sake, someone make it stop... put an end to it," Briggs bellyached from his bent position, sickened by its existence.

"How do you propose we kill something that should already, technically be dead?" Jeffries surveyed the crowd, open to any suggestions.

"The brain, damage the brain." Walter coughed. "Ever seen any movies?"

"Yeah dat's what does it," Willy assured them. "We found dat head shots stopped Frosty cold."

"Good one, brudder." Elmer was rolling.

As Jeffries speared the brain with the branch, a spray of black liquid projected from the wound, signaling the end of its tortured existence.

Davies, disgusted, approached the brothers to revisit something they'd said before the corpse washed up. "So, you mentioned someone was armed to the teeth? Do you think they would join us in our crusade to take down the establishment?"

"Dose girls were crazy. One wanted to beat us with a bat and da other threatened tuh shoot us. Uh-uh, no sir. We're not going over dere."

Davies made a mental note of the camp's position as they continued their walk. He intended to return once he was armed. *If those women are alone, they might need help if nothing else*, he thought as he watched the light fade into the distance.

Thinking of those women alone in this situation, and the image of that creature on the beach... made him think of his wife and daughters. *Alone on that bus, afraid and helpless...* Davies' guts turned over, he placed his hand to his stomach. It felt like the bottom was falling out as he bent and dry-heaved, only bitter yellow stomach acid dribbled into the snow.

Now on his knees, he stifled the sobs that were welling in his chest. The cold of the snow seeped through the knees of his pants as he hyperventilated, the grief suddenly too much to bear.

"Whoa, you okay, man," one of the guys asked as he doubled back to check it out. "When's the last time you ate something?"

"I, I don't know," Davies stammered, his speech burdened by heartache.

"Here," he pulled a protein bar from his bag. "Nibble on this while we walk; I think we're almost there. I heard one of those brothers say, "it's just up da hill eh'," in fact I think I can see the roof from here."

"Thanks, sorry." He smiled weakly as he apologized, amused by the impression of the brothers.

"No worries, we've all had our moments. Add fatigue and hunger to an already burdened psyche and you are bound to break down."

"What's your name?" Davies tried to get to his feet. He surveyed his new friend, this brother in arms, as he composed himself. A little older than some of the others, he had a seasoned appearance. A mock turtleneck peeked from behind his quilted jacket. He projected a demeanor more sympathetic than the others, who definitely seemed more gung ho and ready to roll.

"Cory."

"First or last?"

"First, I'm tired of being called by my last name. I trusted the army...my government... anyway, now I'm just Cory."

"I, too, have left the old me behind," Davies admitted. "I'm going by Mitt these days," his name a tribute to the beloved toy of his precious Lila.

"Let's catch up with the others, Mitt, see what those brothers have to offer."

Cory led the way as they hiked quickly, reaching the house last.

The other men were already packed inside, boisterously commenting on the Jarvi's stockpile. The brothers had produced several crates filled with all manner of ordinance and weapons.

Double barrels, semi-autos, handguns, a rocket launcher, the grenades... Elmer and Willie truly were armed to the teeth.

"Holy hell, this must have taken years, look at the amount of ammo alone." Cory and Davies were amazed.

"We've been preppin' for a long time. We always new da day would come when we'd have tuh be prepared, but we're more dan happy to pull out dese guns and share wit ya, especially after we so selfishly tried tuh steal da firewood."

Davies couldn't help but grin the same purposeful, eager grin as all the other men. The cache meant the promise of reprisal for Steve Landis and his ilk, and that was gratifying. "I think you've more than made up for it."

Chapter 15
Christmas Surprise

"Go away. Go away or I'll ventilate your torso!"

"I heard there were some women..."

"Want my women, do you?" Pop's hackles were up. "Lot of fucking nerve asking about women, what you getting at?"

"No, that's not what I meant. I heard there were some women, and I was worried they might need help, but now I see you're here."

"Oh, a chauvinist. Don't think women can take care of themselves?"

Davies rubbed his face. Pop was purposely giving him a hard time. *Change the subject,* he thought.

"I'm with a group up at the Jarvi's, and we're planning to overthrow Landis. I just walked over before we headed out to see if you're interested in joining. Aren't you tired of being in the dark? Doesn't it make you angry that the governor sits in his heated office with his hot showers and Christmas lights and you are out here trying to survive this winter."

"He'll run out of power eventually, and we'll already be used to roughing it. If you ask me, he's just delaying the inevitable." Pop turned and nodded his head, assuring his family that he was right.

"Even so, don't you want to stop his tyranny? He has killed hundreds, maybe thousands of innocent people. He has murdered and lied to pad his own way of life."

"Yeah, murdered on the buses."

"How'd you know?"

"Only an idiot would get on a bus controlled by one man during a crisis of this magnitude." He turned back toward the family again. "What did I say, see, goddamn bus, straight to the gas chamber!" He turned his attention back to the crack in the door. "I'm sure your motives are solid, but my motive is to get my family through this alive, and following you into town, well, it makes my balls twitch, so... No. Sorry, now fuck off!"

Davies stood at the closed door, feeling truly stupid.

Even this nut job knew not to trust the buses...the governor.

"I know you're still out there, I can hear you breathing. Go away, I'll shoot, I swear to Christ!"

"I'm going," Davies assured the hostile resident as he backed off the porch.

"Is he gone," Doolin whispered, his hands over each one of the boy's mouths.

"Yep, I can see him walking away. What an idiot... he shouldn't go into town. I wouldn't, not for anything, especially on Christmas Eve. No good Catholic would ignore such an important holiday."

"What if you run out of cigarettes?" Elle was positive that's all it would take to send her grandfather out on an errand.

"Nnnno." He hesitated, not certain he could say it. "We have everything we need right here."

189

"Do your balls and or ball hairs, twitch, or tingle? You can't seem to keep it straight." Elle loved to give him a hard time.

"Twitching, tingling...it's all the same. It's my spidey sense, my little voice. A warning bell if you will." He shifted, making a grand display of rearranging his testicles.

"Ahh! Geez! Pop!" The crew groaned an uncomfortable chorus as he grinned and adjusted his warning bells.

Laney was not amused. "The kitchen is almost empty, and what if that guy comes back again, or the guys who tried to steal the firewood before." She was frazzled, her hand on the pill bottle, which was now home to only one tiny tablet. "It's Christmas Eve, we're running out of food, I don't have gifts for the kids...Thanksgiving... we had canned vegetables." She rambled, the pitch of her voice rising with each sentence. "We still had power then, the pump still worked. Things didn't seem as bleak. Now, we have to worry every minute about where the water is going to come from and how to get food. I, I, I...I need to lay down."

She ran upstairs, desperate to be alone, what little control she had left quickly ebbing.

"I'll be right back." Doolin trotted toward the stairs. "We should have told her about the door."

"She stomped off before we could tell her, remember. Just let her go, she wants to be alone. I think we did pretty well... over a month with just the stuff we gathered. I admit it was a little lean these last few days, but we had the oatmeal..."

"Yes, lean. I gave the boys my share of the kidney beans the other night. I couldn't believe they ate them. They must be starving." Doolin regretted not telling his wife about the shelter already.

"Okay, let's liven things up around here and celebrate the birth or our Lord and savior; let's make some holiday preparations. Deck, go outside and haul in some firewood, let's get the place toasty. Dory, be a dear and go upstairs to the attic and pull down that box of old Christmas décor, it's not much, but it'll do. Ma, have Elle help you get some water boiling, and boys," Pop called, "you come with me."

"Where we going?" they asked with excitement in their voices.

"Through the magic door, boys."

They followed closely, Doolin right behind.

Pop furnished the key and held it up, letting them take a close look.

"Wow, I've never seen a key like that before."

"Me either." Ian leaned over his brother to look.

"It's a skeleton key and it opens the magic door." Pop put the key in the hole on the tabletop and turned. The lock made its usual robust click. With one hand he lifted and revealed the opening.

"Could you get the light, son, I can't tell my face from my ass in this dark."

"We have lights?" Ian was confused. "Why haven't we used them?"

"Saving it for a special occasion. So turn it on Dooley...my ass."

Sean and Ian found their grandfather's language more entertaining than any video game. They giggled as they followed him down the ladder.

"Holy hell," Ian swore.

"Yeah, what he said," Sean added.

The hallway to the bunker made for a magical adventure. Caged lights were placed every few feet and cast a dim glow lending a theatrical feel to the utilitarian space. They ran their hands along the rough concrete of the poured corridor walls. They arrived at the bunker ahead of their father and grandfather, and pounded on the steel door.

"This is the coolest ever," Ian complimented, the ringing of the metal tearing through the small space in waves.

"Yeah, what he said," Sean added.

"Let's go inside and pick something for dinner, then you can haul some of this up for the next week." With the door now opened, the boys absorbed the glory that was their Pop's shelter.

Terry and Doolin took a moment to enjoy the boy's excitement.

"Holy cow, this place is great!" Ian darted from corner to corner, observing all it had to offer.

"Yeah, really great!" As usual, Sean's thoughts were the same as his brothers, Ian, as usual the dominant twin.

"Can we sleep down here?" The boys bobbed their heads, hoping the motion would entice their grandfather.

Pop pulled one of the pre-packed food crates and another powdered milk container and told the boys to get them to the kitchen. "I'll think about it, now get this upstairs."

"Got it, Pop." They commenced to lug the sizeable containers to the surface.

"Dooley, come over here with me. I have a few things that might work as gifts for the kids?"

"That would be great; Laney would really be pleased."

Pop revealed an overhead bin filled with unopened board games and playing cards. "We figured being holed up down here might get boring. I also have some scarves and gloves, you know, spare outerwear. They're brand-new, maybe Elle would like a scarf?"

Doolin placed his hand on his father's shoulder. He was never the warmest guy, but he always provided, and right now he was providing more than just material needs.

"This is amazing. I can't wait to tell Laney."

"Well, before you go running up there, maybe you could round up a tree."

"Yeah, and I'll have Elle dig through the old newspapers; maybe there's a comic or two in there that could serve as wrapping paper."

"You've gone all Martha Stewart on me, come back to manhood, my son." Pop wasn't one for sentiment and had to deflect with an insult.

"Okay, Dad, Martha Stewart, very funny."

With their goodies in hand, including a carton of smokes tucked snugly under Pop's arm, they returned to the surface.

The boys had carried the food into the kitchen where Nan was teaching Elle how to light the wood-burning kitchen stove. "Run upstairs and fill the kettle with water," she translated aloud from her grandmother's gestures.

Nan gave the thumbs-up, the translation spot on.

Elle trotted off to fill the kettle, while the boys dug through the crate and tried to decide what to have.

"It's soooo hard to choose," Sean had the packages spread out on the floor.

"Yeah." Ian licked his lips, trying to read the labels in the dim light of the lantern.

"Ooh, the beef stroganoff looks good." She conveyed her intentions by pointing enthusiastically.

"Yeah it does, Grandma, I mean, Nan," Sean corrected.

"Yeah, let's have that," Ian agreed.

Elle wandered back into the kitchen, the water sloshing in the large kettle.

"The tub is almost empty, just thought you'd want to know."

"I bet Pop has a magic place to pull water from too." Sean was certain his grandfather was capable of anything.

Nan placed the kettle on the now-heating stove and took a seat at the kitchen table.

While she spent time preparing food with the kids, Deck was outside splitting a few logs. He swung the axe, cracking the oak and maple with ease. As he swung he thought of Dory and the intimate moments they'd begun to share. Walks in the woods, late night meetings in the shed, stolen moments of privacy in a situation that afforded very little.

Dory took a peek from the upstairs window, filled with the same romantic thoughts. She knocked, to catch his attention. He smiled and gave her a little wave before returning to his swing.

Quickly, she climbed the ladder to the attic. She peeked her head into the space. "Not quite high enough to stand in." She crouched as she reached for the decorations; it was the only box up there. "Plegh," she spewed, as she wiped her hand past her mouth. An ancient cobweb had snagged in her hair and trailed across her face. Now web-free and with the adornments in hand she tiptoed down the hall, not wanting to disturb Laney.

She paused at the door and peeked into the crack. Laney's covered feet were visible as she hummed her little tune, the sound very faint.

"You all right?" Dory was worried about her friend.

"Just tired." Her voice was weak, the stress evident.

"We're going to put up some decorations I found in the attic."

"Okay."

Dory lingered a moment, hoping she would climb out of the bed.

She returned to humming, the tune taking on an eerie tone.

I'll just let her rest; she backed away, disturbed by the melody.

Laney wasn't resting at all: she was stewing. Her thoughts raced as she lay curled in the musty quilt, the aluminum bat cradled in her arms.

No food for my kids, no gifts. Left my house, left my car...my dad bought me those, his generosity, his insurance money...

Her gauge swung wildly into the red. *Had to leave...*

She bolted upright, the bat clutched in her grasp.

"Landis," she whispered.

With her sights set on the University, she crept to the landing.

Sounds of her family drifted up, their holiday spirit audible as the kids rummaged through the Christmas items Dory had procured from the attic.

Unable to exit the house from the downstairs without being noticed, she made her way to the window at the end of the hall. It was positioned above the porch roof.

Warm clothing. She made a mental list. *Extra socks, a hat...* She scavenged the upstairs rooms for protection from the elements, her jacket and accessories hanging downstairs. Luckily, everyone wore their boots all the time. Without central heat, the floors in the house were cold, so at least she had those. After some compromise, she felt she was equipped to make it to town. Wearing two sweaters, one of which was hooded, over a thermal undershirt and some of Pop's wool socks as mittens, she flipped up her hood, hoisted the bat over her shoulder, and climbed out the window.

~~~

"How's the wood coming?" Doolin stopped to inquire before setting out in search of a tree.

"Almost done," Deck huffed between swings.

"I'm getting a tree… Pop's idea." He shook the hack saw he'd pulled from the tool box.

"Need a hand?" Deck put down the splitting maul.

"No, how hard could it be?"

"See you in a bit then," Deck nodded.

Laney waited, the sound of Deck splitting creating a fine cover for her jump to the ground.

She crouched, eyeing the drop to the snow bank below, her legs tiring from her position. *Just kept talking, made me wait,* she thought, her leg now cramped as she prepared to jump.

Trying to scoot forward, she slipped, the bat getting away from her as she lurched to catch herself. It rolled, the barrel ringing as it hit the snow-covered ground.

She dropped without hesitation, landing softly in a pile amassed by the boys and their attempt at shoveling.

Wanting to depart before the noise attracted investigators, she darted into the woods and followed what would be the path (if there wasn't any snow).

Deck stopped chopping, certain he'd heard something around the corner. "Huh, just hearing things, I guess."

"There a problem?" Doolin peeked around Deck, who was peeking around the corner.

"Shit!" He jumped. "Don't sneak up on me like that."

"Ready to go in?"

"Yeah, just let me grab a load of wood."

With their spoils in hand they moved toward the house.

Doolin yanked as he pulled the Spruce through the front door. Snow and needles sprayed everywhere as he struggled.

Deck was close behind, his arms filled with the split hardwood, leaving him unable to shield himself from the flying debris.

"Jesus," he winced.

"Wonderful!" Pop sang as the two hauled in their bounty.

"Deck, get that fire roaring, and Dooley, let's find a way to get that tree upright."

"Let me go tell Laney about the food and the gifts first."

"Why not just let her rest and we'll set everything up. You can call her down when dinner is done?"

"Yeah... sure. Maybe a Christmas surprise would be nice."

"Just so you know." Elle popped around the corner. "The bath tub is almost empty."

They'd been filling it with water from the lake, purified in the makeshift filter.

"Guess we'll just have to spend more time running water through the filter. We should probably get er' filled before the freeze. Once the ice-pack on the lake moves in, we'll be boiling snow."

Elle seemed concerned. "Won't that be slow?"

Doolin did his best to comfort his daughter. "Yes, slow but adequate. We won't go thirsty."

"I think I got it," Pop had the tree wedged in an old bucket, rocks holding the trunk in place.

"Put this around the bottom," Elle handed her grandfather a checked throw from the sofa.

"Oh, that's lovely," Pop exaggerated, hands on his hips.

"There are some lovely old ornaments in this box." Dory rummaged, Deck nestled next to her. "Help me with them?" She motioned to Deck and the kids.

They hung what few there were, stepping back to admire the way they reflected the light of the lanterns.

With a wave Nan beckoned her crew to dinner. She placed the steaming pot on the table, resting it next to a large pitcher of warm milk.

"So, how did the two of you meet?" Dory couldn't remember the last time they'd had a normal, friendly conversation over a warm meal.

"Actually," Pop stood, his chest puffed out, "I dated her sister first, but she had a big mouth. I preferred the quiet one." Nan batted her eyelashes and gave her husband a smile.

The boys screeched with delight at the food before them. "This looks amazing."

"I'm going to get Laney." Doolin climbed the stairs two at a time, eager to show his wife that everything was okay. *Well, for now*, he thought, uneasy with what the future might hold.

"Laney? Laney, sweetie?" he called gently as he reached the door.

"We have a surprise for…" he stopped cold. "Laney," he called again as he turned to the hall. *Maybe she's in the bathroom*, he thought, well aware that with the pump out, it was unusable.

"Hon," he threw back the curtain, the steel tub empty except for the dregs of water left behind. *Where could she be*? He was worried.

He stood in the short upstairs hall, all three doors open, and all three rooms vacant.

A faint whistle followed a cold and creeping breeze.

Doolin turned to the small window. It was open just a crack: just enough to allow the December wind to howl through and land at his feet.

"Oh shit!" He ran down to his family. "Is she down here?" He searched frantically as he looked out each window, then out the back door. "She's gone...her and that goddamn bat."

"I thought I heard something earlier," Deck now aware it was probably the aluminum.

"It's been what, an hour maybe. How far could she have gotten?" Doolin needed to believe it wasn't that far.

"If she's moving with purpose, unimpeded," Pop calculated," she could be in town by now."

"Boys, stay here. Elle, look after them." Doolin threw on his outerwear and hastily headed for the door.

"We'll come with you." Deck stood as he volunteered Dory and himself.

"Arm yourselves, for Christ's sake, before you go out there," Pop barked. "Put extra rounds in your pockets." He stuffed, helping to prepare his son. "Shoot first, ask questions later, do you hear me. It was desperate out there before; five weeks in, it's murderous."

Doolin nodded as he stepped into the cold night to search for his wife. "Watch each other's backs," Pop shouted as they walked away, following their prints in the snow.

Chapter 16
Crossed Paths

"I'm coming for you, Mr.Landis," Laney whispered as she followed the bike path into town. "I have something...a gift for you." She dragged the bat on the ground, the unshoveled path muting the noise.

"It's a shame, really, that I have to kill you on Christmas Eve... and such a beautiful night too. Look," she pointed to the trees lining the path, "isn't it beautiful the way the snow frosts the trees. It's almost magical the way it sparkles in the, well, I was gonna say moonlight, but the clouds are looking pretty dense." With her face turned skyward, she extended her tongue as she tried to catch the swirling snow, a fluffy flake now stuck to her eyelash.

She blinked rapidly trying to discharge it.

"Who you talking to, lady?"

"The governor." She was unfazed by the menacing group loitering near the tunnel.

"You can't cross without payment. We take anything but cash, because as you know, it's worthless now."

All his friends laughed, their whole situation a movie cliché—the leader and his followers.

"All right." Laney placed the bat over her shoulder. Her petite stature, combined with the fact that she was clearly over forty, disarmed the young men, lulling them into a false sense of security.

She acted as though she were reaching for something in her pocket. Instinctually they all looked down to see what she was retrieving. In that split second she threw both hands on the grip and swung, the aluminum barrel meeting the side of his head with a dull thud.

"Whoa," Laney laughed in pain, the vibration of the strike pulsed through her palm. She commenced to do a little dance as she shook it out, "That one stung a little." Amused by her antics, they watched as her manically elevated actions took on an animated quality.

"You're nuts," the dented delinquent uttered between groans. "There are four of us, and one of you little woman." He was hurt and pissed off.

"Oh, Victim One can count, how cute." She hoisted the bat and continued to play with her new friends.

"And I think I'll call you Victim Two, and you Victim Three, and you Victim Four."

From the ground, with his hand cupped over his split and bloody ear he demanded justice, "Don't just stand there—get her!"

The delinquents paused to consider the request of their fallen leader. A consensus via eye contact brought Victim Two forward.

"Just show us if you have anything good in your pockets, and nobody else needs to get hurt."

With her left index finger she tapped her chin in contemplation. " Hmm, I think... I think I'd rather **knock your fucking block off!"**

Chest first she lurched, causing Victim Two to jump back, but she wasn't aiming for him. Instead she swung low and furthered her assault on Victim One with a satisfying crack.

Victims Two through Four kept a safe distance and watched as she picked his pockets.

"Junk, junk, junk." His belongings were discarded into the rising snow.

"Aha! What's this?" She shook the flask, "Just what the doctor ordered." She removed the cap with her teeth and began to pull from the bottle, the minty liquid warming her insides.

"Ahhh, good stuff."

The light flurry had thickened, and the now heavy snowfall was blanketing their motionless friend.

"Oh my god, his head." The hoods gathered; their friend was bleeding profusely.

"Oh yeah," she pointed to the blood staining the snowy path, " Thanks for that release, it felt great! Oh, and for the booze." She gave them a nod.

"You're a crazy bitch!"

"Yeah, yeah," she called back with indifference as she walked away, her hand waving them off, "I've heard it all before."

"Okay, Mr. Landis," she breathed into the cold night, "Had a brief hold-up, but it's all cleared up now, and I'm on my way."

Laney walked, and sipped, taking practice swings with the bat as she hummed her favorite tune.

Distracted, trapped in thought by her manic mind, she didn't notice the band of armed men cross the trail behind her.

Going in a different direction than Laney but on the same path, they too were hell-bent for the governor.

Chapter 17
Just Dropping In

"Psst. Psst." Davies beckoned to the tower. He and his newly formed militia had taken a position behind a thicket of trees where they struggled to gain the attention of Johnson.

Johnson and Barker were parked below the tower; their eyes peeled on the trench, they were preoccupied.

"Frit," he whistled between his teeth, another attempt at contact.

Johnson turned to search the shadows as he tried to locate the source of the sound.

"We have company," he whispered to Barker as he walked toward the woods.

They watched him approach when Walter announced, "I could've just radioed." Briggs waved the two-way at Davies.

"What ya see?" Chalmers was curious as to why he was taking a walk.

"Just want to piss without you gazing at the goods."

As he walked, he glanced back to be sure no one was following. Barker ran interference, engaging Chalmers, keeping him occupied.

"We're here and we're ready to go." Davies dragged his sleeve past his nose: it dripped constantly in the cold.

"Have you gone mad? You can't just drop in…roll up to the trench tower and declare war. It's Christmas Eve."

Johnson scanned the crew, amazed at the numbers they'd pulled already.

"Hey, we know you." The Jarvis pointed to Johnson.

"Hey," he returned with pleasant recognition. "Haven't seen you in a while, been out at the house?"

"You know it." Willy gave a thumbs-up.

Davies shot Elmer a look, clearly frustrated by the interruption.

"We know him though, cause we're from da same…never mind," he trailed off, discouraged by Davies' scowl.

He tried to get back to business. "You said you had someone on the inside; I want to talk to him."

"Christ." Johnson rubbed his head, forcing his hat to shift back and forth. "I thought you'd go out there and make friends, you know, talk it out first. I didn't think you'd be back a day later ready to take down the establishment."

"They were ready, I'm ready… they were already plotting when I got there. They just needed weapons. Which thanks to your friends the Jarvi brothers," Davies pointed (they gave a nod) "we are now packing and ready to fight."

"What's your plan?"

"No plan, just sneak attack. Hopefully many of the others will be like you and welcome the chance to take him down…join us, not fight us."

"Holy shit, that's nuts." Johnson rubbed his head some more. "Wait here."

He wandered back.

"What did they want?" Barker brushed snow from his hat. The flurry now thick, visibility was very low.

"It's that guy Mitt. He's amassed a small army; they're locked and loaded. They want to speak with Brady...they want to take Landis down, tonight."

"Huh, ballsy to just drop in like this, and fast. He must really want the Chief dead. So, how do they plan to do it?"

"Wing it." Johnson shook his head, still unable to believe it.

"They won't expect it, that's for sure."

"Frosty!" J.R. shouted from the tower, his finger now pointed to the tree line on the west side of the trench. "Christ, must be a dozen or more."

A flurry of gunshots rang out as the watchmen picked off the creeping and haunted forms. A dark and bloody mist erupted from the bullet-punctured heads. It floated gently to ground with the white of the falling snow.

"Haven't you seen any horror movies, you have to aim for the head." Barker was amazed by Chalmer's density, his shots hitting center mass and doing nothing to stop their progress.

"They make a horrible noise, don't they?" Johnson reloaded, ready to clean up Chalmer's mess.

"I've got it." Brady hoisted his rifle to his shoulder, Frosty in his sights. "It's got kind of an animalistic sound to it... the Frosty. Clicks and whistles, terrifying." He shuddered as he took aim; their articulated stop motion was unnerving and unmistakable. "You'll never mistake man for a Frosty. I thought maybe, in the shadows, or heavy snowfall, we could have mishaps, but naw. Nothing moves like they move."

Everyone agreed to that observation as he fired on the last few.

One had wandered all the way to the trench's edge, where it fell and impaled itself on the sharpened posts below; the torn but attached tissue of the puncture sites quivered as its dark liquid oozed into the snowy ditch.

"Well, that's a first." Johnson and the others shouldered their rifles and peered down at Frosty; it wriggled, speared and mindless, its motion perpetual. "They've fallen in before, but we shot em', they didn't get speared like that."

Johnson pulled Brady from the trench's edge, taking advantage of the distraction to fill him in. "Say, remember that guy we talked about, well, he and some of his men are tucked back in the trees," he motioned to the left, "they'd like to talk to you about a mission, and your possible knowledge of certain persons."

Brady turned and walked toward Davies and his men without another word.

Chalmers swiveled. "Now where is he going?"

Barker was quick to intercede. "Stop being so goddamn nosey, Chalmers."

Brady approached, his rifle in both hands.

Davies immediately recognized him, and, although angry, he rationalized, *you need him, he's your guide to revenge.* He searched Brady's face for recognition, but soon realized he had no idea who he was. Brady had already been despondent by time he'd intercepted Davies at the dome and didn't remember him, even now face to face.

"What's this?" Brady motioned toward the crowd.

"We're about to walk into the U.P. and take Landis down."

"Yeah and Hatch too." Briggs was ready.

"And don't forget dat prick McGovern," Willy Jarvi chimed in.

"No plan...just walk up and go at it?" With the tap of his foot he looked at the eager faces and contemplated.

"We need you to lead us to the target; you know where he sleeps." Davies hoped he would sign on.

"Well... I like it, I'm in. It's a hell of holiday gift."

He waved to draw Johnson's attention.

With a nod Johnson understood—Brady would join the fight.

"Well, here's the moment of truth," Johnson started, now faced with vetting Chalmers. He grasped his rifle and wrapped the strap around his wrist.

Chalmers stepped back, suddenly certain that Johnson was sick of his grating humor and ready to shoot him. He placed his hand on the radio, the Alert button under his thumb.

Each of the watchmen on duty were issued a two-way equipped with an emergency button, just in case they were breached or overrun, so others could arrive to assist. Chalmers was starting to feel overrun, right now.

"Easy," Johnson took on a soothing tone, before he took a step forward. "I just have to run something by you, take your finger off of the button. We don't know who we can trust out there, this is just between us."

Chalmers was hesitant. "Okay." He took his hand off of the radio and placed it back on his weapon.

"Brady is joining some men, to take down Landis. Barker and I, well, we agree with that policy. The question is, do you?"

Barker stepped up, his weapon ready but not aimed.

"Goddamn right!" Chalmers shouted. "Bastard has it coming. My brother hasn't been heard from since the separation. We think he saw something he shouldn't have when he was called from the militia for some special team...he never returned."

"Wow." Barker was surprised by his answer. "No offense, but I didn't see that coming. Seriously, I thought we'd have to shoot you."

Johnson nodded in agreement before directing a statement toward their newest recruit. "We can't all leave. Someone has to watch the trench."

Chalmers looked up to the tower platform. "I'll stay with J.R."

Barker placed his hand on Chalmers' shoulder, "Remember to aim for the head. And above all else, keep my boy safe."

Johnson got on the radio. "We're taking the Chief tonight. The U.P. isn't safe. Pack up, tell Mrs.

Barker, head to the safe house. Keep it quiet, we don' t know who we can trust in the settlement."

"Roger that."

Josh put down the radio and took charge. "Mom," he spoke gently, "Dad wants us out and at the safe house."

Chapter 18
Fed Up

"Who's a good kitty? Who's my perfect little man?"

Ahh Christ, who's a perfect idiot? Lance was sickened as he watched the governor coochie-coo his cat.

"This is a spectacular night. The snow is falling, the Christmas lights, thanks to the generosity of the citizens below, are lighting my tree beautifully, all is well in my self-contained paradise."

Lance glanced at the snowfall. It wasn't falling gently. It dropped quickly in heavy, thick flakes. He couldn't see across the quad. And the lights, well, Steve had confiscated them and draped the entire floor, the multi-colored glow now cast on the disgruntled people below.

"Don't you think it was a bit cruel to take their lights the day before Christmas, just to hang them in your building?" Lance hated the idea, worried it would further anger the already touchy population.

"Nonsense, the people of the Zone love me. They are safe and want me to be comfortable, just like they are comfortable."

"I don't think you've been paying attention. There's a lot of chatter about missing persons and severe food rationing; maybe you should reconsider..."

"I said nonsense. Now, what's for dinner? We must have a lovely Christmas Eve feast, isn't that right, Mr. Mathers?"

"I've had a turkey breast stewing in the crock pot all day."

"I prefer it roasted, Lance."

"I know, but we don't have a real oven. It will still be nice, I promise, and Mr. Mathers will love it too. You both liked the chicken before."

"True, it was nice, even the second day."

"See. I'll go check on it now, it should be just about done."

Lance made his way to the kitchenette, cursing Steve the whole way.

"Prissy, rotten, son of a filthy... really getting tired of being his bitch boy." Lance grumbled down the hall, complaint turning to self-reflection. *Got what I asked for, let my ego take me here. Thought working for the governor was prestigious... You were wrong, Lance.*

He flipped the light on in the kitchen. *Cooking. What do I know about cooking?* "Been faking it all right so far," he shrugged in the reflection of microwave door.

With the lid off of the slow cooker he checked his boss' stewing meat. *Smells okay, seems soft enough... microwave some potatoes, then some veggies....* he mentally itemized as he plotted his mundane chore of feeding the tyrant, and the governor.

"Tis the season hmm hmm hmmm hmm, set the table for the ca,at. Fa la la la la..." Lance sang as he placed dishes in the apartment.

"I must say Mr. Sisto, you've outdone yourself."

Lance stuck his finger in the shredded turkey, the gravy thickly coating it. With a swirl he stuck it in his mouth. *Just once more,* he thought as he sent his spitty digit back for seconds. *Enjoy a little essence of Lance.*

Satisfied with his taste test he added the finishing touches to the dinner table.

"It's going to be good." His stomach growled as he traveled the hall to retrieve his diners.

Governor Landis was standing at the window, the cat over his shoulder. He was mid-stroke.

"Dinner's done," Lance peeked around the corner into the office.

Mr. Mathers jumped to the floor and ran toward Lance, well aware that he was his meal ticket.

"Seems my kitty knows where his bread is buttered, hey Lancey."

He cringed internally. *Great, a nickname.*

Mr. Mathers led the way, his nose pulling him down the hall toward the poultry.

Steve and his ego made a grand entrance. With his arms spread wide, he complimented the help. "Looks beautiful, Lance. I'm starving."

He grabbed the spoon and began to serve himself one heaping helping after another until the crock was almost empty.

Being the butler for the governor had come with quite the weight-loss plan. *That bastard,* Lance thought as his stomach ached with hunger. *Nothing but scraps for weeks. Sneaking snacks at night...that goddamn cat eats better than I do.* Lance's once tight jeans now had plenty of room.

"Something about that scene," Steve motioned to the people struggling down below. "Something about that just really stirs up an appetite."

Lance eyed him, *You're a sick man*.

Dispirited by the greed of Steve Landis, he placed the remaining turkey on his plate and decided it wasn't as much as he would have liked, but paired with the vegetables, it would do.

Lance mashed a potato onto a plate for the cat and dribbled what gravy and meat bits he could scrape onto the top.

"Give Mr. Mathers your plate, Lance, his looks so sad."

He looked at his plate, the already minuscule portion dwarfed by his employer's.

"Why don't you just give him a bit of yours? You have the most. Just share." Lance could feel himself losing it. Some long overdue selfishness took control. *Eat it before the cat gets it.*

He started to scarf, eating the slight meal in two mouthfuls.

"How dare you." Steve was appalled. "What will my fine sir eat now that you've done that?"

Lance snatched the cat's plate and ate his too.

Worried his was next, and unwilling to share with his own pet, Steve cradled his plate, taking bites while glaring judgmentally.

"That's it! That's it! I'm all done. I'd rather sleep out in the tents and eat snow than take your shit for one-more-minute!" Lance stomped toward the door, hell-bent for change.

Forever the politician, Steve transitioned to damage control. "You are just stressed. I know you didn't mean to get out of hand. You're so good to us, would you mind greatly just taking my little man and finding him something."

Using diplomacy on demand, he redirected under pressure. Instead of escalating, he changed course, unable to blow his top due to years of public training.

"Yeah, I'll take care of it." Lance doubled back to scoop up the cat. He stifled the urge to lash out as he hauled the cat away. *So irritating the way you avoid conflict... sooo irritating.*

Mr. Mathers was unpleased with the rough ride Lance provided, and began to scratch him, once again digging in with the front claws and kicking wildly with the back.

"You miserable..." Lance pinned the cat to the hall floor with both hands, smashing him flat until his feet were splayed out under him.

With his right hand now firmly grasping Mr.Mathers scruff, he carried the cat like a briefcase, keeping all his sharp parts far from his person.

Steaming mad, he skulked angrily toward the exit. "You're a hungry little kitty? Think you should eat my dinner? I'll show you what cats should eat, in fact, I'll whip up a feline fricassee and feed it to Captain Crazy back there too. If he eats it, you'll eat it, and believe me; I will let you both have it all."

With the cat swinging carelessly from his fist, he marched, entering the tunnel that led from the offices to the science building.

"It's creepy down here, like something from a horror movie," he shared with the cat, who just kept swinging, a low growl rumbling in his throat.

The long corridor was dingy. Colorful school pride paintings applied by different student organizations graced the industrial build of the concrete tunnel. The images were hard to make out in the dull emergency lighting.

Now through the fire door, they climbed the short staircase to the ground floor. "Look at this," he whispered as he walked. The classrooms and labs had been cleared of their usual furnishings and were now filled with squatting families. Like a New York tenement, hand-washed clothes hung on makeshift lines, and debris littered the halls. Dirty kids and ragged-looking mothers moved listlessly through the once-purposeful and studious space, their living conditions clearly not as glorious as they were promised.

Squalor. Squalor was the only word running though Lance's mind. *You'd be better off in the woods. If only you could see how well your dear Leader was living.*

Each floor the same story, each room filled with families, the hall busy with parents and kids, trying to make do in a desperate situation for the holiday. Christmas trees were scattered randomly, some rooms better dressed than others. Somewhere, somehow, one of the fathers had procured a Santa suit; its presence causing quite the stir as the tots formed a line to meet Mr. Claus in person.

A string of lights was strewn here and there despite signage that read, "Please conserve energy, no unnecessary power usage."

Sad, he thought as he passed through each corridor.

As he reached the end of the third-floor hallway, he was once again excited about his plan. *I'll give the Governor a snack he and that fucking cat can choke on, unless the office has been used too.*

He opened the Anthropology department's door; it was empty except for the many people of the many lands in the professor's photos.

Lance closed it with his foot. He looked around and was pleased to find everything untouched.

The cat was still dangling precariously. He lifted him, bringing him eye level, "I hate you, but I'm pretty sure the feeling is mutual."

He dropped the cat on the floor and moved through the office. The stillness and familiarity suddenly flooded him with a deluge of emotions. He ran his hand across Dory's desk, her jacket still hanging on the back of her chair. He lifted the wool coat to his face and breathed deeply, the smell of her still trapped in the fibers.

Her purse strap protruded from the desk drawer. He pulled at it, lifting it to the desk's surface. Assured by his mother that a purse was a woman's private world, he'd never ventured inside of one before. "What secrets do you hold?"

With guilty pleasure, he dug; its contents providing a thrill as they passed through his hands. Keys, breathmints, tampons, all the things one would expect to find. With her wallet flipped open he slipped her license from its plastic sleeve. He rubbed the picture on his face. "I'll just keep you right here... she'll never need it again, none of us will."

With her I.D. tucked in his pocket, he realized how quickly his life had changed. This office was a reminder of who he once was, and whom he'd left behind.

"I'll never talk to Dory," this fact saddened him, then he remembered who he really missed. "I'll never talk to my mother again..." With clenched fists he pounded on the desk. *I'm sorry, Mom, so sorry.*

"What was that?" He moved to the study, something was making a terrible racket.

"What're you doing?"

Mr. Mathers, with great precision, pawed at the slides, pulling them from the box. Excitedly, he batted the thin glass, which broke easily on the table. Attracted to the smell of the blood, he kept digging, licking the fragments at his feet.

"Ahh Christ, don't eat that, you stupid thing." The wastebasket now in his hands, he swept the broken slides into the trash with his palm. "That's enough Mongolian snacks." He lifted the slide box and placed it on the wire shelf to his left.

Lance opened the fridge and started to toss sardine cans onto the table. "Let's see how the governor likes these. Maybe a little bleach will make them tastier."

The tins landed on the table with a clatter, "Miserable prick, always giving my food to the cat, let's make his food cat food." His mind was on punishing the governor and not what he was pulling from the fridge.

His trance was broken by the sound of breaking glass. Not the same crunching the slides had made, but the very distinct sound of shattering.

He turned to find Mr. Mathers walking through the contents of the vial. The very vial that arrived so ominously labeled some weeks earlier.

"Ahh shit, kitty, now you're covered in black goo. Great! Now I'll have to give you a bath."

Mr. Mathers had stopped under the table and commenced grooming, vigorously licking the tarry substance from his paws.

"Here kitty kitty," Lance sang as he crawled, face first under the study table. Grabbing the cat by the scruff, he dragged him out into the open,

He emitted a low, deep growl; his whole body trembled.

"It's okay, Mr. M," Lance soothed as he scooped the cat into his arms.

"Yuck." Lance tried to avoid the tarry substance clinging to the cat's coat.

He escorted him into the professor's private washroom and flipped on the light. With his arms extended, he reached to place the cat in the sink's basin. The cool white porcelain met Mr. Mather's feet with a jolt, which caused the volatile cat to lunge. Before Lance could react, Mr. Mathers was clinging to his face, his goo-covered claws sunk deeply into his flesh.

"Oww, get off me—get off!"

With a final violent yank, he pried the cat from his now-bleeding head.

"Holy shit, that's gonna scar for sure." He leaned in for a closer look, his vision suddenly blurry. He rubbed his eyes, only to find his hands suddenly uncooperative. They shook, the joints cramping. "Oh god," he cried as fell to his knees, his back now in a spasm. The pain bent him until he was on the floor. "Awww," he screamed, his nerves on fire, every tendon twisted as he writhed, his back now arched and cracking.

Lance's screams of agony echoed down the corridor, attracting attention.

Residents made their way into the office, seeking out the source of the dreadful cries of agony.

"You okay, man?" the curious tenant inquired as Lance seized and convulsed, dark liquid now running from every orifice. The small crowd took a collective step back as he tensed, every bone cracking, as his form changed...shifted. Then, silence, his broken frame now still.

"Is he dead?" A few bystanders stepped closer. They leaned over, looking for signs of life.

Santa gave him a nudge.

"Wait, I think he moved." He inched closer to investigate.

The transformation was complete. His rearranged form now an efficient machine. His legs, now the perfect springs. His cracked and distended neck angled perfectly to forward his now-exposed teeth. With lips pulled back to the gums, he had no interference when moving in to bite.

He lunged, his nerves and muscles acting on impulse, his reanimated form springing into action.

"Holy shit! Holy shit, run, run!" People pushed and shoved... mass panic now incited by the horrific creature charging toward them.

With acute animalism, his swift movements made easy the task, as he took Saint Nick down, a bite to the neck infecting him, so he too was now shifting.

Lance moved on.

One after another, he tore into their flesh with relative ease.

Terrified, they scrambled, tapped into their natural instincts, desperate to flee.

Running, screaming, terror coursed the corridors as he attacked, leaving in his wake a path of infected victims. That status was brief, for within minutes of his seemingly venomous bite, they too had turned.

The numbers grew quickly, spreading at a high rate of speed; the accumulation of infected, like the evening's snowfall, was exponential.

Chapter 19
Road to Redemption

"I've been lost," Brady admitted as he led Davies and his ragtag army toward the Administration building that served as the governor's quarters. They were close. The University's campus was a block ahead. Quietly, they hiked, their crew now over forty strong as they gathered others in for the fight. Snow had dumped steadily, the flurry heavy and limiting visibility.

Brady trudged, still feeling the need to explain himself. "I was duped, sucked into the governor's promise of safety and comfort. He really sold it, and I bought it...buyer's remorse."

"I tried to recruit, out near the lake, a guy who apparently had some weapons, and after speaking to him, probably some skills." (Davies recalled his threat to ventilate him.) "He said it seemed to him that the governor was just delaying the inevitable. He's right, I suppose. Supplies will run out, and eventually even Steve Landis would be shitting in a bucket. Even if he removed the entire population of the settlement, eventually he'd be roughing it, just like everyone else."

"Good. He should suffer."

"He will."

Blake Davies was the guy to help him do just that. *I'm coming for you Steve,* he thought, *my gun is loaded.*

"Why are you so ate up about ending this guy? I mean, I supervised the mass death of half the county... what's your beef?"

"I trusted my government. I trusted my army leadership, and blindly followed protocol, dropping my wife and babies off at a checkpoint bus, assuming I would just see her at the end of the day. Our house was two blocks over. Just two blocks outside of the Static Zone."

"Wait. You seem familiar to me." Brady searched his face. "You were there. You saw the crates. Oh my god," he dropped to his knees in front of him, "go ahead, do it. Do it, end me." He pulled the barrel of Davies rifle to his head.

"Jesus Christ, get up. Get up right now. If I wanted to end you I would've done it at the dome. Now let's get this prick and his cronies." Davies used his best command voice to motivate his guide.

Brady hopped to, doubling his pace, making time toward redemption.

"That bastard will never see this coming." He was thrilled at the idea, the crusade to end Landis filling him with purpose. *Righting the wrongs*, he thought, *righting the wrongs*.

"What's this?" a belligerent voice called sarcastically from a dark side street. "Shome short of angry mob? I want in."

"You all right, miss?" Davies was concerned.

"She sounds smashed." Brady walked toward her. "You been drinking, hon?"

"Nah, wellsh, maaaybee jusht a little." She pinched her fingers together, a visual measurement of her consumption. She wobbled, leaning on the bat for support.

"Is that blood?"

"Yeah, but they ashked for it, shooo it's okay. So, I wash going to kill the govnerrr, but, there's lot's of buildings, and I've already loooked in a few, but now I'm tirred, and out of pillsh." She shook the empty bottle before tossing it in the snow, quickly followed by the empty pint of schnapps she'd lifted from the hoodlum at the tunnel.

"I'll lead you to him, get in line."

"Spechtachulaaar." Her speech was slurred, but filled with intent.

Brady was amused by her behavior. "She's destroyed, wonder what she was taking? I want some."

They moved on, Laney falling into the patrol.

Davies looked back; she was following along, whispering to the Jarvi brothers.

"Reememmmber my bat," she rolled it in front of Willy. "It reememmmbersh you and your brother." She jabbed at Elmer with the barrel. "Gonnnaaa," she exaggerated the word, drawing it out, her tone building with anticipation, "getcha!" she shouted, causing them both to jump. "Shettle down," she laughed, "I'm jusht meshing with ya." She had recognized the brothers, but what she didn't know was Johnson, the father of her daughter's boyfriend, was taking up the rear.

"Keep it down, we're almost to the first guard point."

"My bad." She ran her fingers across her lips, shutting an imaginary zipper.

They approached the entrance to the University. A bit of blood was splattered on the ground. Davies signaled, fist up; everyone halted.

He crept around the back of the large sign that marked the campus's start. It wasn't lit, part of the governor's plan to conserve energy.

"Holy shit, he's in really bad shape."

"Someone got to him before us." Brady nudged him with his foot.

He groaned, but remained still.

"Think we should further subdue him?"

Laney snuck up behind them. "Should I whack him again?"

"You did this?"

"I told you he desherved it."

"Do you hear that?" Davies turned toward the buildings grouped behind him.

Chapter 20
Frantic Zone

"What's that ruckus?" Steve Landis looked out the window to find a commotion in the courtyard. Without concern for the disturbance below, he questioned aloud the whereabouts of his cat and butler.

"And where is Lancey with my Mr. Mathers?"

With his silk paisley robe now donned over his shirt and pants, he traipsed down the hall, looking for his assistant and his cat.

"Here, kitty kitty," he called through doorways and into corridors. "Mr. M, where are you?" He made his way from one floor to the next. Finally landing at the first floor entrance.

"Hey! Hey you! Open the door, open the fucking door!" A young man frantically shouted, a small child clutched in his arms. The toddler was crying, the warm tears steaming in the cold of the heavy snow. He continued to plead with the governor to let him in, his terror muffled by the glass of the locked security door.

"What's the commotion?" Hatch asked, making his way to Steve's position. "This guy wants in, with his kid I guess, seems pretty panicked."

"He's waking up the whole building." They stood, oblivious to the scene unfolding before them, their pompous indifference eluding them from the danger that lurked outside.

The squelch of Hatch's radio echoed through the hall, "Sir, Sir?" a voice called, his tone unsettled. "There's a situation in the quad. I think they're infected, sir."

"Roger that. Hold for instruction."

"That would explain his panic." Hatch's demeanor was still calm, his indifference intact. "Thoughts?"

"No. No way. We're safe...static." Landis refused to believe it.

He watched as the horrified man shrieked at the window; he changed his mind.

"Ahh, how did they get in? All the reports claimed they were slow, frozen. I want someone's ass!"

I wonder if... Hatch knew there were weak spots, places along the divide less than secure. *I can't worry about that now.* He forced himself to focus on the crisis at hand and not the possibility that he might be responsible for the breach.

"Make the call." Hatch held the radio, finger on the trigger, ready to bark orders.

"Sound the alarm, call everyone in. We need to fight, end this thing quickly. My Zone must remain intact."

"Roger that." Hatch lifted the two-way to his lips, giving the order to rally the troops. "This is a recall, rally point Common, this is not a drill. All threats, shoot to kill."

With more people now at the door, their faces filled with fright,

Hatch backed up. "We better hunker down." His tactical training was telling him it was about to get ugly.

The mass of panicked humanity beat at the door, sheer will to survive driving their efforts.

With the governor in tow, he trotted down the hall toward safety, the door breaking open just as they reached the end.

Horrified, they poured in, shouts to make haste ringing out.

"Hurry, hurry up, close the fucking door!"

As they secured the entrance, the alarm blared, the signal tearing through the air as it wailed from every speaker. This alert, meant to draw help from all stations, had unintended consequences, as it further agitated the infected. Like a dog roused by a doorbell they snapped, lathered by the ringing. The monsters rallied, their frenzied state even more horrific than before.

Still in retreat, Hatch and the governor watched as the frightened citizens leaned against the now-broken door, trying in vain to keep it shut as the twisted and frothing creatures thrashed against the entrance. Lured by the intoxicating scent of fear-tinged sweat wafting through the broken glass, the tortured, afflicted souls amassed. With flattened noses they sniffed at the crack, their bloody teeth bared and pressing as they inhaled deeply. One after another they came, the efforts of the citizens no match for the collective power of these rabid creatures.

Bent arms darted through the broken window, joints and bones popped as the gnarled forms clawed at the opening.

Groans, shrieks, and clicks escaped their foul mouths as they pushed, the desperate humans inside losing ground.

"It's sliding," someone screamed in fear, "we can't hold it much longer, run!"

Terrified, they scattered, a few brave souls stayed, wedging themselves against the compromised door to hold them back.

The others headed for the fire door that separated the corridor from the stair well.

"Open it! Oh my god, open up!" they clamored, pounding on the door. Some tried to gain entrance to empty offices lining the hallway; those doors were locked as well.

Steve stared blankly through the glass.

The same child-riddled fellow was demanding entrance.

"Open the door, you bastard!"

He didn't.

While the governor watched from the safety of the stairwell, the battle to keep the entry door closed was about to be lost.

"Oh my god! Run! Run!"

They'd lost their hold, and the infected poured in, taking down one victim after another: those few brave souls at the entrance the first to be turned. The governor watched as his Static Zone crumbled, somehow breached by this terrible plague.

"How could this be?" He hurried back to his floor, mumbling frantically. "The trench, the towers, all these people in my pocket, how could they fail me? It was perfect, the Zone was perfect."

Looking over his shoulder, afraid and abandoned by Hatch, he made his way back to his quarters.

Riddled with disbelief, he locked his bedroom door and climbed under the comforter, his head buried. "I'll just be still and wait it out."

"Landis!" There was pounding on the door. "Landis, open the fucking door."

"Why must everyone use that language?" he whispered.

"Open up, you coward, I have a weapon for you."

Steve crawled out of the bed, taking the covers with him. With the down comforter draped over his shoulders like a cape, he cracked the door and took the gun. "Is that all?"

"Would you like to join us?" Hatch was irritated and now placating him. "We are all going," he motioned to the crowd in the hall behind him, which consisted of Hatch's wife and McGovern's family. "We're going to grab some of the confiscated snowmobiles and head out of town. By all reports the infected encountered at the trench were slow; we can wait it out, shut down the utilities to the settlement, give these things some time to refrigerate."

"What if Mr. Mathers comes back?"

"We'll keep an eye out for him on the way."

"What if we can't get safely to the vehicles, we could all be attacked by those things."

"We need to move to survive." Hatch started to walk away.

"Alright, just let me grab my coat."

Hatch lifted the radio to his lips, "Cut the power. Shut it down."

Chapter 21
Worried Sick

"Where could she be?" Doolin peeked around the building's corner, his back flat against the brick as he searched.

"Dooley…Dooley," Deck was now tugging on his sleeve, "Something's coming."

They strained to make out the eerie shapes as they approached through the veil of heavy snow, their erratic movements preceded by a choppy shadow that stretched and shuddered on the white ground.

Doolin turned to find that Dory had already backed past them, putting them between her and the horde.

"Oh my god…" The fear in Deck's eyes the catalyst for their hasty departure.

Doolin passed Dory, and was now firing on their aggressors. "They're moving too fast."

Deck took aim, landing body shots with no effect.

"What's that horrible noise?" Dory looked back, emptying the rifle; not one shot landed.

The mutated forms groaned, shrieked, and clicked; the sounds more terrifying as the creatures moved in, their speed increasing, enticed by the sweet smell of fear.

"We have to find cover." Deck scouted doors and jiggled handles.

"Here!" Doolin held an open door ready to provide them with shelter. Now ducked inside, they leaned against the wall. With labored breath they squatted, trying to collect themselves.

"Shhh, I hear something." Dory raised her hand to signal silence.

"I hear them, they're almost on us."

Weapons in hand they stood, as they braced for the incoming threat, the shuffling getting closer...frenzied.

"Follow me," Doolin scurried, trying to make it to another door in the hall. "Locked... stand back." With the PMR aimed at the lock he fired, only a loud click discharged. "I'm out, burned up trying to make it in here." Frantically he reloaded, as the afflicted moved in.

"So am I." Deck fumbled in his pocket for another magazine. Frustrated by his gloves he pulled them off with his teeth discarding them to the floor.

"An axe." Dory used the butt of her Pop-issued .22 to smash the glass and retrieve the implement, trading it for the rifle.

Shadows stretched the length of the hall as they approached, their jagged forms searching for targets.

"Oh my," Dory trembled. "Deck, fire," she urged, a fine veil of perspiration now coating her body as terror took hold.

"No conserve, we'll need any remaining rounds to get out of here. Crack the door."

Dory's hands trembled as she split the door from the jamb.

With one push, Doolin forced it open. "Flip that table over. We'll block the entrance."

With backs to the table, they hunkered while the rabid mob, worked their way down the hall. Deck took the axe from Dory and rested it across his lap.

Drawn to the trio by their keen sense of smell, they breathed heavily at the crack. The sound was unsettling.

"Are they...sniffing?" Dory mouthed with a slight whisper.

Deck threw his arm around her, his mouth pressed to her ear, "We're safe for now, they can't get in here."

No sooner did he finish his sentence, the door began to shake, the frame threatening to give under the weight.

With soles flat to the floor, they pushed against the unrelenting force of impending death.

"Time to GTFO... let's take our chances outside."

Deck and Doolin kept pushing, as Dory quietly cranked open the window.

"What if the ruckus they're raising draws the attention of more to the open window?" Dory was filled with dread, her usually sassy and confident demeanor now wrought with hesitance.

"Go first, help her down." Deck was the strongest and wanted Doolin to get Dory out while he held the door.

"Move quick," Doolin instructed Dory as he surveyed the yard below. "We'll get out of sight when we slip around back."

He jumped out first, landing softly in the fresh snow.

"Hurry," Deck was losing ground.

"Come on." Doolin reached up, his hands a guide for Dory. The drop was low, but still brought uncertainty when danger waited on both ends.

She wriggled backward, her arms hanging from the ledge. She could feel his hand brushing her foot.

"Drop. Drop it isn't far."

She let go, but was snagged, her jacket caught in the mechanism on the sill.

"They're in!" Deck wielded the Swedish style axe, splitting heads with ease. Black blood sprayed and dripped, running down the handle and onto his hands.

"Let go," Doolin whispered, pulling at her feet.

"Go, Dory," Deck now added, peeking past her to the ground below.

"I'm stuck she growled, yanking her arm, trying to break free.

With a final pull she slipped, but the jacket remained, hung up and waving above her.

Now backed to the window, a heap of bodies at his feet, Deck prepared to depart. "I got it." Deck wrestled the jacket, trying to tear it free.

"Leave it." Doolin could see the erratic forms of the infected jerking through the heavy snow. They started to creep closer, their noses in the air.

Deck jumped, the axe still gripped in his hands. "Let's move it." He grabbed Dory's arm, dragging her as Doolin led the way. Once around the corner they were out of sight and able to duck under a delivery truck.

"Ahh Christ." Deck scrubbed the blood from his hands with the snow. "I can feel it...moving."

"No, you're just freaking out."

"Maybe." Deck kept scrubbing.

"What now?" Dory was freezing, her jacket left behind.

"We wait, we...is that Laney?" Doolin watched as Davies' militia entered the commons, a familiar form in the mix. He scrambled, trying to quickly kick his way out from under the truck to intercept his wife.

Deck dropped a hand, holding him back.

"Ash, what the ..."

"Do you want your kids to be fatherless too? Are you sure it's even her? How could you recognize anyone through this white out."

The snow fell in a heavy and steady flurry.

Paralyzed by the immediate presence of the infected and the fear of leaving his children orphaned, Doolin held his position as his wife charged head first into the fray.

"Oh, seems like something's happening," Laney pointed, the living fighting the infected as people screamed, running in a mass exodus from the university commons.

She hoisted the bat and paid no mind.

"On your guard," Brady instructed in his best military tone.

They slowly advanced, weapons at the ready.

She broke off from the group.

"Frosty?" Willy questioned as he took aim on the approaching horde of ravenous beasts.

The pop of the Army's expended rounds could be heard amidst the screams as the men crept into the settlement. Now, in the thick of things, the threat was evident.

"Aim for the head, that's what works at the trench." Brady squeezed off a few, putting them down to demonstrate.

"Look like howlers, like in dat lycan movie," Willy decided.

"Not too frosty right now." Elmer had one in his sights.

They popped up as fast as they could shoot them, the bitten turning before they could clear the ones already charging in their direction.

Cory was in trouble. "No, no, no, no," his jammed rifle leaving him exposed. Consumed by the infected mass, all were engaged in a battle for their own lives when Cory fell victim. With his face now torn open, he dropped to his knees. As the pathogen coursed through his veins, his attacker moved on. He grasped at his shredded flesh as blood poured into the fresh powder.

His fellow soldiers watched as he quickly transformed into an implement of dissemination. Without bias they fired upon him; it didn't matter that just moments before he was one of them.

"Frosty never hauled like that," Willy's semi auto pumped as fast as he could aim.

"Fall out." Davies could see they were close to being overwhelmed.

The men scattered.

As they ran, the infected followed, clearing the area.

With the immediate threat removed, Doolin lifted his head to peek from under the vehicle. "Where'd she go?" He whipped around as he tried to find her location, his vantage point limited by the rear axle.

"Maybe it wasn't even her." Deck stuck to his narrative.

~~~

Laney had missed the fight. She'd already entered the admin building looking for her target.

With bat held high she crept, exploring the building her husband had recently escaped, hoping to find her foe.

"Who's there?" The dimly lit hall was disheveled; blood and debris littered the floor.

"I hear you moaning, I'm gonna find you."

Her slow and steady pace was suddenly halted.

"Brraaahgg!" Its joints and bones cracked as it charged.

"Take that, you freak of nature." She beat it again and again, the joy of ending it's miserable life somehow soothing. She slipped into that dreamlike place, but this time it was a conscious euphoria, leaving her still aware of what was going on around her.

She began singing, "Such a feelin's coming over me. There is wonder in most everything I see…"

She left its lifeless corpse in the hall swimming in a pool of its own black tarry blood before she climbed the stairs to floor-two. Her bat soon met the cranium of another then another, the song still on her lips, "Everything I want the world to be, is now comin' true especially for me. And the reason is clear, it's because you are here, you're the nearest thing to heaven that I've seen..."

She kept trucking, the bat kept swinging; she was undeterred.

"I'm on top of the world, looking down on creation, and the only observation I can find..."

In this chaotic time, while men and women were fighting and fleeing for their lives, and mass chaos filled the streets, Laney Riley had finally found some peace.

With the building cleared, she trotted down the stairs and headed out the exit.

Unafraid and feeling invincible she clubbed her way through the swarm, avoiding attack while cracking skulls. Violence became her, her movements almost elegant.

Doolin watched from under the truck as his wife dished aluminum to the infected. He grabbed the axe to assist and moved toward her.

"Laney, hey Laney."

Whispers seemed to float on the wind. She swiveled, her bat stilling the last howler as she tried to locate the source of the beckoning.

"Ugh," she groaned as she was swept away— brought to the ground unexpectedly. Doolin pulled her under the truck.

"Its me honey...us." Doolin brushed the hair from her face, just happy to see her alive.

"I'm so glad we found you Dilly, it's terrible out here. My god I'm so happy to see you, I'm so sorry I abandoned you, I hope you can forgive me."

Deck apologized, spilling his guts, thankful to have the chance.

"What the hell are these things?" Dory whispered, not wanting to pique their attention.

"Been calling 'em howlers," Laney grinned, amused by the label."And this other guy, Jarvi, you remember Jarvi, he called 'em Frosty, but he said it was just when they're frozen."

"But these aren't frozen." Dory shivered, almost frozen herself.

Laney explained, "These ones didn't cross from the Western Outlands, they were Static Zone-bred. Infection to transformation is fast, two minutes tops."

Deck was in shock. "We saw people drop after being bitten, then hop back up biting machines."

"Yep," Laney agreed. "A good crack to the head works best. Huh... just like zombies, damage the brain. Who knew all the crap the kids watched would turn out to be useful. Speaking of the kids, we can't hide under here forever, we need to go. We need to warn Pop... get to safety."

Now thinking clearly, her quest for the governor wasn't important. Returning to her children was. "Where will we hide? The numbers are building fast, what will we do?" She would have been bent at the waist before, a pill bottle in her hand, but this fight eliminated those issues, that anxiety. No pills, no gauge. *Holy crap, I get it, I get you, baby brother*. She realized why her brother had spent so much time behind his gun.

"I do," she blurted, as she reached over her husband's back to touch her brother's face. "I do forgive you."

"That's touching, really it is, but we need to get the hell out of here." Dory was undone. She'd begun to shiver, her body temp dipping lower.

"Laney, you left before I got to tell you, Pop has a bunker under the house filled with supplies and survival gear. If we play it right, we'll all be fine for a really long time."

"What're we waiting for?" Dory was now impatient and ready to go.

With the axe still in his hand Doolin slid forward, the snow, mixed with his body heat made for an easy and slippery exit. With great caution he stood, his back flat against the side of the truck.

"Very quietly," were his instructions. With visibility still low, his eyes were locked onto the only howler in sight, about fifty yards away.

One by one, they slid out from under the trailer.

Deck wrinkled his nose, "Bet he's an ugly mother."

Doolin led the way, moving swiftly around the vehicle, checking their path to the back of the building, once again assuring the coast was clear.

Dory was last; her muscles tensed as she tried to will herself to move. Locked up with fear and the early stages of hypothermia, she tripped, slapping her hand against the rig for support. Her palm met the cold steel with a resounding echo.

Stimulated by the sharp sound, the howler snapped around and moved with swiftness, not yet encumbered by the cold.

Deck turned, expecting to see her.

Doubling back, he worried, *what's taking so long, she was right behind me?*

With his question now answered he stopped dead in his tracks.

Dory was still at the truck, her shoulders pressed against the container wall. With her eyes slammed shut, and her lips clamped together she stifled the urge to scream. The howler was in front of her, nose to nose.

It smelled her, prodding at her like an animal getting her scent. It inhaled, getting closer each time. She peeked, its grotesque form a horrific sight.

Deck watched, mystified by its seeming interest in her. *Why hasn't it attacked yet?* He slowly, quietly reached for his gun.

Dory watched it investigate her, and suddenly felt sorry for it. *This was someone once, this was...Lance?*

She could see the sheen in its mangled hair, and the remnants of the LaCoste polo, the alligator insignia covered in slime, but still intact.

"Lance." With the whisper, her warm breath escaped her lips.

"Brraaahgg." The bark caused her to flinch.

Deck lurched to save her; Lance was immediately on him. Deck didn't have time to draw his weapon; all he could do was keep the distended, snapping jaws from tearing into his flesh.

Now on the ground in the fresh powder they wrestled, Ashleigh Decker no match for the animalistic strength of Lance Sisto.

Doolin and Laney doubled back to find the struggle. Doolin handed Laney the axe as he took aim with the PMR.

Deck rolled, the howler now positioned above him, his locked elbows the only thing protecting him from his protruding teeth.

A shot rang out, and Lance fell to the side. Black brain matter and its thick, molasses like blood pooled into the snow.

"Take that, you disgusting, clicking, gurgling..." Laney's line of insulting   adjectives kept streaming, just like the goo that oozed from the hole in its skull.

"Yech!" Dory ran to Deck's side. "You know, that's not the first time he's caused me to make that noise. Oh, Ash... your arm!"

His right arm was oozing blood.

"Fuuuckk!" he yelled, as the axe fell, Laney acting without hesitation.

"What? It always works in the movies," the axe was back over her shoulder.

Hot, red blood squirted into the fresh powder, steaming on contact.

"Christ." Dory squeezed, her hands wrapped tightly around the site.

"Tie it off with this." Doolin pulled his belt off and tossed it to Dory.

Gun at the ready, he returned to keep watch, while Dory tried to stop the bleeding.

"Mind not pointing that at me?" he shivered, the blood loss causing his temperature to drop.

"Can't risk it, bro." Doolin looked at his wife, not willing to lose her again.

Dory hustled, her undershirt now off and headed to Deck's aid. "Right here, right now?" Deck flirted jokingly as he gazed upon her satin bra. She shot him a look as she pulled her sweater back on.

"Lets get out of here, you pervert." Dory helped Deck to his feet, his arm belted off and tied in her shirt.

Laney was concerned about her brother. "Let's move, he won't last long; he's lost a lot of blood."

"I'm sooo cooold," Dory's teeth chattered. Her one sweater offered little warmth for her already chilled core.

"Here." Laney rested the axe between her feet and removed a layer.

"Thanks." Dory struggled to pull the garment on. Not only were her hands stiff but Laney was considerably smaller.

"That's it, that's why he didn't attack; she was cold." Deck shivered as they walked.

"Interesting theory, what makes you think that?" Doolin was eager to hear his hypothesis.

"She was already cold, hypothermic even. He didn't act aggressively until she opened her mouth to scream."

"Hardly concrete, but interesting. Let's get moving, our ruckus here has drawn some attention. I can hear them coming." Doolin tried to get everyone to follow closely.

"Did he learn those hand signals from you?" Dory teased as they watched his brother-in-law point ahead, his wrist snapped forward, his forearm at attention.

Deck's teeth chattered as he offered a weak grin. "How could you joke at a time like this?"

"Shut up, keep moving." Doolin's head was on a swivel as they advanced.

The yard was empty, all inhabitants had scattered, the infected in pursuit. Screams for help could be heard in the distance, an awful accompaniment to the guttural cadence of the howlers as the disordered chorus drifted with the flakes of the heavy snow.

The chaotic shadows of the infected danced through the faint ambient light of the winter moon as they hunted the living. Random gunshots punctuated the already hectic evening. "Thankfully, with time, the infected will freeze, limiting their movement." Doolin walked along, praying for a long cold winter.

Chapter 22
Cat-Scratch Fever

"Well," Brady scanned the Governor's apartment, a flashlight taped to his rifle, "Looks like he enacted plan B and headed for the safe room. We can get there through the basement tunnel. It will lead us right to West Science and down to the target." Brady stepped back into the hall, "I'm really not looking forward to going back out there." He stuffed his hand into one of the many pockets on his pants, another magazine for his rifle now in his grasp. "Lock and load, we can't live forever."

"Lock and load," Davies returned, his nose pointed toward the stairs.

With all the diligence of a military mission, they patrolled, retracing the treacherous hallways they'd already cleared on the way to third-floor room of the governor.

"Twitcher," Brady shined his light on one of the previously shot howlers, not quite subdued.

Davies stooped, and gracefully pulled a knife from a sheath on his thigh. He jabbed it between the eyes of the still quivering creature. The black blood seemed to crawl from the wound pushing up past the blade. "Done." He wiped the sharp steel on the howler's shirt before returning it to its position on his leg.

"So far so good," Brady stepped into the first-floor stairwell. The lower floors were tricky because the doors and windows were compromised, allowing the infected to stroll in at will. Initially lured in by smell and sound, they now lingered, all previous targets already compromised. As soon as they caught wind of fresh meat, there was nowhere to hide.

Davies peeked through the window and into the stairwell that led to the lower level. It was their connection to the tunnel system. "Really hard to see what's down there with the lights out."

"Well, no guts no glory." Brady pushed open the door, taking a moment to listen. "Sounds calm, no groaning or gurgling."

"How about clicking, I can't stand that clicking noise they make. Like someone shaking a box of broken bones." Davies stepped forward, scanning the landing with his light.

"Last one down is, well, I guess only an idiot would purposely walk headfirst into this situation."

"Very funny." Brady tapped Davies on the shoulder. "I don't hear anything, so I say, let's just trot down the stairs and worry about what's at the bottom when we get there."

"Solid plan, I like it; throw caution to the wind." Davies took the initiative and led the way, dropping down quickly, their gear raising a lot of racket.

Once at the bottom they froze, scanning and listening.

"Seems clear," Brady shined his light along the corridor. "No movement."

"All right, then." Davies took the first step, now working down the tunnel.

"It's amazing that the whole university is connected by these underground passages. Clearly it was constructed with the weather in mind."

"Makes sense, the winters are harsh. Who wants to switch classes and risk frostbite."

Davies lifted his fist. Signaling, they halted. With the rifle pointed he shined his light on a mass at the end of the tunnel. Difficult to make out from this distance, he suggested they proceed quietly and with caution. "Cover me," he whispered as he approached, rifle at the ready.

Now over the body, he recognized the figure. "It's Hatch," Davies inspected the corpse. "Not turned, just dead. Gunshot to the head."

"Maybe he was bitten." Brady was indifferent. "Well, one less for us."

"Mrs. Hatch?" Brady wondered as they passed a female body, just a few feet from the General.

"Think so, she was infected though, look at the discharge from the eyes."   They both looked, their lights pointed at her face. "Looks like cat scratches, right. Too sharp for human nails." Davies cocked his head as he investigated.

"Yeah, four razor-like scratches, I'd buy into cat claws." He too investigated. "He got her in the temple." Brady waved the beam of his light over the wound. "Not much of a looker is she." His observation was cold.

"Yeah, even before she shifted. She always had a bit of a bulldog quality. I first saw her in the settlement when I was moving furniture. You think

Hatch would've had better taste in women…Oh, she's a twitcher."

Mrs. Hatch lurched. The tips of her fingers flicked as her eyelids fluttered.   Davies   pulled his knife and gave her the treatment, his blade between her eyes.

"So, just to speculate." Davies shared his theory as they walked. "She turns, infected on the way down somehow, and bites him. He shoots her then himself."

"Possibly, but I didn't see a gun."

"Did you actually look?"

"No."

"Then my theory stands."

"Enough. Back to work." Brady switched back to tactical mode, the pair now facing the door to West Science.

"He really was clever. The admin building connected to science, where he put a safe room, just in case."

"Changing your mind, want to be friends with him now?"

"Stop giving me shit, Brady. I'm just stating facts."

They cleared the door to the science basement and walked on high alert, signs of a struggle evident. "Blood." Davies pointed to the floor. "Cat tracks?" Paw prints were stamped in the gruesome trail.

"Roger that." Brady shined his light, the trail ended at the bend in the corridor. The safe room is around that corner."

"Of course it is. It's around the corner, in the dark, and the bloody trail leads the way. Why should it be easy?" Davies was amused. "It's like a horror movie down here."

"Shh, I hear something." They crept forward, the crimson trail shining to lead the way.

Once at the corner, they paused, their lights now dimmed.

Brady pressed his lips to Davies' ear, afraid their voices would alert whatever was shuffling out of sight.

"Sounds like a few howlers, I can hear them."

Davies whispered one word, "Clicking."

Shoulder to shoulder they pivoted, stepping into the hall's opening and flipping on their lights ready to fire.

Five forms stood facing the wall at the other end.

Now sniffing loudly, they turned, disturbed by the light and ready to attack.

"Ahh, Christ, kids. That's fucking disturbing." Brady winced as he fired, putting down the two adults.

"Nice, leave the little ones for me." Davies hesitated, unable to shoot.

The three children sprinted in their direction, their small, contorted bodies clicked as they charged. With pale complexions and blood-streaked faces, they approached, the whites of their eyes now gray and bloodshot.

"Fire! Fire goddamn it!" Brady took aim, eliminating one as the other two moved in, quickly becoming to close to shoot. "Shoot now or we'll end up bare handing it!"

Davies got a round off; the tiny howler was clipped in the head and fell where it twitched on the floor. His vision went blurry; the situation too much to process. Pushed into an anxiety attack, he fell to his knees, once again expelling his own bile.

"Could use some help here! Mitt! Some fucking help!" Brady wrestled with the remaining howler, who, although young (about twelve), had found extraordinary strength in the transformation.

Davies struggled to find his feet, pulling his knife as he approached his partner. Without thought he drove the blade deeply into the young boy's skull, the blow rendering him motionless.

"That was a close one." Brady pushed the boy's body aside and stood up. He checked himself for injury, paranoid about infection.

"I wasn't prepared to see kids like this. I lost it, so sorry, man. I just, I saw little kids and couldn't look past it."

Brady clapped Davies on the back before stepping over to the tiny twitcher. He looked at the little girl as she flinched and quivered. Her neck was bitten and torn revealing the tendon, and Davies bad shot had cleared the right quarter of her skull, exposing her brain. It had partially oozed onto her flowered night-gown.

Brady took aim and shot her between the eyes. "Let's get that door open, achieve our objective, and get the hell out of here."

With a flat palm Davies slapped the steel door of the janitor's closet, hoping to appeal to Steve's desire to be saved.

"Governor Landis, we've cleared the threat, open the door."

Brady nodded, impressed by the convincing impromptu line.

With a loud click the recently installed deadbolt shifted, and the door gave to reveal a small crack. The governor's eye scanned their faces. "Have you been bitten...scratched?"

"No sir, we're fine, here to bring you to safety."

"Did Martin contact you from the garage?" Steve's eyes darted, he was clearly nervous.

"Yeah," Davies nodded, with Brady following suit. "He was concerned when your party didn't show." Davies gave the door a shove, tired of the chit-chat. He and Brady stepped in.

Steve ran across the dim, industrial room. An LED lantern illuminated the sad space. A cot lined the bottom of the large shelving, which had once held the many cleaning supplies required to keep the university tidy. The shelves above had been stocked with food and bottled water.

"Quite the setup you have here, but doesn't look like it would keep you long."

Brady walked around, scoping out the makeshift safe-room. Feet were sticking out from behind a heating and cooling unit. It was large, and provided a separation from the front of the room.

"Who's this?" Brady asked as he walked around, curious who was stretched out on the floor.

"We got in together, after the trouble in the hall. He stumbled in then I locked the door. He started to change...shift. I, I, shot him with this." Steve produced the pistol given to him earlier by Hatch. "I got him in the chest a few times but he kept coming, then I finally hit him in the head. I'm not a very good shot."

Brady flipped on his light, "It's McGovern."

"What trouble did you have in the hall?" Davies put his light on him, wanting it to feel like an interrogation.

"We were headed to the campus garage, I have some vehicles, snowmobiles, stored there. We couldn't make it. The snow and the infected...it was too hard to travel efficiently with the women and children in tow. We ducked into West Science to escape attack. Luckily I found Mr. Mathers, whom my assistant had absconded with earlier. Anyway, we made it down here to wait for the infected to freeze. Well, it would seem the general's wife somehow fell ill, and, well, it spread from there."

"Well, I guess that just leaves you." Davies took a step forward, bridging the gap between Landis and himself.

"Yeah, just let me grab a couple of things." Steve rushed toward the shelves. Davies raised his rifle, ready to act.

"Wait, wait, I'm just grabbing my book and Mr. Mathers."

Steve was now in a submissive pose, the book tucked under one arm and his other hand raised and pointing to the top shelf.

Davies and Brady looked up, and sitting on the shelf was a skinny gray cat, his once-pristine coat tarred with the gooey blood of the many infected he'd traipsed through.

"Just let me get him." The governor stepped on the shelves, using them to reach up. "Here Mr. M, let's get down."

Davies put it together. *The scratches, she fell ill...they shifted...the cat.* "Leave that thing there, it's contaminated."

"Nonsense, he's my little man." Steve slipped his beloved brown book on the top shelf, and pulled the scrawny thing to him, placing it over his shoulder like a baby.

Davies stepped back, and was now shoulder to shoulder with Brady. "The cat scratches... it's covered in infected blood... he's been transmitting."

"Sweet Christ." Brady raised his rifle, Mr. Mathers the target.

"What are you doing?" Steve became agitated; the cat sensed his stress.

"Let's just do them both now, I don't want to drag this out and end up shifting because of a cat scratch." Brady took aim. "Feline first," he said, his finger now on the trigger.

His light was now directly in Mr. Mathers' eyes. Unnerved, and with his ears pinned back, the reflection made him look evil. The cat lunged, using Steve's shoulder for leverage. Brady fired as the governor dropped to the ground, the cat's dirty nails delivering the pathogen, the shift already under way.

"Holy shit, what did I tell you, the cat—the fucking cat scratched him with contaminated claws."

Steve writhed on the ground, his arms stretched up toward the cat. They twisted as he looked for some comfort.

Mr. Mathers kept his distance as he watched judgmentally from his perch on the shelf above.

With the cat in his sights, Brady called it. "You get him, and I'll pick off the cat."

They opened fire. Davies put one in the governor's skull, right between the eyes, the contents of his cranium now splashed on to the closet's interior.

"Missed him, he's on the move." Brady looked for the feline.

Davies and Brady scanned the dingy room, rifles at the ready.

"Of all the shit I've seen, this cat is the scariest." Brady took another step.

"The cat actually did him in." Davies chuckled, "The irony."

"Where could he be, this room is only so big." Brady rounded the corner, now at the head of McGovern's body.

"He's here," Brady stopped cold. Mr. Mathers was hunkered down, buried between the Colonel's legs, only his diabolical eyes visible in the limited light.

Brady fired and Mr. Mathers lunged, burying his claws deeply into his arms as he tried to escape the small space.

"I'm hit." Brady fell to his knees; the rifle crashed to the floor.

Davies turned the corner to find his partner on the ground, the shift clearly underway.

The scratches burned, as the infection tore through his bloodstream. His hands cramped as he reached into his holster. "Righted the wrongs, we righted the..." Brady put the pistol in his mouth and pulled the trigger.

Davies gasped as the contents of his new friend's head dripped down the wall. Thinking tactically, he squeezed past Brady's body and picked up his rifle. "You made it right, my friend. I forgive you. Rest in peace."

He pulled the extra magazine from Brady's front pocket, mindful to avoid any spilled blood.

"I'm coming for you, kitty," Davies pivoted, exiting the back of the room and ready to hunt.

Mr. Mathers, his delicate nerves now shattered, once again cozied up to his owner looking for comfort. He was curled in the governor's armpit, grooming himself as he had probably done hundreds of times before; except, this time, Steve was dead.

Davies kept an eye on the cat as he moved toward the shelving and the coveted brown book. Carried everywhere like a security blanket, Steve Landis never left home without it. Now he could see what all the fuss was about.

In the dim light of the small plastic lantern, Davies flipped through the pages of the old book. The original text was filled with tips on how to build shelters and start fires. A whole chapter was dedicated to what plants to eat in the wild. Some orderly notes had been scrawled in the margins, small ideas, lists of necessities, etc. There was something about separating yourself from the population, and establishing shelter. Thinning your burden by including closest family only.

Then there was the manic, loopy scribbling of a lunatic: grandiose ideas like demolishing bridges and eliminating the population. There were doodles of trenches and tanks, explosions, and a cat in military dress.

Davies closed the book and slipped it right back where Landis had left it.

Now filled with pity for the pathetic feline, Davies backed up to the door and, with the cat in his sights, left.

Landis and his survival guide were now static, entombed with his cat in a janitor's closet.

Satisfied, he walked the long corridor.

Chapter 23
Lying in Wait

"We've gotta stop, he isn't going to make it." Dory couldn't hold Deck up any longer; he was putting too much weight on her.

The houses were few and far between as they approached the forest path. Town was behind them, along with the many tidy rows of residences once filled with families and hope.

The snow was still falling, the heavy blanket now even thicker as it continued to pile up. Doolin cupped his hand over his brow, trying to peer through the flurry to find a place to hunker down. He squinted to find smoke rising from a small chimney in the distance.

"Follow me." he led the way, plowing through the ground cover.

Nervously they trudged, the horrific sounds of the twisted predators still carrying through the cold night air.

"Stay here, let me check it out."

The others stayed back, leaning on a woodpile behind the shed, as Doolin approached the small house. Obscured from view by the hilly landscape, it was cleverly tucked between two mounds surrounded by a thicket of trees. As he approached he could see the dull glow of lamplight spilling from the windows.

"I'll just knock and pray they feel like being civilized."

Doolin raised his hand to tap on the door when it flew open.

"Tell me why I shouldn't kill you." Josh Johnson held his .22 to his nose.

"Mr. Riley?" He cocked his head, surprised to find his girlfriend's father at the safe house door.

"Josh?" Doolin had only seen the young man one time before when he'd dropped off Elle. He was a strapping young man, handsome in a rugged, Scandinavian kind of way, with coarse blonde hair and blue eyes. "Ahh, thank Christ it's you. We're in real trouble out here."

"Yeah, come in. Is Elle with you?" He looked around, hoping to see her.

"No." Doolin's answer was short. "Frit," he whistled calling the others to the house.

"A little help?" Laney quietly beckoned, as she and Dory tried to haul Deck up the snow covered hill.

"What happened to him?" Josh backed out of the way as they led him inside.

"He was bitten, so I chopped his arm off." Laney placed the axe on the floor, leaning it against the wall with a thud.

"Where'd the bat go?" Doolin was surprised by its absence.

"Traded it in for the axe."

"Bitten by what?" Josh couldn't stop staring at the bloody stump that had replaced the arm.

"Not quite sure I can quantify that. People. Infected people," Doolin's answer only caused more questions.

"Infected with what? What are you talking about; I thought we were in the Static Zone. My dad said all the infected were slow, and frozen. He had me evacuate the settlement, bring Mom and Celia here. He never said anything about Frosty. I thought he was just getting ready to oust the governor."

"That's true, and I did see a patrol entering the quad, but I found my wife and once I snagged her we spent the rest of our time just trying to escape town."

"Did you see my dad, was he still alive?"

"I didn't but maybe Laney did."

"I don't know your dad kid, and I was pretty out of it...wait a minute. Wait one goddamn minute, I know you, you're the little shit that's been violating my daughter." She charged toward him, her hands extended in a choking motion.

"Wait, wait," she calmed down, "that was the old me. I will not lose it and then put my hands on you. I'm going to act in a calm and measured manner. Where's my axe?"

"I'm sorry Mrs. Riley, I love her."

"If we didn't so terribly need shelter, I'd kill you myself." Doolin gave him the hairy eyeball, disturbed by the development.

"Josh," Barker's wife Celia entered the room. "Your mother is worried about you...disturbed by all the commotion, she wants to see you."

"On my way," he scurried, hurrying to her side.

"Celia Barker," she introduced herself to the room of strangers. Celia was a stocky woman of about fifty. Although not thin by definition, she was firm and proportionate. She wore a red flannel hat with a brim, and her friendly eyes peered out from behind wired rims as she surveyed the guests.

"Deck, Dory, Laney, and I'm Doolin," he introduced, pointing everyone out.

"Three D's. Parents had a thing for that letter?" she was amused by the alliteration of first names.

"Actually, Laney's name is Dylan and Deck's name is Ashleigh. So she would be the other D and he would be an A." Doolin shook his head, embarrassed by his rambling.

"Very confusing." She was even more amused.

Laney got involved. "Deck, or Ash and I, rather, are brother and sister. Doolin is my husband and Dory, is well, she's with Ash."

"Children?" Celia asked, all the while hoping her boy was all right. He was still at the trench keeping watch; she hoped he would get back to her safely.

"Yeah, two boys, Ian and Sean, they're eleven. And our daughter Elle, she's seventeen."

"My son J.R. he's twenty, he's at the trench. I haven't heard from him or his father in hours."

"Its crazy out there, but I'm sure they have it under control." Laney stepped closer, placing her hand on the worried mother's back. "We left our kids out in the woods with Dooley's parents. I'm worried too, but I'm sure we'll get there and find everything is fine. Just like your boy will get here, and he'll be fine."

Celia nodded, her Midwest mom hair bobbing beneath the hat.

"Mom needs a drink," Josh waltzed in to fill her plastic cup with water.

"Is she all right, have her come out so she can meet us; you're dating our daughter after all."

"She can't, she's bedridden." He slid the straw back into the cup's lid before returning to his mother's side.

"MS, I think, or something like it." Celia filled them in. "End stages maybe. She is weak. It's been tough here without electricity, but Bret radioed and said get out of the tents."

"Good thing, too. She's better off here. Not too many people are left after the attacks." Doolin looked to Deck.

"Is that what happened to him?" She swallowed hard at the sight of his arm, or lack thereof.

"Yeah. Be glad you're here. We haven't seen any out here yet."

Chapter 24
Cross-Contamination

"Josh! Josh open the door!" J.R. beckoned from the porch, his father in his arms. "Josh!"

Josh rose from the floor at his mother's bedside. With his rifle in his hands he crept to the door.

Doolin was already armed and waiting.

"Josh, Jesus Christ! Let us in!"

"It's J.R." Josh informed Doolin who took a step back so he could open the door.

"What happened?" he asked as they stepped in, Celia now emerging from the back room.

"Oh my god! What happened, are you okay?" She cradled her husband, guiding him to the floor.

"We were attacked on the way here. A firefight broke out, and the infected were everywhere. Dad was hit with a stray bullet."

"Friendly fire is better than bitten." Josh motioned to Deck, who was lying on the floor in a pool of sweat. "His sister cut his arm off."

Even Barker sat up to look at Deck and his missing limb.

"Let's take a look," Doolin shuffled over. "Where'd it get you?"

"Left flank," Barker winced as Celia pulled open his jacket. His shirt was soaked with blood.

"Pull that up, let's take a look."

Doolin investigated the now-exposed wound. "Through and through. Let's get it clean and dressed. As long as the bleeding stops and you can avoid infection, you might be okay."

Barker winced as he strained to talk. "There's a kit under the sink, get it, son, so we can take care of this thing."

In the lamplight of the dated kitchen, Doolin used his latent scouting skills, and became a medic."

" Think you can do something for Deck? He's looking really bad." Laney watched her husband work.

"Clean and dress it, maybe. What he really needs is painkillers and antibiotics. So does Barker here, for that matter."

"In the back... in the bathroom. We stocked up in case of emergency. J.R., you know where." Barker set his head down; the wound sent pain through his back in waves.

"Jesus Christ! Ouch!"

"I'm almost done," Doolin squeezed the saline one last time, wiping the fluid with gauze. "There, all patched up." He fastened the last piece of tape.

"Here." J.R. handed over a box filled with bottles. "FishMox. Well, that'll work." He dispensed the antibiotic to Barker. "Looks like all there is for pain is ibuprofen."

"I'll take it," he choked down the fish meds and the pain reliever.

As his wife offered him sips of water, Doolin approached Deck.

"How's it going? You look like shit."

"I used to look better when I had both arms."
He shivered; a cold sweat coated his body.

"Let me see what we can do with this magic
kit," he unwrapped the stump; the shirt had started to
stick. "Awww!" Deck writhed in pain as his brother-in-
law removed the fabric.

"Okay, here comes the tricky part." Doolin
loosened the belt, ready to stem the blood flow if
necessary. "Oh, looks like it might have stopped, just a
trickle, that's good." He commenced the task of
cleaning it. "This might sting a little."

In the flickering light of the tiny living room,
Doolin cleaned and dressed the wound while Deck
screamed. He kicked his legs violently, his shoes
scraping the old wood floors.

Everyone watched as he suffered, his cries
filled with agony.

"Done." Doolin looked up, Deck now still. "Ash.
Ash," he tapped him on the cheek.

"Oh my god, Dooley, what happened?" Laney
was now over him, calling his name. "Ash! Ashleigh
Decker! **Deck**!"

Dory was on the aged and flowered sofa, sitting
above his head; her legs were pulled to her chest as she
rocked. "Is he dead? Oh god, is he dead?"

"No, wait, he's moving. I see his eyelids
fluttering."

Deck's eyes popped open; the whites were
gray, deep red lines trailed from his pupils. Black liquid
pooled in the corners as he began to shake violently.

"What's happening, Jesus Christ what's
happening!" Laney moved in, her hands on his

shoulders. "Deck! Deck!" she screeched until foam collected at the corners of her mouth.

"What's going on out here?" Mrs. Johnson emerged from the bedroom, her weakened frame supported by a walker.

"Mom, go back to bed, you shouldn't be out here." Josh rushed to his mother's side.

She eyed Celia and her husband on the golden linoleum. She became worried. "Where is Bret? Was he with you?" Barker looked away.

J.R. looked to his father, wondering if he was going to tell them.

"He didn't make it. We were attacked on our way back from the trench. We had gone to get J.R. after the infection broke out. The team got split up, many of the men turned. Bret and I decided to warn the tower, grab J.R., and head for the safe house. We were overcome on the way here. He helped me protect our boy. He was bitten... I took care of it."

Barker was visibly shaken. Sickened by the memory of putting down his best friend. "I couldn't protect J.R. alone, I was weak... already shot."

In the turmoil of it all, the group lost sight of Deck and his struggle. Only Laney, Doolin, and Dory were still paying attention.

"Back away from him." Doolin tried to pull his wife clear, gravely aware that he was mid-shift.

Dory remained on the sofa. Her rocking increased as she tried to deal with the horror unraveling before her.

"It worked, it worked; he can't be turning. It's been too long. Why now, why is he turning now?"

Laney searched the room for answers, for clues as to why this was happening.

Doolin speculated, digging for an explanation, afraid his wife would snap. "Maybe the tourniquet had somehow kept whatever traces of the contaminate out. Maybe there was cross-contamination from Barker's encounter with Johnson when he turned. I don't know!"

Deck's violent shift was nearing its end, his once chiseled and athletic form was now twisted and grotesque. This once-virile young man was now an animal, determined to carry out its one objective...infect.

Reanimated, Deck jumped to his feet, unimpeded by the loss of his limb.

Doolin tried to comfort Laney, unaware that he'd risen, ready to attack.

Dory rocked, her face buried in her folded arms while he lunged, Josh's mother the easiest target. In a split second she was on the ground and mutilated, her neck torn open by his powerful jaws.

Her severed artery pumped, spraying blood onto Josh who was just inches from her.

"Mom!"

Seconds ago, he was trying to calm her from the news of his father. Now she would join him.

The spray quickly turned from red to black as the pathogens invaded. Her once weak form became powerful as she got to her feet. The small space was now a battle Zone, two howlers in close proximity.

A loud pop rang out as Josh put down his mother, the .22 driving a bullet into her brain.

Deck, had already made quick work of tearing into poor Celia, who'd decided to shield her injured husband. Now she was on the floor convulsing, her transformation imminent.

Laney, now with the axe in her hand, approached her brother. With his nose upturned he moved toward Dory, the smell of her fear drawing him toward her.

Just as she lifted to swing, another shot rang out, and Deck collapsed, his head blown wide open by Doolin's PMR.

"My mom!" J.R. called out.

Without hesitation, Doolin turned and popped her too.

"Anyone else?" he was tired of the whole situation.

"It's on me, I can feel it moving," Dory was freaked. "Christ, it's on me, I'm gonna turn."

Laney tried to keep her calm. "No. Wash up, you'll be fine."

Dory rushed to the sink where she poured water onto her hands from a plastic carton. She rubbed frantically to remove the creeping crud.

"You son of a bitch! This is all your fault!" Barker was now sitting at the table with a gun in his hand. "Bringing him in here when you knew he was compromised... She's dead, she's dead, and you did it!" He took aim and shot Doolin in the shoulder.

"Are you fucking crazy!"

Laney decided to shift into crisis control.

"Ahh Christ, Josh, get the first aid kit."

"Dory, Dory you all right? Get yourself together, we're getting the hell outta here."

"Yeah, I'm good... clean."

Laney poured all the alcohol from the kit on her hands, then packed the wound in her husband's shoulder with gauze.

"Good news, it's up high, I don't think it hit anything important. Bad news, bullet's still in there."

"I'll live for now, let's get home." Doolin got to his feet.

Barker was at the table with his head slumped. He was grief-stricken and filled with remorse over shooting Doolin.

J.R. had taken the gun and worked to console his father.

"I'm coming with you." Josh was ready, his jacket on and his backpack in place. He looked at his mother, her body almost unrecognizable. "I've got nothing left here."

Desperation

Chapter 25
Rescued

"Don't look at me like that, I don't know where they are." Pop paced, watching each window. Nan brought him his coat and pushed him toward the door.

"I don't even know where to begin. Ahh god," he trotted in place, "my ball hairs are twitching something terrible." He could see the desperation in her eyes. "Okay, I'll go. I don't want those kids to wake up in the morning without their parents either."

With her finger hooked in his belt loop she pulled him close, her lips to his ear. In breathy tones she whispered, "Or the parents wake up without a kid."

Pop looked at his watch. They'd been gone several hours; he was just as worried as his wife was.

"I'll take the snowmobile, it'll save time." After arming himself he stepped to the door, ready to depart.

She was pleased, nodding in agreement. With a hug she sent him out, her hands pressed together over her lips in prayer.

He looked back, uneasy about leaving his wife and grandchildren unprotected.

"There's a loaded shotgun under the downstairs bed. Use it if you have to. Shoot first, do you hear me."

She nodded, her messy bun bobbed up and down, as she gave thumbs-up, prepared to do what she must.

Nan watched from the back door as he walked to the shed, her thin arms crossed for warmth.

With the doors thrown open he wrestled in the dark with the large canvas drop cloth that covered the machine. It had been sitting for quite some time. "Probably should've checked on this sooner. With my luck, it won't turn over."

As he pulled the line, the old Arctic Cat wheezed and whined. He tried a little sweet talk. "Come on, you old bitch, start up for Daddy."

Taking a step back, he tried to compose himself.

"I will get on you, and you will ruuunnn!" His composure quickly dissipated as he stood before the snow machine, his arms flexed in their usual manner.

Furious but determined, he grabbed a helmet from the seat.

Now buckled and with the goggles pulled over his eyes, he straddled his old Cat one more time. He grasped the cord, and with sheer determination and the choke wide open, he yanked.

"Ring ting ting ting ting ting," the engine screamed, ready to roll.

"Ahh ha ha ha." Pop tore out of the yard and through the heavy ground cover, as the fresh powder kicked up and dusted the trees behind him.

With the throttle cranked he ripped along the trail, the path obscured by mounds of snow.

Footprints, he thought as he sped along, *there are no footprints, all of this snow is undisturbed; they haven't made it back.*

Now just a couple miles from the edge of town, he could see two forms dodging into the trees as they attempted to avoid his oncoming vehicle. He slowed, certain it was his son. *Only two, they didn't find her, something bad happened.*

Now at a stop, he peered into the trees where the evaders were hunkered twenty feet in, their prints easy to see in the white of the snow.

"I see you out there," he shouted over the Cat's idling engine.

"Pop," Laney was now on her feet and moving toward the trail. "Is that you?"

Dory joined her, trudging back toward the path.

"Where's Dooley...Ash? I only see two of you." He swiveled around, looking for the missing member.

"Dooley's hurt, he's back a bit. He wanted me to get home safe to the kids and then send help. He was just worried he was slowing us down. I shouldn't have left him." Now in her father-in-law's presence, in light of all that had happened, she broke down.

"Get on, I'll run you back and then pick them up."

"Just leave me, go get him now."

"No. He wants you safe. It'll only take a few minutes to run you back." He cranked the throttle, the Cat screaming in response.

Laney and Dory climbed aboard and were whisked to safety, the ride much easier than the long trudge through the deep snow.

"Get in the house, I'm going back."

"They are tucked just inside the tunnel on the edge of town." Laney hugged him. The smell of nicotine and exhaust filled her nostrils. "Be careful, the infected are everywhere."

Pop saluted his wife, who was now at the back door, before taking off in search of his injured son. She rushed to collect Laney and Dory as she watched him ride away.

Landfall? He thought as he sped along. *Crossed the trench? Washed up in the lake?* He looked to his right, the water breaking in the distance. *If they can swim, how will we defend the lakeshore?*

As he drove, he not only worried about his son, but now the infected and all the points of entry they could breach.

Construct a perimeter. When the snow melts, we'll wall ourselves in.

Chapter 26
Tummy Trouble

D avies scanned the large garage; his mag light illuminating the many university vehicles and confiscated machines.

He crossed the floor to the snowmobiles and checked ignitions for keys.

The scan was interrupted, "Freeze," Martin flipped on his light, the beam directed at Davies eyes. "Where do you think you're going on the governor's snowmobile?" His words were garbled by the spoon full of food tucked in his cheek.

"Think it's a good idea to cause a commotion, they're everywhere." Davies nodded toward the windows, the infected always on the prowl.

"They're slowing down now, cold's getting to them." He chewed the spoon. "My partner was infected, he's out there barely moving now."

"The ones outside aren't fast. The buildings haven't all reached freezing yet. If they travel out, they'll still have some fight in them." Davies had just experienced such and encounter as he fled West Science.

Martin spit the plastic utensil on the garage floor, his rifle now raised and pointed at the back of Davies' head.

"I didn't think of that... anyway, the governor..."

"Well," Davies explained, "he won't mind, because he's dead."

He recognized the familiar click of the safety being released. "If you could lower your weapon, I'd like to get out of here."

"Since when?" He was now perplexed by his prisoner's report.

"Since I put a bullet in his skull."

Martin contemplated the news. "He was an idiot, but I can't let you go, I've got Hatch and McGovern to answer to still. "Hatch radioed a while back and said to gas 'em up, they were on their way."

"Well, they were all infected and then killed, so they aren't coming." Davies decided to take his chances, and take a seat on the nearest sled.

Martin lowered the rifle and doubled over.

"You all right?" Davies found himself asking.

"Yeah, MRE's, they hate me." Martin returned to his upright posture, rifle at the ready.

"Why should I believe you? You'd probably say anything to drive out of here." He winced as another gas pain tore through his colon. "Silent but violent." He gave Davies a wink. "Incoming."

Davies cringed as the smell drifted in his direction.

"Never mind that," Martin waved off the flatulence. "I'm going to have to detain you."

Davies was incensed. "These aren't even his. He took them from people he killed." The anger bubbled up. "And I refuse to die in a garage, killed by the world's gassiest guard. Not after everything I've been through today."

Martin stepped closer, the rifle now in Davies face. "Get off, and head toward the office."

"I tink you should head to da office." Willy Jarvi put his barrel into Martin's back.

"Yeah, ya hoser. Drop da rifle and move it, eh."

Willy and Elmer were welcome sights.

"How'd you find me? Anyone else out there?" Davies hoped others had survived.

"Saw da dueling flashlights, but it's just us. It's been a hairy night. We popped lots of Frosty though, or, well, howlers. I guess dey should be Frosty by tomorrow though, eh?"

Elmer nodded in agreement with his brother's analyses.

"How 'bout you?"

"Popped a few, they got Brady. But, the governor, Hatch…"

"Dat prick McGovern?" The brothers were hoping for the best.

"All dead. Hatch shot himself and McGovern was infected… killed by Landis."

"Jesus Christ pajamas!" Willy beamed, delighted by the news.

"Yeah, what he said." Elmer was just as pleased.

"Let's lock dis prick in da office and drive back to da house. I could use some refreshments."

"Did you say Brady? Sergeant, kind of grisly?" Martin seemed to know him.

"Yeah, you knew him?"

"He sent me on a goose chase for the governor, some guy named Decker."

"And?" Davies waited for the punch line.

"Nothin'. Small world, is all." Martin was deflated, certain his anecdote would have meant more. Maybe keep him from being locked up.

"Okay. Well, yeah," Elmer checked his watch, "I could go for some God's Breakfast." He ushered Martin to his makeshift cell.

God's breakfast...I'm afraid to ask. Davies checked for Frosty before opening the overhead door while Willy inspected the machinery.

"Hey let's snag the SkiDoo, we can use it for parts when one of ours takes a shit."

"Solid plan, brudder." Elmer saddled up, leaving room for Willy to sit."

Davies mounted a sled, ready to get out of town.

"What ya ridin' dere, Mitt?" Willy scoped his machine choice. "It's a green one." He looked for a name, unsure of what brand.

"Polaris. I'd rather push my Doo dan drive dat."

"Can we just go?" His patience with the Brothers Jarvi was wearing thin.

Willy waved Davies off, as his SkiDoo whined, the track scraping the cement of the floor on the way out.

Davies followed.

The racket of their departure attracted Martins' infected partner and other Frosty in the area.

Some of the freshly shifted ran like dogs after a car, trying to catch the snowmobiles.

Fast, they came close enough to give Davies and the brothers the fear, but eventually the machines won out.

Martin wasn't so lucky.

Locked in the office he hunkered quietly, aware that the garage door was wide open. "Still and quiet, that's what I'll be."

He found that task difficult as he cramped, his meal ready to eat now ready to depart.

Not now, he thought. He rolled to his side, and pulled his knees to his chest as he tried to control his insides.

The patter and clicking of the local Frosty drifted under the office door, their approach slow and methodical. Roused by the racket they shuffled into the garage.

Ahh Christ, Martin was worried, his sphincter no match for the pressurized liquid of his recently digested meal.

Not now, not now, his thoughts filled with anxiety. Sweat dripped down his back; he was unable to hold on any longer.

Slowly, quietly, he tried to pull down his pants. Ducked under the counter of the coffee station he squatted, trying to relieve himself into the wastepaper basket.

The MRE's rocketed from his behind in a flurry of spits and spatters, followed by an odor of epic proportions.

As he held the rim of the can for dear life, he noticed the shadows of the infected drifting closer to the window.

"Shh, shh, shh," they sniffed at the door. With great force they rattled, as they clawed and pushed, lured by the smell of Martin's... fear.

Chapter 27
Santa and His Helpers

"How much-ch-ch longer?" Josh's teeth chattered in the cold.

"Not long, I bet they're almost there, and then Pop will come for us."

"What if they don't... do you hear that?" Josh swiveled, trying to separate the sounds of nature from the sounds of death heading their way. "They're coming." Fear filled his eyes. "What if we can't fight them all." Clumsily he clutched the rifle, hypothermia affecting his motor skills.

Doolin watched as Josh shivered, reminded of Deck's theory. "Let's head into the trees, and bury ourselves in snow."

With great caution they crept from the tunnel's opening. "All clear." Doolin led the way, only groans and distant shadows visible.

"Its so deep," Josh's muscles were burdened by the cold.

Doolin was even slower, his status complicated by the gunshot wound.

Together they plowed their way into the nearest thicket of trees and dropped, trying to wiggle down into the fresh powder and cover up.

"They're right there," Josh trembled as the pack shifted closer, clearly slowed by the cold and snow.

"They're slow."

"Shhh," Doolin shot him a look.

With upturned noses they sniffed, their exposed teeth glinting in the moonlight, the snowfall now dissipated.

Loudly they breathed, some scent drawing them, they were attracted.

Please work, pleeease work, Doolin prayed internally, as the creatures crept nearer.

With sickly anticipation they moved in, their clicks and moans now audible.

Josh clamped his eyes and mouth tight, afraid they would see a reflection of light in his eyes or his breath swirling in the cold air.

Doolin was locked on. He couldn't stop looking at what approached. *It's Santa, that one is dressed like Santa.*

Santa's jolly appearance was no more. His suit was soiled with the blood of his many victims, and his beard was cock-eyed and littered with gruesome bits of human tissue.

The approaching infected used the path cut by Josh's and Doolin's footsteps, lessening the burden of movement and increasing their speed. They were now only feet away.

They reached Josh first. He was barely visible; the snow covered most of his body. They scooted by, uninterested, his humanity, his scent, shielded by the cold.

Doolin was afraid. He was cold and buried, but he was injured.

He watched as the pack caught on, the cold not enough to suppress the smell of his wound and the fresh blood that had soaked through the gauze. Unable to run, he gripped his gun and prayed for speed and accuracy.

With teeth distended and snapping they moved in. Slow but deliberate, they poised to attack.

"Take that, you ugly mothers." One dropped, his black blood a stark contrast to the white hillside.

"One down, six to go." He fired again, missing the headshot.

With his heels dug in he scooted, trying to put more distance between himself and the encroaching threat.

Josh turned, alarmed by the horrific scene unfolding before him in slow motion. Doolin was outnumbered, just a few feet between him and infection.

He fell back, as he fumbled with the rifle, his hands numb from the cold, as he aimed, trying to avoid his girlfriend's father as he fired.

"Good one," Doolin was filled with hope as Josh dropped another Frosty into the snow.

They both fired, each picking off another.

Doolin scooted back again, as the last three closed in.

Josh struggled to reload, his .22 jammed in the snow.

"Can't get all three before they get me," Doolin aimed as he decided which one posed the most immediate threat. He fired, the target nearly point blank, fell after the bullet passed right through to ricochet off a tree. The speeding and now infected bullet passed just inches from Josh. Startled, he tripped, and fired, his feet cut out from under him by buried brush.

"Arrg," Doolin shouted out in pain. The sloppy shot was now buried in his leg.

Frustrated and pissed off, he emptied his clip, firing wildly at his aggressors.

The firing continued even after he was out of ammo, Pop sniping the rest of the infected from the seat of his snowmobile.

Josh peeked up, lifting his head from the snow, checking for the all-clear.

Pop took a drag from his freshly lit cigarette. "Are you two done fucking around with Santa and his helpers out here, its cold, let's go home."

Josh helped Doolin down to the trail, and onto the back of the Cat.

"Son..." Pop kept smoking, his eye on the blood as it dripped onto Doolin's foot.

"I was shot."

"Better get back and have a look at that. Laney said you were hurt, how long has that been bleeding?"

"This, oh this just happened, she was talking about the gunshot wound in my shoulder."

"Had a bad night?" He looked around, Deck not in attendance. "Who's this? Where's Ash?"

"Deck had a bad night, too." Doolin's body language said it all.

Pop hugged his son. "Shh, ahh, take it easy." He patted his father on the back, "My shoulder, remember, I was shot."

"I'm Josh, by the way," the oblivious youngster interrupted.

Pop eyeballed him but said nothing for a moment, his intentional silence meant to make the teen uncomfortable.

"Okay, enough of this roadside outpouring of emotion. If we hurry, we might even get home before the sun rises. Climb on." Pop cranked the throttle, making haste toward the homestead, his son's leg bleeding the whole way.

Chapter 28
Mr. Incredible

"I hope he found them?" Laney stared into the flames, the fire finally removing the chill from her bones.

Dory was still shaken, her knees once again pulled to her chest. With tear-filled eyes she stared at the ornaments hung from the tree, her thoughts focused on Deck. *Just hours ago, his hand placed that there.*

"I'm going to check on the kids one more time," Laney bounded upstairs; every glance at their sleeping faces brought her a little more peace than she'd had before.

She returned to the living room, "I can see Ash in them—in the boys. They remind me of him." Laney choked back the tears, unable to grieve her dead brother while her husband was absent and in danger.

Nan lifted her finger before moving quickly to the window. The faint ring of the Arctic Cat's engine could be heard in the distance, the headlight now visible as it bounced through the trees.

"It's them!" Laney led the way as she and her mother-in-law charged the back door.

Dory remained on the sofa, her gaze fixed on the ornaments.

"Dooley, oh my god, I was starting to wonder if I'd ever see you again."

The trio dismounted the sled, making their way toward the porch.

With her arms wrapped around his neck she smooched, his face now peppered with kisses.

"Okay, okay, I'm all right." He winced as he stood, his leg still bleeding profusely.

Nan pointed to Josh.

"We picked him up along the way," Pop put his arm around his wife.

"He's a gift for Elle," Doolin limped to the house, supported by his wife.

Nan shrugged, her shoulders asking the question.

"He's her boyfriend. His father was...you know what, later. I can't explain right now." Doolin dropped to the sofa across from Dory.

"Can I see her?" Josh was broken down and looking for some comfort.

Laney quietly nodded. "She's upstairs, but don't wake the boys."

"I don't trust him," Pop watched as he ascended the staircase. "He looks shifty. I know what I'd be looking to do if I was seventeen... Better keep all your parts to yourself."

Josh gave Pop a salute. Terrified of the grisly man, he wouldn't dare touch her.

Doolin rolled his eyes, "You're still looking to do it now." His father was a long-standing and outspoken pervert.

"I just have a healthy appetite."

Nan shot him her signature look of disapproval.

Pop defended himself. "This is no time for deconstructing my character. Our son needs assistance. Do you think you can get down to the shelter?"

"No, Dad, I'm in pretty bad shape, I'll never make it down that ladder."

"Will do, I'll just run and get a few things, and then we'll fix you right up."

He produced the key and opened the door, which provided quite the thrill to Laney, who was not yet privy to the clever entrance.

"Laney, would you help me, I need an extra pair of hands?"

"Yes, right behind you." She stepped into the barrel, astonished by the man she thought she knew.

"Incredible," she put her hand on his shoulder. "This is just incredible."

"This is only the tunnel, wait till you see the bunker."

He thought of Deck and how he and Dooley had joked that he'd have to turn sideways. Once again, Pop found himself giving out spontaneous hugs.

Although taken aback, Laney reciprocated.

After a moment, she tapped out, "Can we get to the supplies, we should probably hurry."

"Yeah, yeah, sorry." He ran his sleeve past his eyes.

Was he crying? She glanced at his face certain she saw moisture around the eyes.

Deeply moved by his vulnerability, she teared up as well, neither of them saying a word.

With a sniff he piled the last thing in her arms and called it. "I think that's everything."

With one last look around, she realized that they really could make it, *all thanks to Pop.*

With the last of the supplies handed up and out of the opening, he closed the door, and locked up, the key once again tucked safely inside his shirt.

He cracked open the medical kit. "Are you ready?"

"As ready as I'll ever be." He slid to the floor. Nan tucked a throw pillow under his head.

"Don't." Dory was white as a sheet. "You fixed up Deck and he turned. He attacked people. Just leave it."

"He was exposed...bitten. We were in a house with others who'd been exposed." Doolin flashed back to the scene, trying to pinpoint the source, trying to find something concrete to give her. "I'm sure it was some sort of cross contamination. He had a severe wound."

"I've got it," Laney cradled his head in her hands, as she choked back the tears. "If he so much as jerks wrong, I'll take care of it. Pop, I need a weapon."

"Don't hesitate, think of the kids, of Pop and Nan," Doolin made Laney promise.

"I promise," she rubbed his cheek.

Nan retrieved the double barrel from under the bed.

"Drink this," Pop produced a quart of whiskey from the med kit, "you're gonna need it."

Doolin started his liquor intake, and Pop lathered on some hand sanitizer.

As Doolin sipped, Pop began probing the thigh injury with Q-tips soaked in Solarcaine.

"Holy hell," he took another gulp.

"As soon as the anesthetic takes hold it'll become more comfortable. Not as good as being put under, but livable."

"Ready?"

Doolin gave a nod.

"Who shot you?" Pop dug in the wound, the bullet eluding him as Doolin squirmed and bled onto the floor.

"Josh got me with his .22, friendly fire."

The pain was building. All his muscles tensed.

"Feeling the pressure?"

Doolin held his breath while he answered, "Yeah, yeah, Dad, there's some pressure."

"What about this shoulder?" He moved north, the leg already treated, the slug now resting in Nan's hand.

"Angry husband."

He raised an eyebrow before snatching the bottle from his son and taking a swig himself. "A little medicine for the doctor... Something you want to tell your wife?"

Still holding his breath he answered, "Funny, but he wasn't angry because of that."

Now self-medicated, he returned to digging in Doolin's shoulder, his son extremely uncomfortable and pale.

"You don't look too good, how you feelin'?" Pop grabbed his face, and gave him the once over.

"It would seem your combat medic skills are rusty. You're taking too long. Good field doctors are fast ones." With a shiver he passed out, his body went limp.

"I told you, I told you." Dory backed up. She stumbled over the dog as she wedged herself into the corner, the rocking again present.

Spencer opened an eye, only to return to his nap, the hour too early to be awake.

"Let's not overreact; he was in a lot of pain, he probably just blacked out." Pop snapped his fingers by his son's ears, and called his name. "Dooley, Dooley, wake the fuck up, you're freaking everyone out."

"Ma, grab the salts from the kit."

With steady hands she produced the smelling salts, showing every confidence that her husband had it under control.

She placed her hands on Laney's, and with a gentle nod gave a quiet cue to stay calm. She reached over, and pushed the loaded gun just a little farther away.

"Get a whiff of that." He waved the stick under his nose. "Oh, there he is, that's right, wake up."

Doolin's nose twitched as the powerful scent pulled him back from his unconscious world. "Stop waving that thing," he grabbed his father's hand, "I'm starting to feel a little green."

Nan clapped her hands together and brought them to her face, once again striking her prayerful pose, clearly thankful that he'd pulled through the ordeal.

"It's all over, I've patched you up to the best of my abilities. We just have to keep you infection-free." Terry took another pull from the bottle, the booze helped smooth the frayed nerves.

Doolin spoke weakly from the wood floor, "FishMox. They had fish antibiotics at the other place, when I fixed up my shooter."

Pop reached into his self-built med kit and produced a similar product. "FishPen. You can't buy prescription antibiotics for personal use, but the aquarium stuff, I pulled it right off the shelf, and it's the same thing people take, no script."

"Huh, so when you were preparing for the end, you knew that and stocked up."

"Yep."

"He's all right, Dory, it's safe." Laney approached with her arms extended.

"I don't know how you are holding it together." She bent over, resting her head on Laney's shoulder. Now in the arms of her friend she sobbed. "I loved him, I loved your brother. I'm sorry he's gone...Oh god, he's gone."

Doolin could hear the grief spilling from the other side of the room, and was now concerned for his wife's well-being as Dory opened the emotional floodgates.

Numb and in shock, Laney just wanted to sleep. "It's been a long, long, long, long day. Let's rest, let's just get some rest."

Dory moved to the downstairs bed, now that Doolin and Laney would have the sofas where she'd previously been bunking with Deck.

"I'll stoke the fire, get this place warm. Dooley is chilled to the bone." Pop threw a few large logs on the already roaring blaze.

He agreed with his father, quietly shaking his head, as he tried to meditate the pain away. "Pain relief? Anything?"

Nan produced a bottle of Vicodin.

"Its from a tooth she had pulled. There are only a few left. We stuck it in the kit." Pop pulled one from the bottle and placed it on Dooley's tongue. He quickly washed it down with another sip of the Jack Daniels.

"That's enough of that." Pop snatched the bottle and took another drink before capping the bottle. He whisked the med kit back to the bunker while Nan wrangled her son, helping him to the sofa and off of the hard floor. Now next to him, her thin frame leaned over and whispered.

"Love you too, Mom." He closed his eyes, unable to stay awake any longer.

Laney joined him, taking up residence on the adjacent sofa while Pop and Nan moved upstairs.

Pop stopped outside of the kid's door. "I'm checking on that boy, he better be keeping it in his pants."

Josh was on the floor, curled up next to the bed Elle was sharing with the twins. He never even woke her; he just camped next to her.

Chapter 29
Sneak Attack

"**W**hat happened here?" Davies pointed from his idling snowmobile, the seven contorted forms splattered and spread in the pristine snow.

"Looks like a pack of 'em went after da wrong guy." Willy hopped off of his sled to observe the scene. "Quite da struggle, someone was hurt though, look."

They turned their attention to the track marks cut into the snow by Terry Riley's Cat. A red drip line ran down the center.

"Another machine's been through here."

"Yeah, musta encountered dese fellas here." Elmer wrinkled his nose, the contorted faces even more horrific in the light reflecting off of the snow. It cast shadows on the forms, every wrinkle and crease deepened...more frightening. "I tink dat one's still movin."

Davies dismounted and flipped the latch holding his knife in place as he trudged, the twitcher his target.

"I've never seen one do dat before," Willy watched as Davies buried the knife in its head, the bullet wound in its temple his entry point.

"Seems like you have to destroy enough of the brain, or the right section, to really stop them from moving. I haven't seen one actually stand and ambulate, but had a few continue to quiver... can't take any chances. Ahh, Christ!" He fell back, tripped up by a hand as it gripped his ankle, the infected arm covered in a plush red coat. Now splayed into the mess, he scrambled to extricate himself. In a violent flurry, he stabbed, nailing each one in the head. Adrenaline coursed through his veins as he crossed the trail and plunged his hands into the bank next to the Polaris. He scrubbed feverishly to remove the bits of bone and tarry brain matter. He swished the blade in the snow to remove the excess gore before he sheathed it.

Wide-eyed and exhausted he plunked himself back into his seat, ready to depart, unaware that in his haste to still the twitchers, he'd left one intact.

"Let's go, I'm parched, and da sauna is callin me. Some shine and a steam is on da schedule."

Elmer scooted up, his hands now on the throttle. He cranked it, the engine screaming with each twist of the wrist. Willy hopped on as his brother accelerated. Caught off guard, he shouted, "Slow down ya son of a bitch," the whine of the two-stroke drowning him out, "my ass is hangin off."

Davies grinned, the antics of the brothers a welcomed distraction from the horrors of the last twelve hours.

As they approached the turn-off to the Jarvi's camp, he took a deep breath, relieved to be safe and out of town.

"Pull it in here," Elmer waved him into the pole barn. "We'll keep 'em out of sight."

"I'm ready for bed." Davies walked toward the door.

"We should unwind. Let's get cooked in da sauna and have a little God's breakfast first." Elmer clapped his hand to Davies back, "Ever have it before?"

"Can't say I have."

"You'll love it. It's better den beers, I tell you what."

He nodded, enticed by his new friend's enthusiasm.

"Ya know, we really got dumped on. I bet there's two-three feet of fresh stuff out here. We'll have some shovelin tuh do tomorrow, well, later tuh-day," he corrected as he looked at his watch.

"Yeah we'll just have to trudge our way to the sauna," Willy pointed to an outbuilding a hundred feet behind their main house and opposite the barn. It was a small saltbox in design, the front taller, and the roof longer in the back. It was sided in brown asphalt shingles and had an old tin roof with a stone chimney rising from the top.

Elmer huffed and puffed, "Hard to get up this incline through all of the snow." Fatigue was making the task even more challenging.

"Think about how good it will feel to get inside." Willy brushed the snow from a sandstone, which rested in the rotten window box. The key was stashed underneath.

The lock was quickly manipulated. "Behold, da Jarvi sauna." He fidgeted in the dark. Years of familiarity guided him as he retrieved a match and lit the gas lantern that hung from a large hook at the entry. With that lantern lit, he moved to light another, the tiny house now illuminated. The small dwelling had three rooms. The front room was a rustic living area with a table and chairs and an old dusty sofa.

To the left of that, was a changing room, equipped with wooden benches and iron hooks for towels and clothing. Through the changing room was the sauna itself. The cedar-lined room ran the entire length of the building and was lined with a two-tiered pine bench. The bench resembled bleachers, and was held back by a railing that ran the entire length of the seats. The sauna stove was massive; it inhabited the front quarter of the space, its open top filled with large soap stones. Its unique design was reminiscent of an old car, as though it were constructed of a hood and quarter panels. Although it was a flat, dark gray, bits of red peeked from beneath chips at the edges.

The floor was poured concrete, which sloped gently toward a large brass drain. Resting at the base of the bench was an assortment of galvanized tubs and, buckets. The buckets were beneath the tap that provided the water to be thrown on the rocks by a long-handled scoop, and the tubs provided space for bathing in the traditional way. A decorative wooden rack graced the wall at the end of the bench, draped with loofahs and back brushes.

"Very impressive." He moved back to the front room and looked around. "Uh, what's in there?" Davies approached an igloo drink cooler. The ten-gallon dispenser was parked on the midcentury dining table, its modern orange exterior a strange contrast to the faded green of the tabletop. Piled along side was an assortment of jars and mugs, apparently for whatever liquid was lurking inside.

"Dat's da drink of the righteous. Da beverage for all dat ails ya."

"Let me guess, God's breakfast?"

"Fill him up, and I'll get dis place heated." Elmer started the sauna stove, "its a handmade Finnish design, super-fast and super-high heating."

"What about in here?" Davies sat back onto the sofa, dust drifted into the air. "It's a bit chilly."

"A jar or two of dat, and da heat dat'll start building from da Iron Maiden in dere, you'll be plenty toasty."

Davies sipped the fluorescent yellow liquid cautiously, its appearance a bit off-putting. "Wow! That's stiff." A light sweat broke as an inferno worked through his insides.

"Still cold?" Willy took another long pull from his Ball mason jar.

Davies inhaled as he answered, an attempt to cool his burning insides. "Nope."

"See, God's breakfast… Gatorade and moonshine…distilled from an old family recipe."

"That explains the color." Davies held the jar at eye level, the electric beverage already fogging his senses.

Time began to pass in pockets, reality now filtered by the Jarvi's homemade liquor.

"Stove's hot," Willy's naked behind disappeared around the corner, and Elmer followed.

Paralyzed by booze and exhaustion, Davies simply turned and placed his feet on the couch, unable to move any farther.

The sauna stove had indeed heated the entire building; his face was now red from the radiant heat of the brother's handcrafted stove.

"You comin?" Elmer's naked form appeared, his milky Scandinavian skin now bright pink from the heat.

Davies waved him off, too tired to speak.

He drifted off hearing the jovial banter of the brothers in the background as they basked, seemingly unaffected by the turmoil of the previous day.

Chapter 30
Twitcher in the Woods

"Braaaagh, braaw- aaagh." The twitcher stirred, stiff and layered beneath the other corpses. Driven by impulse, the creature clawed at the snow, its drive to infect coursed through its tarry veins.

"Braaaagh, braaw- waaagh," the shriek echoed sharply as it pierced the early morning air. Like a wolf calling to its pack it screamed, a signal that prey were near.

Sound traveled swiftly through the thin frosty air. All infected in ear-shot, echoing the cry, commanded by their impulses.

Rallied by the signal, they attacked, their noses their guide as they broke through windows and doors, hunting their way out of town.

Energized by the fresh blood, their numbers grew as they traveled, the roving horde snowballing as it rolled through town.

Slowed by the deep snow, they struggled until they reached the trail cut by the snowmobiles, the packed throughway now a funnel to the families hiding in the woods along the lakeshore.

Random shrieks and screams were bellowed; the twitcher in the woods responding in kind, calling them in.

Now on its feet, it stepped down from the forested mound and crouched on the trail, its nose pressed to the snow as the faint scent of blood, metallic and mineral, was detected. Frozen into the path the scent was faint...hard to follow. Once again upright, the light wind passed through its nasal cavity and over its exposed gums.   It inhaled deeply as the pungent pheromones of man wafted in waves on the winter wind.

Titillated, its distended jaw shuddered and the teeth chattered, as thick and gelatinous sputum dripped from the fleshless mouth.

It powered forward, nose in the air as it followed the sweet scent, sure to call out as it went, compelled to draw others.

Nose to the wind, they skulked, with every fiber pulling them toward the call. No longer burdened by thoughts of their own, their only compulsion was the spread.

Chapter 31
Silent Night?

"**B**ow, bow, bow, ow, ow, ark, ark, ark!" Spencer stood at the door, a narrow strip of fur from his shoulders to his tail on end, his hackles up over what lurked outside.

"Grrr, ruff, bowwww, ark, ark, ark!"

"Ian, Ian," Sean, roused by the yap of their elderly dog, looked out the tiny second-floor window. "Ian, I think Santa's outside."

Irritated, he grumbled from the bed, "No such thing. Now shut up, it's too early."

"Really, I can see the suit." With his hands pressed to the glass to cut the glare, he peered, trying to make sense of the figure.

"Move it, let me see," Ian pushed, eager to prove his brother wrong.

"Holy shit, I see it; I see the suit!" The red jacket, trimmed in white, stuck out among the others in the dim light of the emerging dawn.

"You're going to see my finger in your eye if you don't quiet down in here," Pop stood in the doorway, a cigarette already lit and between his lips.

"Sorry, Pop," they climbed back onto the bed.

With two fingers he pointed at the boys, then at his eyes, then at the floor on the other side of the bed. "You watch him, while I go downstairs to see what that fuckin' dog is barking about."

Curious, the boys slid across the bed and climbed over their sister to look at the floor.

"Elle, Elley." They smooched the air loudly while shoving her.

"I swear to god," she lifted her hand and swung wildly. "Gross, why are you sweaty?" She wiped her hand on their shirts, one after the other.

"I guess it's hot in here from all the body heat," Ian pointed to the floor, before the two commenced another smooching duet.

~~~

"Is the dog barking?" Laney turned to her husband, who was sleeping soundly on the other couch, clearly drugged and exhausted from his ordeal.

Laney sat up, her feet now on the wooden floor. "Christ, it's hot in here." She stumbled past the tree and toward the dog.

Irritated she started to scold, "You never bark. You haven't opened your mouth to so much as growl for years and you choose the one day when we really could use some peace to open your giant, stupid..." Pop covered her mouth before pointing her head toward the window.

Frozen with fear she gawked at what approached. Eerie and familiar in the breaking light of day, they were defined by the shadows cast by their unmistakable forms.

With her finger hooked in the dog's collar she pulled him back, uncertain how to react.

Pop, with his mouth at her ear, went into action. "I'll get them, you get them, we'll all go down there."

Although cryptic, she understood to gather the others and head down to the bunker.

"Dooley, Dooley," her mouth was turned sideways as she kept her eyes locked on the door. His deep slumber left her with no choice; she had to break the silence. "Doolin Terrence Riley, wake the fuck up!"

With great difficulty he sat, his chin now over the back of the sofa. "What is it, did Santa come?" He was tired and sarcastic, unhappy with being bothered.

"We have company," she pointed at the door as she continued to back up, "I'm going," she motioned, her head nodding to relay that she was getting Dory.

With his attention now turned to the lurking threat, he could hear them shuffling and sniffing. They must have just arrived, for they hadn't actually climbed the porch, yet.

Now on all fours he crawled, wanting to open the door to the shelter. Dehydrated and wounded, his head pounded, worsened by the stifling heat of the cottage.

As he fumbled with the key, he dry heaved, his shoulder and leg throbbing from his climbing blood pressure.

"Shhh," he could hear her beckon, trying to keep Dory quiet as the panic took hold.

"Grrrrr," Spencer rumbled under his breath as the infected climbed the porch, the door now rattling with the sounds of impending doom.

"Hurry Pop! Hurry up, they're at the door!" Doolin flipped the hatch to the passage.

Glass exploded as their warped arms punched and flailed, the windows of the small home no match for the voracious need to infect and feed. A fresh feed meant mobility in the cold, and mobility allowed for the spread.

Like piranha they swarmed, pushing and bumping against the doors and windows, teeth exposed and snapping.

"Oh god!" Elle ran down the steps escorted by Josh, her reunion now overshadowed by fear of death. With her hands clamped over her ears she screamed, the sound of their gnashing teeth and seething groans too much to take.

Josh doubled her efforts to block out the noise and placed his hands over hers. With his arms around her, he pushed her toward her father and the safety of the tunnel entrance.

The wood of the doorframes and window casings creaked and snapped, the weather-worn lumber no match for the force of what pushed from outside.

Although time had seemed to stand still as Doolin watched his family rush to safety, only moments had passed from initial contact with the house to the breach.

Splintered and frayed, the door and its frame imploded, the horde now in-fighting to attack first. Only this moment of inter-mass conflict allowed Elle and Josh safe passage as they flung themselves down, assisted by Doolin, who had given his horrified daughter a shove.

With the boys in hand, Nan and Pop had just cleared the last step when the infected entered. Now back-to-back, with the boys sandwiched between them, they rotated, Pop armed with the PMR and a ball pein hammer he'd kept at the table for insect smashing, and Nan was now armed with the fireplace poker she snatched mid spin.

Almost to the safety of the entrance, they were attacked,

Pop was protecting his son and grandsons, two-fisted, squeezing off rounds with his right and pounding skulls with his left.

Nan got turned around. She jabbed repeatedly, lodging the poker deeply into an eye cavity. It collapsed, the hooked poker caught and taking her down with it. With his back turned, hunkered between the sofa and the barrel, Doolin guided the boys to safety, but couldn't see the trouble his mother was in.

Ian did. With his eyes just clearing the drop, he realized she was about to be overpowered. Without thought for his own safety he leapt from the entrance, over the barrel's lip and under the gunfire of his Pop. With newly found strength he ripped the poker from the gnarled skull.

"Take that, you frosted freak!" He drove the tip of the iron implement into his Nan's attacker.

The haste of his youth blinded him to the danger he'd put himself in.

Overrun by beasts, his one defeat was hardly enough to save the day. As he basked, the peril swirled around him, closing in.

Sean, now at the barrel's lip, looked for his twin as though he'd dropped an appendage. Horrified to find him surrounded and fighting for his life, he too climbed from safety and tried to help his brother.

Doolin, slowed by his injuries, aimed the shotgun, unable to take a shot that would miss his children. In these seconds, he lost all hope. A dozen infected crawled through the house, some faster than others. If it hadn't been for the cold walk from town slowing their movements, the whole family would've been infected by now. But now, with Frosty inside and out, they were swarmed and ill prepared to fight.

Doolin pulled the twelve-gauge to his good shoulder, and with his eye to the sight he inhaled, *hit the target, or miss and save my son the horror*…

The blast echoed, drowning out the pop of the PMR. The boys dropped to the ground, the noise tripping their instinct to duck.

On the floor face to face, they smiled at each other past the creature, who twitched between them, the top of its head gone.

Ian, who had been missed by the blast, was hit by the black splatter of brain and bone. Sean cringed as it dripped along his brother's face, "That's gross, dude, it's dripping toward your eye."

With his tongue sticking out in disgust he raised his hand to demonstrate where his brother should wipe.

This brotherly moment was interrupted by a flurry of gunfire, which was only paused by a large explosion. The yard had become a war zone, and while the battle raged out there with some unknown army to the rescue, the occupants fought on, trying to survive.

Holed up in the small downstairs bedroom, Laney and Dory were trapped, driven back in by the encroaching pack. Paralyzed with fear, Dory hid as

Laney plotted and searched for a weapon. "This is your fault. If you would have just moved, we could be in the shelter or at least out there fighting."

Cured of her anxiety by the bat, she yearned for it now. "Yes!" She was delighted, the idea to use the tall, turned, wooden lamp at the bedside her solution. Its shape although much more ornate with its dips and curves, was just a wooden club. With the cord now yanked from the outlet she wrapped it around her wrist, and with the shade and bulb removed she walked toward the door. Dory remained cowered, tucked in the corner of the brown paneled room, her face buried in her crossed arms.

Frosty scratched and clawed, the small bedroom window, high set and hard to reach, prohibiting their easy entry. The room door, being solid oak, had held so far, but rattled continually, threatening to give at any moment.

"I'm going," she placed her hand on the knob. "I tried, Dory, but I'm fighting...leaving you."

"Well it's your fault Deck's dead." Dory's voice was quiet, obscured by her arms. "We were only in town because of you. You went crazy, needed to be the center of attention, now your brother is dead. Your fault."

Enraged, she channeled the emotional energy, and like a bull in a china shop charged from the room, clubbing her way through the twisted crowd. The lamp base proved effective, splitting Frosty skulls with ease.

Davies and Elmer could be heard calling to the Riley's. "Hold on, we're coming." They continued to battle in hopes of sparing their neighbors the same fate Willy had suffered.

Nan crawled toward the boys, as Laney plowed through, driven by her favorite tune. "I'm on top of the world looking down on creation and the only explanation I can find..."

With Davies and Elmer stemming the tide from outside, and Laney's voracious appetite for death, they could almost make their way to the barrel.

As these last few moments of mayhem occurred, one infected form managed to hurl itself into the barrel's opening.

Josh and Elle scrambled to located weapons in the bunker.

"Here," Josh found a stash in a box under the bunks.

"We have to go up there...help them." Elle was anxious, ready to join the fight.

Years of militia exposure had been useful. He was familiar with all manner of weapons and quickly readied two guns.

She hoisted the firearm without hesitation, "Its heavier than I thought it would be." She grabbed the handle ready to exit into the hallway.

"Wait," Josh pressed his ear to the door, a familiar shuffle and groan present. "I hear one."

Elle fingered the trigger, and nodded.

Locked and loaded, they opened the door, one Frosty blocking the corridor.

Josh called it, "I've got it." It was a clean shot to the head.

Concerned about his eager girlfriends inexperience with firearms, he gave pointers on the fly. "Heads or knees," he instructed as they climbed the ladder, "we want them dead or immobile. Also, squeeze the trigger, don't pull it. "

The sound of her family in trouble filled her with courage, so she emerged with her finger on the trigger, the M9 in the lead. Josh was close behind.

"Ian! Oh god, Ian!" Sean bawled as his brother convulsed.

Nan pushed him out of the way, as she cradled her grandson, trying to wipe the infected blood from his eye.

She screamed, her face beet red, as only an airy squeak escaped.

Distracted by the crisis Ian was in, she didn't notice the twitcher next to her revive and lunge, its snapping teeth now buried in her leg.

The pathogen coursed, her collapse immediate as she too now convulsed, her bones breaking, changing just as her grandson's were. They turned together, eyes, ears and noses, filled with the black blood of the infected, teeth exposed and extended, they stood ready to bite.

Elle and Josh began shooting, their presence helping to turn the tide, the room now under control as Davies and Elmer fortified the doorways, the approaching Frosty chilled and slow.

"Dad! Daaad!" Sean screeched, the blood-curdling cry unlike any he'd ever heard before.

With attention turned, the family looked on, devastated by what they found. Nan and Ian, freshly turned, eager to spread.

Pop shook as he took aim, Nan his unfortunate target. She snarled, her voice still absent as her joints and bones clicked and popped, her teeth chattered as she snapped her jaw.

Now just inches from her husband of forty-four years she lunged, and Elle shot, quickly choosing to fire on her Nan and save her pop's life.

Hit in the lower back she dropped, her legs now cut off from the needed impulses of her spinal column. On her arms she dragged her lower half, a streak of black sludge smearing as she pulled, her teeth gnashing.

With each slap at the floor she scooted closer. He stepped back, just trying to absorb this reality.

Doolin was focused on Ian. "Oh god," he raised the rifle, as his infected son sniffed and drooled, his new form horrific and heartbreaking. Enticed by the smell of his brother, he bent his now deformed legs, ready to jump.

"Fire," Laney shouted, "Fire, or we'll lose Sean too!"

With his attention now diverted by the shouts, he ran, his mother the new target.

As Pop held his gun to his wife's head, Laney bludgeoned her own son, the lamp base crushing his skull.

The circumstances left them no time to deal with the complicated feelings brought on by this tragedy.

Frosty had gathered once again, the smell of the humans drawing them in as it drifted through the air like a holiday turkey, their travel eased by the deep and firm groove groomed into the snow via the snowmobiles.

The bedroom door creaked as it slowly opened, Josh took aim.

Dory crept out, not wanting to be left alone.

Laney, riddled with anger and resentment, eyed her, the blood covered lamp still tied to her hand.

With emotions on hold, they scrambled, stepping over the corpses of the many infected, including Santa who found his end under the tree.

"I know you," Laney pointed her weapon at him. "We went after the governor together." Her tone was defeated as she swirled the gore-covered lamp in his direction.

"Thought I scared you off?" Pop eyed Davies. "Good to see ya now. We'd all be oozing that black shit if it weren't for you and your friend. And what is that fucking smell? It's like smashed assholes mixed with fermented garbage."

Davies offered his analyses, "Just the pleasant aroma of the infected."

Pop stood above the barrel's opening, personally shuttling everyone to safety. He probably would have found Davies sarcasm entertaining if he hadn't just shot his wife in the head. Instead, he was just pissed and ready to lock the shelter door.

"Move your fucking asses before I have to euthanize someone else!"

Davies nodded as he followed the crew into the barrel.. "Ahh shit," he recognized the festive corpse.

"What?" Elmer inquired as they quickly descended the ladder.

"Festive Frosty up there, under the tree... he's the twitcher I stabbed back at the trail head."

"How..." Elmer was at a loss for words.

"Not enough of its brain or the wrong area. It's like he rebooted and walked on."

"What you two flapping about." Pop locked the bunker door and pulled the bottle of Jack Daniels from the medical kit.

"Talk," he shot them a look while he drank, the liquor helping to wash down the death of his wife and grandson for proper processing.

Davies looked at the disheveled group, aware that they needed to discuss what they all knew about this plague.

"It seems inappropriate to talk about Frosty at a time like this, when we all want to be mourning our losses, but it might be what keeps us alive in the future.

Santa, upstairs..."

"Yeah, Josh and I saw him in the woods at the trail head. We shot him."

"Well, when the Jarvis and I drove through, he was still moving. Have any of you encountered a twitcher?"

"Ian and I saw one upstairs, it's the one that got Nan." Sean buried his head in his father's lap and cried, his forehead bumping the gunshot wound.

"Aww, watch it, pal." Doolin rubbed his son's back.

"Well, in my patrols I've encountered them a few times, and I always would push a knife into their heads, or double tap, that seemed to work. But Saint Nick up there, he still walked here, even after I gave him the treatment. I think you have to destroy a certain part, or enough of the brain to really stop them. Yesterday… was it yesterday?" Davies asked Elmer, "that we saw the thing in the lake?"

He shook his head in agreement.

"The other guys and I saw one of these things wash up on shore. It was eroded, for lack of a better word. Its appendages were gone, and so was the front of its head and chest. Its brain was hanging out and the stumps were quivering. It was still trying to move, running purely on impulse. Also it would seem that the pathogen just has to be introduced to the bloodstream. I saw people turned by a cat scratch."

"Ian got, blood, in, his, eye." Sean hyperventilated between each word.

"Okay," Pop sipped as he stood, before passing the bottle to his son. Deflated, his usual cocky posture slumped, he walked to what looked like a large breaker box mounted adjacent to the door. With a flick of his wrist he opened it, the bunker's command center exposed.

"Here you can see the temp down here, and the temp outside. This shows the pressure and wind direction. These switches control the power and monitors the batteries charged by the solar panels. No one should touch this but me, capisce. Unless I'm dead, then Dooley takes the helm. We stay, down here, until the deep freeze, then we gear up and start an elimination. If they are exposed to sub-zero temps for a few days, they should almost be immobile. We'll just wait 'em out."

Chapter 32
Nicotine Fit

"How much longer?" Dory was in her usual corner.

"Well, we haven't had any consistent truly zero days." Pop retrieved a book from the shelf at his bunk. "According to the almanac, the average dates for sub zero weather occur end of January through beginning February. It's just been a little warm this winter. Well, if you consider thirty warm."

"But you are welcome to leave now." Laney's sarcasm was as blunt as her club.

Dory retreated to her folded arms, with the rocking close behind.

"So, what did happen over at your place, you and your brother seemed so close?" Laney had waited to ask, but now seemed like the right time.

Elmer slid his chess piece, leaving Davies to contemplate his next move.

"We came back from town with Mitt here, and convened in da sauna for some booze and a steam. And it was going pretty nice, da Iron Maiden was really cookin and da moonshine was flowin like wine, eh."

"Who's the Iron Maiden?" Pop couldn't wait to hear this; he could use a sordid tale.

"Oh it's da sauna stove Willy and I welded from our father's old Buick. He called her da Iron Maiden, always said she was a bitch tuh get warm in da winter, therefore a torture to drive. Anyway's we stripped her when Da died and built the cooker for da hot house. We thought it was kind of ironic, da cold bitch now a stove."

"Huh, sounds like your brother had a real sense of humor." Pop didn't have the starch to bust his balls.

"Well, Willy and I, oh excuse me," he paused, as he blew his nose onto his sleeve, thoughts of his dear brother proving difficult. It had only been a few weeks since the attack. "Anyways, we got pretty ripped and passed out eh, in da sauna. So, we wake up and Frosty's at da door. Well, we got mobbed trying tuh.. get tuh.. da barn and da weapons. Willy was infected trying to save me. Mitt and I could hear you firing, so we tore over on da sleds. I finally got to use the Limonkas ... Sorry you missed it Willy," Elmer raised his chin, an apparent nod to his brother above.

"Oh, its okay," Davies soothed his sad friend, who was now sobbing into his chest. "Oh my," he was a little disgusted by the string of drool that now stretched from his shirt to Elmer's lip.

"Oh, how embarrassing." Elmer ran his nose over his sleeve again.

Dory peeked up from her self-made cocoon. "More of us will die before this is over."

"Well, miss britches, this thing will never be over. This shit is forever. Even if we worked for ten years and cleared the Static Zone and fortified the divide, and kept the water secure, we would be it. Very few spots in the country, let alone the world, have the conditions necessary to freeze and eradicate the infected. Then you have to consider disease and injuries and shit, it will be a fucking miracle if we make it to spring!"

Sean quietly sobbed. Laney reclined next to him, heartbroken for her son and herself as she held him. "Nice, Pop, he's already hurt. Think you could think before you speak, for let's say, the next year or two?"

"Listen, we're all hurting here. You think Mitt isn't hurt about sending his family to the buses or Dory about Deck or her family. I lost my wife!" He rubbed his head trying to compose himself. "It's time to buck up and fight on, or just end it now." Angry, he pulled a firearm from his bunk. "Who's ready to throw in the towel?" He gripped the barrel, and offered the butt of the gun to everyone in the room. "No, no takers. That's what I thought."

With the gun now wedged in his pants, he crossed another day off of the calendar and plopped next to Doolin.

"It's been a few days since we've cleaned it, how's it lookin?" He peeked at the bandages protecting the gunshot wounds. The lights had begun to dim, the batteries running low.

"Shit." Pop looked up.

"What?" Doolin scanned the ceiling for clues.

"Panels must be covered...batteries aren't charging."

Aware of what he needed to do, he looked around at his family as he contemplated his next move.

"You all right, hon, you look a little green." Laney touched Elle's face from the bunk, trying to comfort both children at once.

"I'll live, but I think the smell of that chemical toilet is getting to me. Or maybe it's the constant accidents of our old pooch."

"You been slipping it to her?" Pop was suddenly suspicious and in Josh's face.

Intimidated, his voice quivered; her grandfather was scary. "No sir, keeping all my parts to myself, just like you said."

"Sure? The last thing we need is to have a pregnancy on our hands. Can you imagine trying to keep that thing alive in these conditions."

"I'm just sick, is all; it's stale down here, and the food is all starchy. I need fresh air." Elle was undone... stir crazy.

"We're all a little green, but we really should hold out for colder weather, just to be safe." *But we're almost out of power*, he thought.

Elle crossed the room and put her ear to the door. "It's quiet, they're gone."

"That is not a sufficient test of Frosty status." Pop was stir crazy himself, and severely nicotine deficient; he moved toward the controls to glance at the temperature.

"What you doing, Pop?" Doolin winced as he shifted, the wounds still sore.

Without explanation he donned the holster and pulled on his coat.

"Stay here, we're safe here." Doolin wasn't ready to lose him too.

"Elle's right, it's stuffy down here, and I need a smoke." He pulled open the trunk and stuffed a pack in his coat pocket.

"They could be in the tunnel or in the living room, the house was compromised, the doors are fucking broken."

Doolin was angered and not pleased with his father's plan.

"That's why I'm taking the back door."

Hurriedly, Pop emptied the pantry. A broom, a tool box, toilet paper, soap, hand sanitizer; a wide variety of dry goods and toiletries were tossed to the floor.

In their absence, a ladder was visible.

"If I'm not back in thirty minutes, don't come looking for me, stay here."

Already up the ladder, he climbed, his narrow behind now obscured by the hatch that led outdoors. Air locked, the seal helped keep the moisture out and the safety in. "Dirty whore," he reefed on the stubborn wheel, "should've opened you once in awhile, you stubborn bitch."

"Need some help up there?" Davies peered up the hole.

"Even if I did, we won't both fit in here."

"Back down, I'll give it a try."

"No, if it breaks I want it to be me."

"How about some leverage?"

"Yeah, fucking brilliant. There's a flat bar in that toolbox."

Davies procured the implement and passed it up.

Now armed and determined he twisted, the flat bar doing the trick as the hatch opened. "That's right, open up, you frigid hag, let me through."

Slowly he lifted, now clearing ground level; a fire pit that rested in the middle of the yard obscuredthe entrance.

Filled with snow, it floated down the ladder and into the pantry. "Looks like we've had a storm."

His head still in the pantry, Davies relayed the information as he brushed the falling snow from his head. "He says we had a storm."

Cold, fresh air from the open hatch drifted and settled in the bunker.

Spencer sniffed, awakened by the cool breeze.

The yard was desolate; snow had drifted over the porch and covered the entrance. No new footsteps were visible.

Feeling secure he pulled himself up, and exited the fire-pit, a cigarette already in his lips.

Davies motioned to Elmer; they followed behind.

It was bright as the snow reflected the diffused sunlight of the overcast skies, their eyes had to adjust to the natural light.

The afternoon was still; the air heavy and threatening more snow. The deep ground cover made the patrol difficult as they trudged, careful to survey the property.

The recent storm had added to the already deep blanket, which obscured all exposed objects.

"Its eerie," Elmer's head was on a swivel, convinced that every mound and pile was Frosty ready to lurch, that behind every evergreen and deciduous tree was a threat.

As Davies and Elmer crept, Pop marched on making his way around the house. The exterior door had been ripped off and the snow had drifted into the living room. The interior entry had been destroyed; the splintered frame all that was left.

With his gun drawn he entered, jumping through the drift, certain that whatever lurked would emerge and grab him at any moment.

Now in the living room he looked left, the kitchen empty, and undisturbed. All the dishes and food, right where it had been left all those days ago.

He moved forward and inhaled, smoking hands free, exhaling through his nose. The ash grew long as he stared down, his wife, his soul mate, stiff and plastered to the floor.

"You all right in there," Davies called quietly from the entry.

Pop waved him off, just wanting a moment to contemplate.

I shot her. I just pulled the trigger. It wasn't her anymore...that's why it was so easy.

Still streaming smoke from his nostrils like a dragon, he walked, Ian his next stop. "Ahh Christ. Fuck me." Taken aback by the caved skull of his young grandson, he wobbled.

"Whoa," Davies grabbed him, now on his flank.

"Her own son, she had bash in the skull of her own son. We are done. For the rest of our lives we'll be looking over our shoulders, wondering when it will be us. No more security, no more wishing for warm weather, we'll spend the rest of our lives praying for snow."

He looked around; the floor was littered with dead Frosty.

The house was cold, the interior temp the same as outdoors. What infected were left, were nearly dormant, unable to move with any speed. Now disturbed by the talking and lured by the smell of fresh meat, they stirred, their movements sluggish and erratic.

Pop opened fire, putting two in each skull.

Elmer entered the porch, uneasy about being outdoors alone.

"I heard shots," he paused, "Oh, good, you're both okay. I was a bit worried dere for a bit."

A sigh of relief escaped his lips just as a terrible pain tore through his leg.

"Awww, oh god!" The terrible jaws of death protruded from the drift in the porch and were now tearing at his flesh. Elmer dropped to the floor as the convulsions of change tore through his body.

He struggled against the spasms and pulled a Russian lemon from his brother's brown satchel. His fingers cramped as he gripped the pin, and with one last violent jerk he exploded, his black and tarry bits now flecked onto the porches interior.

Frosty, now somewhat mangled but charged by Elmer' fresh hot blood, emerged from the drift, hellbent for its next target. One arm dangled, severed by the blast and several holes were torn into its already horrific face, shrapnel now protruding and providing a wide side view of its snapping jaw.

"Oh, that's lovely," Pop exhaled as Davies pulled his weapon and shot. Frosty dropped to the floor just inches from the two men.

It twitched, the bullet wound high and to the right.

"See, a Twitcher. It's where I hit it."

Davies pulled his knife, ready to experiment with his theory.

Pop lit another smoke. "Let's wait to see how long, or if it ever rises."

It quivered as the twitching continued for several minutes. Then an arm flailed. Then a leg shifted. With eyes now open, it groaned, its teeth grinding as it sniffed in their direction.

Davies pulled the knife.

"You better not get too close. Might jump up and bite ya."

Pop fired, two between the eyes. Now it was still.

"So what have we learned here today, boys and girls," Pop quizzed Davies.

"Between the eyes."

"Yep, between the eyes... Wonder why? Do you know about anatomy? What part are we destroying?"

Davies took a stab at it. "Frontal lobe of some sort, maybe the part that regulates emotion?"

"Well, I guess it's not so important we know why just as long as we know what we're aiming for."

"Ahh Christ, I thought you were all dead!" Doolin limped over. "We heard shots and an explosion... You scared the hell out of me."

"You shouldn't be in here, it's not safe. Elmer got it and blew himself sky high." Pop pointed back to the porch.

"Oh, that would explain the gory entrance."

Doolin suddenly realized that he'd walked past his dead mother, and just feet in front of him rested his son.

"Oh Dad, I, I can't just leave them here. We need to do something." He fell back onto the sofa, his head in his hands.

"We need to establish a secure perimeter and clear away all the excess snow. We need to know what's lurking beneath every drift and bank. If we can clear the immediate threat, and implement a warning system, maybe build a barrier, we could probably move back in, try to have some semblance of a life." Pop was ready to be out of the hole and above ground.

"Snow blower. I have a snow blower in the shed. Probably should conserve fuel, but I don't know that I want to shovel this whole place, especially with Frosty lurking underneath. Son, head back down and let them know what's going on and then send that Josh up, you're still in no shape to be up here."

"Nonsense. I'll go get him, but I'm helping."

Doolin departed to retrieve Josh and assure the others that all was well, except for the news of Elmer's unfortunate departure.

"Well, while he's doing that, why don't we see if we can get that snow blower running."

It was a relief to feel filled with purpose instead of grief, because, as a doer, Terry Riley had always been task-driven.

With gloved hands they burrowed through the deep drift that had obscured the doors.

"Dig carefully, Frosty could be stashed in here, sitting, waiting for two idiots to dig recklessly. Poor Elmer…But, at least he went out with his boots on."

"I doubt they have the ability to plot." Davies eyed Pop as he delved deeper, certain he'd never met such a character before, well, except the Jarvi brothers.

"That ought to do it." Pop grabbed one door and Davies the other as they pulled the shed open.

It was a large space, some would have considered a barn, but shed was more appropriate considering the lack of animals. A workbench stretched along the left wall, its tools and equipment organized and orderly. Firewood was stacked between two support posts in the center of the structure, creating a false wall.

Pop walked in and around the wood. Behind it were some garden tools, bags of fertilizer, and a large mound covered by a gray tarp.

With the corner in his hand he yanked and revealed the snow blower.

"Holy hell, when you said snow blower I pictured a self propelled unit like I have. You know, the twenty-four inch blower with headlight and heated grips. I didn't expect to see that monstrosity." Davies basked in the glory of the tractor-mounted, fifty-four inch blower. "That'll do."

"I got it for a steal when the base closed." Pop gave Davies a wink while lighting another cigarette, "Let's run these mothers over."

"Breaking out the big machinery." Doolin arrived with Josh.

"Yep," shovelin's too dangerous, too many hidden threats."

"So, what's the plan?" They all waited for his nuggets of wisdom.

"We need to clear a perimeter, and then secure it. We can't really run out to the hardware store, so we'll have to make do with what we've got, and what we've got is trees and snow. So, we'll cut posts to cross and point, try to give a little buffer between us and them. In the summer we'll need room to garden and a safe path to the lake."

"What if they wash up, and wander in." Davies thought back to the quivering blob he'd encountered on the beach.

"Maybe we construct a corridor to the water that is gated off... shit, I don't know, we'll figure it out as we go. First things first, we have to clear the house and deal with the dead. I think we burn Frosty and give Ma and Ian a proper burial."

"Then we can get out of the shelter and stay in the house? I don't think Elle can take much more." Josh looked concerned, his love for her made her discomfort his own.

"Its sweet you're concerned, but we stay in the shelter at night until we've established a perimeter and have removed all the infected from the property. It would probably be a good idea to get everyone involved. Hard work will be a healthy distraction from grief and fear." Pop flicked his spent cigarette and lit another one.

"Should I go get the others?" Josh was ready to help.

"First things first," Pop pulled a box of neatly folded tarps from above the cupboards mounted at the workstation.

With the red plastic crate dangling from his fist he walked into the house and stopped at his wife. "We need to wrap them and store them till spring. They need a proper farewell."

"We don't have a priest, we can't give them a Christian service. They never received last rites..." Doolin was now stressed. Raised a Catholic, he had fallen into the Easter and Christmas trap over the last two decades, but still held onto the doctrine, well, as much as any other Catholic, but now found he was in need of the comfort.

"Horse shit! It was all horse shit. God has abandoned us, probably because he never existed. This wasn't the work of our creator. This is the mad dabblings of nature or science or, Christ, aliens. God wouldn't do this. These things have all but exterminated us. There was a mutation, or earth needed cleansing, or nature's gone mad, but there is no God here."

Shocked by his father's blasphemy and lack of faith, Dooley crossed himself, suddenly superstitious.

"We'll see where that gets you," Pop stooped to wrap his wife's horrific corpse into one of the tarps. Doolin was grief stricken, his dear mother jagged and frozen, was now rolled up.

Saddened by his once-faithful father's rant, Doolin followed suit and commenced to roll up his son's body for storage.

With trembling hands he tried to scoot him onto the plastic, his young frame stiff with rigor mortis and stuck to the floor, frozen to the ground like winter road kill.

"Ahhh," his hands trembled as he tried to deal with the anger and grief, the horror and the disbelief.

A calm hand landed on his shoulder. "I'll take care of it, let me help."

Davies moved him aside, and freed the boy from the grips of the wood floor. With great care he wrapped him, certain to avoid the dark, infected blood.

"Thank you." Doolin wiped his eyes, as he looked at the wall, unable to make eye contact or view the rolled bodies of his son and mother.

"We'll take them to the shed...store them there."

Pop flipped Nan over his shoulder, her thin frame just as light as it had been for the last forty-plus years.

Davies lifted Ian's body, the roll in his arms like a load of wood.

"Wait." Doolin stood, his arms out. "I should do it. I want to do it."

Davies passed him off, the boy now resting gently in his father's arms.

The walk to the shed was a solemn one.

Josh watched as they were laid on the cold concrete, but he found comfort in them lying side by side, "At least they have each other. I can't stand the idea of my parents, out there, dead and alone. But they are together," he motioned to the rolled tarps, "and somehow, that seems better."

Doolin and Terry stood silently as they listened to Josh blather.

"Well, enough of this fucking pity party," Pop clapped his hands loudly, "Back to work. Josh, get the others. They can come up now that they won't see their loved ones splattered in the living room."

Focused on work, and avoiding his feelings, he climbed on the tractor and turned it over, the trusty Briggs and Stratton motor firing the first time. "Oh yeah," he put it in gear and drove, hell-bent, "Running you mothers over!"

"Gross!" Sean was disgusted and thrilled as he emerged, the large snow blower chewing up the snow (and whatever lurked beneath) and spitting it into piles.

Clearing the property with ease, the tractor, in all its gleaming green glory made easy work of the deep snow and, on occasion, would encounter Frosty with a thump. The tractor lurched as the rotating blades sliced and diced.

Soon the surrounding property was clear, and the resulting snow banks were high and infused with minced Frosty.

Pleased to see his grandson outside and smiling, Pop stopped and called him over. "Climb up here, help me out."

Sean scrambled, thrilled at the idea of driving the impressive machine.

"What the hell," Dory yelled as she viewed the grotesque piles of snow.

Pop turned off the tractor and dismounted, leaving Sean to hold the wheel as he pretended to drive.

"We are clearing the property, soon we'll cut back some trees and erect some sort of perimeter."

"You've contaminated the entire yard. Were you planning to garden in this... the pathogen in the soil? We can't climb over it...the dog could carry it, have you lost your mind?"

He was deflated. It never occurred to him the reach it might have. *Could you be infected from other sources? If contaminated soil were to enter a wound, or water for that matter, could they carry the pathogen and transmit it? Could it grow into the food? Deer, wild animals...*

"Ahh Christ," he looked at his feet planted in the snow. "I'll treat it like radiation and remove the top eighteen inches of soil. We have to press on. We have to try, what option do we have? If you wouldn't mind keeping your concerns to yourself, I have to try and keep these people afloat." Now filled with desperation he returned to the tractor, trying to put on a brave face for his fragile grandson.

"Can I drive? Is it great to run them over?" Sean showed his first signs of life since the incident.

"Very great." Pop glared at Dory, irritated that his hopes no longer carried him.

Chapter 33
Home Sick

"I'm leaving." Dory stood in front of the makeshift family, a bag on her back.

"I want to head home, see if my dad made it, I need to travel while it's still cold."

Laney placed the hatchet on the ground, pausing in her task of sharpening the posts cut by Pop and Davies.

She looked at the property as she approached Dory, the perimeter almost complete, the many posts crossed and backed by high banks of snow.

"Why? I know I was cold to you, but I was angry, grief-stricken. Don't go out there, it's suicide. We've almost reached our goal here. We've got a corridor through the snow to the water, and in spring we'll be able to reinforce and work toward a permanent and safe settlement."

Convinced they weren't safe anywhere, and that the pathogen would spread and eventually infect everything; she didn't have the same optimism.

"Listen, I've gotta go. My dad might still be alive. And If I can get to the city, to the lab... Maybe I can find someone, tell them what I know, if they don't already."

Davies dropped his axe and approached Dory. "I'll go with you... help you get there."

"You don't have to do that, Mitt. I couldn't expect you to put yourself in danger."

"They have each other... this place. They'll be fine, but you shouldn't travel alone."

"Well, gear up, I won't turn down the company."

"Let's arm you, at least. Christ you can't wander off without protection. Maybe some snow shoes, you know how deep it is by now, you'll sink and suffocate before you make it to town."

With the pair in tow, Pop led them to the shed giving them their choice of weaponry. "Load up, food, ammo, whatever you can carry."

"Are you sure, you should conserve." Davies was touched that he so willingly shared.

His generosity was less than altruistic, all they could carry was less than they would use during a lifetime of living there.

"If it weren't for you and your rogue runs, we wouldn't even have some of this stuff."

Davies was responsible for the stash. After they'd begun clearing and fortifying the property, he was curious if anyone had made it back to the outpost. After a trek out there, he found the property empty and hauled back the food and supplies they had stockpiled.

Aware of Elmer and Willy's spoils, he took Josh to retrieve their guns and gear, and yes, the Russian grenades as well.

"What route you taking?" Pop made small talk while they fixed the snowshoes to their feet, the many buckles difficult to pull tight over their boots.

"I think back toward town and into the Western Outlands for a start. With the bridge blown, a direct route south to Commerce City is out of the question. We'll have to go the long way around. If I could be sure the straights were frozen, we could walk across, but it would suck to get all the way down there and have to turn around."

"Commerce city?" Davies wasn't familiar with where Dory was from.

"Yeah, ever been?"

"Not yet."

Pop shook his head. "Well good luck. I wouldn't want to be roaming around out there."

Now armed and supplied, they hugged and wished each other well.

The Rileys watched as they departed, the wooden shoes cutting their hatched design in the snow.

She scouted a bank free of minced Frosty, and the frigid February air made for easy climbing, the snow crusted over and firm.

From the top of the bank they looked back, and with one final wave they disappeared over the other side.

"I can't believe they'd leave the safety of the property let alone the Static Zone. I mean big picture, a few winters from now, we might be able to re-establish."

Laney was optimistic, clearly unaware of the possibility of contamination and infection that Dory had shared.

Chapter 34
If the Shoe Fits

"I see the tower," Davies was in the lead, breaking a trail in the deep snow.

"What a sight, isn't there supposed to be a trench here?" Dory approached the wooden structure, the bottom obscured by snow.

"I think this small dip *is* the trench."

Without a team of men tasked to clear the divide, it had become filled and drifted over.

"Stay close, go slow, it's lined with spikes and who knows what other dangers are lurking under all this stuff."

Slowly he stepped, the snowshoes helping to distribute his weight as he inched over the covered trench. The top layer had warmed slightly on one of the sunny afternoons and had now frozen over, resulting in a thin and icy sheet. "Whoa," he spread his arms, as he sunk, startled by the collapse of the fragile crust.

"Ho," Dory stifled a laugh, her heart in her throat. "You scared me, don't do that."

"I scared me." He stretched his arms again for added balance as he traversed the dangerous hole.

"I think we're over." He looked back, the dimple in the snow behind them.

The afternoon was cloudy, the perpetual threat of flurries loomed as they hiked floating feet above the highway, on the deep, deep snow.

"Beautiful, isn't it?" Dory took in the natural wonder around her, the evergreens heavy with white, everything blanketed and peaceful.

Lulled into a false sense of security by the scenery and the fact that they hadn't seen one Frosty, they trudged on.

"I see a sign ahead, we must be on the highway."

The road sign, its usual height lessened by the high shelf of snow, suddenly struck the pair.

"Ha, oh that's fucking hilarious."

"It really takes on a whole new meaning when you're looking at it from this perspective."

The caution sign, which was triangular in shape, had a snowflake filling its center. On a placard below there were two swerving lines, and a suggested safe speed of 35mph.

This was funny because the usually seven-foot-high sign was now at waist level.

Distracted by the hysterical irony, and in desperate need of a good laugh they lingered, the sign providing some much-needed comic relief.

The pause came with a price, for they didn't realize what dangers were lurking beneath their feet.

Roused from an icy slumber by the vibration of footsteps and the boisterous laughter, Frosty awoke.

Arms darted through the snowy cover; one gripped Dory's right ankle.

Anchored by the snowshoe and unsinkable, she fell back as Frosty pulled itself to the surface, its jaws snapping.

Davies rushed to her aid, only to be tripped, his face now inches from a Frosty and its flailing hand. A garden of arms erupted like demented daisies, as they struggled to emerge, their movements slow and jagged.

Dory screamed and kicked trying to free herself from the powerful hold. She discarded her gloves and commenced to remove the snowshoes, hoping to pull away.

"Don't, don't stand without them, you'll sink, they'll get you." Davies struggled to his feet, as he pulled his gun, aiming at Dory's attacker.

"Hold on, you're obscuring the shot." Suspended by the specialty footwear, but encumbered by their drag on his speed, he lumbered to her aid as he avoided the many grabbing hands trying to find a better position.

"No time." She pulled the snowshoe from her foot. With her hands wrapped around the curved wood, and her fingers poking through the hashing she stabbed wildy, forcing the pointed heel of the Ash and leather snow gear through the top of its skull. Black and viscous, the cold infected blood, burst through the wound and sprayed from its mouth. Dory was covered, her hands and legs washed in Frosty's gore.

"Ahh, ahh, Christ, it's all over me." It quivered on her skin, crawling...a life of its own.

She grabbed the snowshoe and stood, using the sign for support as she strapped it back to her foot.

She eyed the sign, and with the blood on her hand drew a biohazard symbol over the snowflake.

"Snow is no longer what makes this road dangerous."

... No end in sight

"**L**ook at this garden grow." They all gathered to admire their hard work.

A warm wind blew causing the foliage of the full trees to shimmy above.

"I didn't think we'd ever make it this far." Laney put her arms around Sean's neck and kissed his cheek.

So far they had avoided infection, and Pop was optimistic that the pathogen had degraded and wouldn't enter their food supply.

As they stood and watched the seedlings sway in the light June breeze the very distinct sound of howlers wafted in.

With an established protocol, they fell into position.

With the perimeter completed and two towers recently erected, they manned their posts, weapons at the ready.

The infected moved in, their usual disgusting and twisted forms clicked and gurgled. Some had been frozen and thawed and were now saggy, their frames holding up their damaged tissue. Others weathered differently, their skin tight and freeze-dried to their skeletons.

"Its amazing, the different manifestations." Pop had a really droopy one lined up. Nan nodded in agreement.

Doolin tapped Laney from their shared seat in the north tower. "Look, I can't believe it," he pointed to a howler with a very familiar tic. She scanned the horde for what he was talking about. "Holy shit!" She laughed as she took aim, the pointed head and bizarre finger movements unchanged by the infection. "Please let me do the honors."

"Of course."

With the finger-flipper in her sights, she fired.

"Nice one." It collapsed, its head blown wide open. Usually, there was a spray of liquid, or the splatter of tissue, but not this time. One tiny trickle of tarry blood oozed slowly... nothing else escaped the massive hole.

Doolin clapped her on the back.

"Huh, I knew there was nothing in there."

They laughed, the stupidity of their old neighbor now verified.